I^NH_{UMAN}

INHUMAN

KAMA FALZOI POST

BOOKFISHBOOKS

Published by BookFish Books LLC.

Copyright © 2016 Kama Falzoi Post

All rights reserved under International and Pan-American Copyright Conventions. No part of this book may be reproduced in any form or by any electronic or mechanical means, including information storage and retrieval systems, without permission in writing from the publisher, except by a reviewer, who may quote brief passages in a review.

Published in 2016 by BookFish Books LLC.
P.O. Box 274
Salem, VA
24153
bookfishbooks@gmail.com

This book is a work of fiction. Names, characters, places, and incidents are either the product of the author's imagination or are used fictitiously.

Library of Congress Cataloging-in-Publication Data
Post, Kama Falzoi--First edition.
InHuman / Kama Falzoi Post
ISBN 978-0-9975283-6-7 (print)
ISBN 978-0-9975283-5-0 (e-book)

Cover Image: © iStock
Cover Design: Anita B. Carroll www.race-point.com
Interior Design: Erin Rhew

Printed in the United States of America

www.bookfishbooks.com

To J.P., who told me I was the only one in any room I'm ever in. Thank you for making Adam real.

PART I

Chapter One

Given the choice, I would have rather taken a nosedive straight into the sidewalk than started my senior year at another new school. The human half of me—awkward, impatient, self-conscious—yearned for the type of mind-numbingly ordinary existence most teenagers longed to escape. But the inhuman half of me... I buried that so deep not even Jacques Cousteau could have uncovered it.

"They're late." I dropped my bulging suitcase by the front door and stood at the window to wait for my ride, twisting the cord to the blinds around the tip of my finger and watching my skin change from deep red to purple. Outside, sun rays glimmered off the dewy grass, and the remaining leaves rustled underneath the cloudless, blue sky. The world outside had never looked so bright—so *big*. Inside our little house, gloomy and sparse and littered with unpacked boxes, my mother sat on the living room floor surrounded by her newspapers, scissors in one hand and obituary page in the other.

I'd grown so used to the *snip snip* of those scissors, I only noticed it when it ceased. When I spun around, she was standing beside me at the window, the sun highlighting the swath of freckles across the bridge of her nose. She reached out and snapped the blinds closed, and I jumped. Darkness swallowed the room.

"They'll be here, Mira," she said in that mother-knows-best tone—the one that made my eye twitch. "Have patience for once."

My finger went numb and turned white. How did she expect me to be patient at a time like this? I had trouble waiting out the last five seconds of a frozen dinner in the microwave.

"You always get nervous on the first day." She searched my eyes, her hands heavy on my shoulders. Usually my mother's panic manifested as a sharp-edged intruder lurking around every corner. But this morning, for some reason, she remained exceptionally calm. I was the one having second thoughts, cutting off my own circulation for the fun of it because as everyone kept saying, *this could really be it*. When I released the cord, my fingertip throbbed.

"Everything is arranged, right?" I asked, nervously swiping through the screens on my phone, noticing only the fluttering birds in my stomach. Meryton hadn't sent me an acceptance letter. My mother told me last week, on a drab Tuesday afternoon, that's where I would start my senior year. That same night, under cover of darkness, we packed what we could carry and headed four hundred miles north.

"They took care of all of it. I don't want you worrying about things like that. Focus on what's important." My mother's green eyes sparkled and lit up the room like they always did when she got excited. With a pasted-on smile, I tried to mirror her enthusiasm, but I had to turn away before she saw right through me.

"I just don't want to get there and find out I'm not even registered. Last time, I had to sit in the principal's office for half a day while they called a hundred places looking for my records."

"You're registered, Mira. That was the easy part."

"What if they ask for my birth certificate or something?" I chewed at my fingernail while a million trivial worries nagged at me. "Because that one time, they wouldn't let me stay in class until I had proof that—"

My mother pulled my finger away from my mouth and held my hand. "It's all taken care of. Relax."

She was always telling me to relax, to find something to distract myself. *Read a book*, she'd suggest. Forget that. The smallest noises made me jump. I couldn't even turn on the television, because we didn't have one. So every night, alone with my frazzled nerves, I paced my bedroom, glancing every ten minutes through the hairline crack in the shade, scouring the yard for movement.

Relax. Right.

I moved the blinds aside once more, and they clacked together. They were yellow and smelled of stale smoke. The paisley wallpaper border and the length of the carpet shag screamed *seventies throwback*, but it's not like we would be here long enough to update it.

"Relax? That's easy for you to say. I'm the one going out there all alone, risking my life for something I'm starting to think isn't even going to happen."

The last three times—Charleston, Cincinnati, Topeka—they were so sure of it. Then we got there in the middle of a semester and found out we were *too late*. After being let down again and again, I'd lost hope.

My mother sighed, heavy and long like she'd taken what I said personally. When she opened her mouth to respond, I held up a hand.

"Kidding," I said. But I was totally serious. I knew my mother well enough to know a set jaw and pursed lips only led to an argument, and I didn't have the energy. Especially because just then, I turned to see the red truck rolling up our long and winding driveway, and the knot in my stomach tightened.

"Well," my mother said with finality, enveloping me in her arms. Her hair smelled faintly of strawberries. Her trembling concealed my own. "Promise me you'll call right away if anything strange happens."

"I promise. Make sure your phone is on." I forced myself to take a deep breath. "The new number, right?"

I wanted to get everything right. Just in case. The butterflies in my stomach alerted me that this time might be different. This time might be real. I liked to think I had a knack for sensing things, given what I was.

My mother nodded. Maybe she felt it too because her hand shook when she handed me my suitcase. Compact, vintage, leather straps. Full of almost everything I owned. She embraced me again, squeezed me hard just once, and then turned me around and steered me out the door. I felt as abandoned as a baby bird being pushed from its nest.

Alone, I stepped out onto the porch into the blinding sunlight and shielded my eyes. The screen door swung closed behind me with a definitive bang that shot my heart into my throat. For a moment, I contemplated sprinting back toward the house, locking myself in my room so I wouldn't have to leave my mother, so I wouldn't have to start another new school.

Larry and Hal watched me from the truck, and with a quick exhale, I resigned myself to the task at hand. I swallowed hard, hitched up my bag, and heaved my suitcase across the driveway. As I approached, Larry gave me an encouraging nod that settled my nerves.

I slid into the backseat next to my suitcase and tucked my legs under me. My mother didn't step one foot out of the house. She stood motionless behind the large plate glass window, only a sliver of her face visible between the vertical blinds. With a lump in my throat, I raised my hand to wave. Hal hit the gas, and we flew out of the driveway so fast my luggage slid off the seat and dumped onto the floor. I fastened my seatbelt, exhaled, and leaned back against the cracked leather.

"He's waitin' for you on campus." Hal caught my gaze in the mirror. "You ready for this?"

I rubbed my clammy palms on my thighs. "I've been waiting seven years for it." Out the window, I studied the vehicles as we whizzed by. The way Larry drove, I didn't worry too much about being followed, but we could never be too careful.

Gigantic sycamores lined the long driveway, tilting toward each other across the road so I could only see patches of washed out sky. The procession of vehicles stretched as far as I could see. I sat straight-backed in my seat, digging my knuckles into the leather.

There were *so* many of them.

Every spot in the parking lot overflowed with packed minivans and SUVs. Bewildered parents stood with their arms full of colorful crates, bedspreads, boxes, and duffel bags. Teenagers everywhere. Teenagers squeezed together in clumps so dense I couldn't see the ones in the middle. In the quad, on the sidewalks, in the grass.

Starting a new school in a new town never got any easier. I thought I'd get the hang of it after a while: seeing the same types of kids, avoiding the same cliques, plastering myself against the lockers like a chameleon to try and avoid the inevitable cracks about my hair. Navigating those hallways without one familiar face had been bad enough. The fact that something very powerful wanted to kill me took high school drama to a whole new level.

"Drive around back," I told Larry. "It will look weird if anyone sees me getting out of this truck." They had secured a Meryton Campus Security truck, or at least they had painted one to fit the role. I never asked where these things came from. From what I'd seen, their network ran far and deep, and when they needed something, they got it. Including bodies.

Once they let me out, I navigated the cobblestone walkway, dragging my decidedly unfashionable suitcase behind me. I'd made a bad choice of clothing: a dark blue cardigan over a black-and-white striped tank top and black shorts. Other girls wore capri stretch pants and spaghetti straps, short jean shorts and flip flops. The sun beat down on the back of my neck, and my underarms threatened to sweat through my shirt. Not a great impression on my first day. I stripped off my cardigan, threw it over my shoulder, and wrangled my hair back into a ponytail.

They told me to look for a boy—tall with dark hair. I didn't need more than that. I'd be able to pick him out based on my instinct alone. Or so I thought.

They'd initiated him the night before. Just once I wish they'd let me watch the initiation. My mother compared it to a flower opening its petals, but Larry had shrugged and said in his gruff way, "It's lyin' there not breathing, and then suddenly it is."

I pulled the map out of my back pocket, suddenly disoriented. I'd never seen a boarding school. I only knew about them from movies and books. It felt a lot like a college campus. Ivy strangled the old brick buildings. Cobblestone sidewalks curved around trees and patches of grass and branched off to different buildings. The Math and Science Center. Brighton Sports Complex. Harris Dining Hall.

Sparrows nested in the leafy growth underneath the windows. On the campus map, Larry had highlighted the way to the girls' dorm, and even though I had it memorized, I checked it three times. On my way there, I scanned the campus with hawk-like diligence for a tall boy with black hair. There had to be a hundred of them. My heart sunk with each step. I should have been better prepared. But there had been so little time.

A girl in a pink headband stood behind a desk in the foyer of the girls' dormitory handing out welcome packets, a bored smile plastered on her face. *Natasha, Resident Advisor,* her nametag read. I wiped the sweat off my forehead with the back of my hand and tried to look casual.

"Mira. Mira Avery."

She eyed me, flipped through the file in front of her, and slapped an ID down on the desk.

"Keep it on you at all times. It lets you in and out of all the buildings on campus. Don't let anyone borrow it. If you lose it, there's a ten dollar processing fee." I could barely hear her over the clamor of girls reuniting all around me.

My face stared back at me from the ID. *Mira Avery, Meryton Preparatory Academy.* "I look like I just woke up."

"Well, you should have sent a picture you liked." Natasha slid a paper across the desk, eyeing my thrift store suitcase before I could tuck it behind me. She had already made up her mind about me. She didn't hang with girls that had frizzy red hair, but I didn't hang with snobs. I had known a hundred Natashas in the schools I'd attended. They all sized me up and dismissed me with the same glance. I got it. On the surface, I didn't look special at all.

"Here's the list of dormitory rules. They're also posted on the bulletin board in case you forget." The rules practically took up an entire wall. Most likely I would end up breaking all of them.

"Thanks." I folded the paper in half, then in fourths, tucked it into my back pocket, and looked up. I could never pull off blue eyeliner like Natasha. Not with hair the color of a Dorito.

"You're in One-Thirty-Seven." She glanced down at another paper. "Rooming with Cassidy Ellis. Swing a left and follow it all the way to the end of the hall. Last room on the right." Her gaze traveled down to my frayed canvas shoes, and she made a face like she'd just sucked on a lemon. I reminded myself once again, I wasn't there to make friends.

I slid my card and waited for the telltale click, and then I turned the knob and entered what was to be my temporary home for the immediate future. Sharing an entire house with my mother felt cramped enough, but this room had just enough space to fit a bunkbed, two small dressers on opposite walls, and two small wooden desks. A great room if we were toddler-sized. My bedroom at home consisted of a mattress on the floor—so it's not like I craved luxury—but I couldn't imagine two people sharing such a small space all semester.

I cracked the window and judged the drop to be about ten feet. Doable, if it came down to it. I claimed the desk near the window and the dresser with the missing knob. After I unpacked, arranged my blank notebooks on the desk, and smoothed down the bleached sheets, I stood back, regarding my work…and frowned. Other girls on the floor had matching dorm furniture, framed art, and Bose speakers pumping heavy bass. I had my father's astronomy books and a drawer full of Meryton-issued uniforms.

"Look here, another ginger! You must be Mira? Mira Avery?" A red-haired woman with a clipboard poked her head into my room.

"Yeah?" She reminded me a little of my mother, if my mother had transformed into a thick-waisted busybody who summed a person up in one look.

"Honey, you're in group two. You were supposed to meet at three. Are your parents bringing up the rest of your stuff?" She scanned my room.

I fought the urge to apologize and shrank into myself. "No, they left. What you see is what you get."

She gave me the kind of understanding nod she probably reserved for lost puppies and poor people and introduced herself as Ms. Hendricks, one of the housemothers. She hurried me out of the room, walking crisply down the hall ahead of me, dictating a memorized list of the rules and regulations of dorm life. I had to jog to keep up with her.

"Do you know if my roommate is here yet? Cassidy Ellis?" Red-and-black checkered carpeting ran along the hallway. Posters and announcements decorated the walls.

Ms. Hendricks stooped to pick up a candy wrapper and sighed. "Cassidy Ellis? I think she checked in. She has to be in the room by eight tonight." She ducked into what was labeled the Common Room and deposited the wrapper in a large trash bin. A giant flatscreen television hung on the far wall. "Do you have the itinerary? It's in your welcome packet. I've got thirty-six girls in my care. We're all meeting here at seven tonight. Tardiness won't be tolerated."

I followed her to the front doors, which she flung open like Moses parting the sea. Outside, a couple of kids turned to size me up, and I tried not to squirm.

"You're over there." Hendricks pointed to what must have been my orientation group, gathered in a tight circle underneath the giant sycamore in the middle of the quad.

"The same sycamore Benjamin Franklin leaned against," proclaimed the girl who led the tour. An underclassman. Everyone knew each other except the freshman, and even they bonded together. I hung at the back, popped in my headphones, and searched for the boy, my stomach tumbling end over end.

Overhead, the large, knotty branches of the tree released a few leaves, which spiraled to the ground in front of me. We stepped out of the shade as a group, and a body slammed into mine from behind. The ground came up fast, but thanks to my lightning fast reflexes, I avoided landing on my face.

When I turned my head, a sandy-haired, brown-eyed boy stood over me, looking down. He wore a plaid shirt and cargo shorts. Despite the pain in my shoulder, I scrambled to my feet and brushed the leaves off me.

"Are you okay? I am so sorry." He tucked a football under his arm and attempted to catch his breath. Sweat glistened on his temples. His deep voice didn't match the boy-next-door exterior. "I didn't want it to hit you. It was headed right toward you. I swear I tried to stop."

He reached out and put a hand on my shoulder. His brow furrowed in concern, but a smile played at one side of his mouth. Everyone looked at me as my face burned.

"It's fine." I extracted a leaf from my hair and adjusted my headphones. *Okay, Earth, swallow me up now.*

The kids in the group lost interest almost right away: some with their heads on swivels taking in the campus and others digging through awkward small talk to try and make connections. Meanwhile, the boy didn't remove his hand from my shoulder. He held me there with some kind of gentle force and continued to inquire about my health.

"I'm fine, really." I rubbed my palms together. "Better than a football in the back of the head, right?"

His smile could have blown out the windows in a church. "And more exciting than the tour, I'm sure. 'Meryton was founded in 1908 by the Reverend Jonathan who-gives-a-crap.' Wouldn't you rather know where you can sneak away for a smoke?"

"I don't smoke."

"Me neither. It's so bad for you." He held my gaze for a beat too long. I shifted my stance. The two girls ahead of me turned to steal a look at us.

"I'm Brandon." He actually reached out to shake my hand. His felt smooth and soft, not sweaty and calloused like I expected a guy's to be. When my neck and ears grew hot, I pulled my hand away.

"You don't look like a freshman." He studied me so close he might as well have put me under a microscope.

"I'm a senior."

"What a coincidence; me too. I haven't seen you before. First year at prep? Let me guess. Your dad's in the military. You move from city to city and never really get a chance to make any lasting friendships? I've heard it a thousand times."

My mood instantly lightened, and I stifled a laugh. This guy had no idea. It was refreshing, and for a few sweet moments, my burdens took a backseat.

"Wow, you're good." The group moved forward, so I moved with them. Brandon bobbed beside me now, all energy.

"Really? I'm usually wrong about people. But I bet I'm not wrong about something." In the sunlight, his rich brown eyes hid absolutely nothing.

"What would that be?" Was he flirting with me? At least five of the girls in the group were prettier than me, skinnier than me.

"You don't care about the history of the rec center." A few freckles dotted the ridge of his nose and the smooth skin under his eyes.

No one in my group noticed, or cared, that I had fallen behind. They carried on with the tour.

"Actually, I can't imagine anything more riveting."

That charming smile made his eyes shine.

"Don't you have somewhere to be?" I asked him. "Like, rescuing girls from errant projectiles?"

"I honestly can't remember." Confidence seeped from his pores. The complete opposite of me. Despite my inexperience, even I knew when someone was flirting with me. I just didn't know why, or quite how to do it back.

"Are you ready to catch up with us?" The perky tour guide had come back to collect me. "Brandon Tate, get out of here. You're distracting everyone."

Brandon turned on his smile like it had a pullstring. "Hold on, I haven't gotten her name yet."

"Mira." I blushed.

"*Mira*," Brandon repeated in a Spanish accent, adjusting his hat. "You know, that's Spanish for 'look'."

"I'm impressed. Someone took Spanish 101." I didn't tell him my name had nothing to do with Spanish. Mira was my father's favorite star.

"You should hear me recite the periodic table." Brandon tossed the football with ease from one hand to the other.

"Sounds fascinating." I couldn't wipe the stupid grin from my face.

"Well then, Mira, I will definitely see you around." He backed away from me slowly—my hero—and threw the ball up one last time. This time, though, he botched the catch. He stumbled after it as it rolled across the grass. When he stood, ball in hand, he gave a quick bow and ran off to join his friends. I put my headphones back in and concentrated on not smiling, but there was nothing I could do about my racing pulse.

In the Math and Science building, just like Larry and Hal had planned, I slipped into the bathroom, hid in a stall, and didn't come out until the rest of the group had moved on. I took a look in the mirror before I left and tried to see myself through Brandon's eyes. Why did he talk to me? My hair frizzed out of my ponytail, my eyes were too wide set, and the freckles clustered on my cheeks made me look years younger. Maybe he was just being nice.

The sign on the heavy metal door at the end of the hall read *Danger–Keep Off Roof.* I proceeded to the roof immediately. It was not what we had planned, but I hoped it might give me a better vantage point.

I climbed the stairs, pushed open the door, and stepped out into the fresh air. The sky was bluer than blue. A huge flock of crows took off from some pine trees to my right. No, not a flock. A murder.

"Hey, what are you doing up here?"

Larry and Hal strode toward me wearing dark blue security uniforms. I hadn't heard them approach, and Hal's deep voice startled me. He stood almost seven feet, with white hair and a tight smile that could have been a frown.

Larry, the shorter, dumpier one, regarded me with kind eyes before waving a finger in the air. "You're not supposed to be up here."

I narrowed my eyes. "*You're* not supposed to be up here. Didn't you see the sign? Nice uniforms, by the way. Very official." They hadn't been in uniform when they picked me up.

"And what are you doing all alone? We already talked about this. If your mother knew…" With his hands on his hips like that, Larry's beer belly jutted out, rounder than ever.

"I'm not alone anymore, am I? Anyway, we covered all this on the drive. I have it under control." They had already warned me about going off on my own, trusting anyone outside of the two of them, watching my back, my front, and my sides, and countless other tips I proceeded to ignore. Nothing had ever come of this in all the years we had been chasing the evil and elusive Conduit.

Hal rolled his eyes and shook his head as if he could read my mind. But he couldn't because members of Orientation, like Hal and Larry, didn't have supernatural powers. They only possessed the ability to initiate, which was gifted to them in what my mother described as "a flash, a dizzy spell, and the sudden compulsion to carry out the wishes of an otherworldly species."

"Impressive view, ain't it?" Larry sidled up next to me and whistled high and long through the gap in his front teeth.

"How should I know? I'm not here for the view."

Although, he did have a point. Beyond the brick and stone of the old campus, the landscape stretched and rolled in gentle green curves for miles before it culminated in the distant soft peaks of the Adirondacks. The afternoon sun amplified the shadows of the valleys, washed out the hilltops, and warmed my skin.

"So how long are you going to keep me in suspense?" Registration, the orientation tour, and now gabbing it up on the roof meant wasting valuable time.

"Why don't you give it a shot?" Larry said. "See if you can tell."

Hal hung back, always on guard. The security uniform suited him, though it stopped short of covering his wrists and ankles, like all his clothes did.

I peered over the edge of the roof, nodding toward the crowd of kids below me, careful to stay out of sight. And to not fall. "You mean he's down there? Right now?"

Larry nodded and cleared his throat like he did when he was nervous or excited.

My heartbeat quickened. I scanned the boys' faces, knowing any one of them could have been the newest Initiate—the one Larry and Hal just brought into a body last night. But how would I know which one? I waited for a warm glow to bloom inside me or a loud voice in my head to shout, *"There! There he is!"* I thought I had that innate ability, based on what my father had told me.

I paced along the edge of the building. So... the boy with the skinny legs? The boy with the black-framed glasses? The one with the cast on his arm talking to three blondes? I felt nothing except the faint glimmer of frustration. And to add to my distraction, I kept sneaking looks at Brandon, who had probably only talked to me on a dare or something and would probably never talk to me again.

"Can you at least give me a hint?"

Hal sighed in the background. "We don't have all day. This ain't a game, you two." I'd always wondered why they'd chosen Hal. Not for his personality.

Larry scratched his stubbled double chin. Flecks of white peppered his once black hair. He constantly commented on how much I'd grown, but the years showed on him too. Soon he would be too old to do what he did.

I surveyed the crowd once more. My head snapped toward a group of boys under a far tree, then to a lone boy reading a book next to the brick wall of the adjacent building. No one stuck out to me. I'd expected this to be easy, but it was taking too long. I chewed the skin around my nail until I tasted blood.

"Oh for gosh sakes," I heard Hal mutter. "He's—"

"Wait." I held up my hand.

Wait.

My attention floated across the multitudes, homing in on the signal that stirred up a slight breeze, a tickle across my skin. Goosebumps. A drumming in my ears. All sound concentrated on one point. On one boy.

"That boy." The boy with the dark hair who stood rooted to the ground, shoulders back, a spot of stillness in the chaos of the quad. He turned his head and looked up at me, looked right at me through the barrel of those eyes. That gaze held me, pinned me. I didn't know how long I had been holding my breath. Maybe forever. Maybe I had been holding my breath forever until that moment.

Then I came back, as suddenly as if someone had flipped a switch.

"That's him." I hitched my bag over my shoulder and sprinted for the door before Hal could stop me with his lectures about how my impatience was going to get me killed. I burst from the Math and Science building, and suddenly that boy, the one with the hypnotic eyes, stood before me.

"Adam," I said. "Welcome to Earth."

Chapter Two

It felt as if the two of us stood alone in the quad—everything quiet and beating, swirling around us just out of the picture.

"Mira," he said.

Time stopped as I inspected him. His perfect olive skin, the freckle at the base of his neck, his hair—dark and unkempt, cut close to his ears and longer on the top so it hung just above his eyebrows. The small bump in the ridge of his nose. His cheeks flushed pink, and he stood a full two heads taller than me. Square shouldered, light blue veins just under the skin of his forearms, smooth knuckles, fingernails. As human as anyone—including me. Perfectly put together. Nothing in his eyes betrayed his true identity, nothing in the way he stood, except the awkward erectness of his arms hanging at his sides. I had the urge to reach out and touch him. To lay my hand on his chest to feel for the revived heartbeat. To stand on tiptoes and peer deep into his black pupils, as if behind them someone bent over a machine, furiously programming.

"You're one of them." I could barely catch my breath. "You look so…"

"Human?" He had a normal teenage boy voice.

"And you can talk." For some reason, this came as a surprise to me.

"They focused on that during training. And I have been practicing on my own." A normal teenage boy voice with a strange accent and traces of a lisp. I didn't remember this about my father. Of course, he initiated before I was born.

"You're going to need more practice." I couldn't take my gaze off him. "People will ask questions." We had searched for one like him for seven years. My mother's newspaper clippings, obituaries, all the relocations, the false leads, and the dead ends. And now, on the campus of a private boarding school, the bait stood smiling down at me. I swallowed hard and looked away to keep from disappearing into his eyes.

I looked around at the other students. "We should go somewhere. Do normal things. We can't stand here staring at each other."

Though I very well could have done that. After all, the human half of me fawned over cute guys just like anyone else. The alien half, though, struggled to make itself heard from somewhere in the depths. A faint echo, that could have become a boom if I'd let it, told me two pieces of an intergalactic puzzle had snapped together as soon as I laid eyes on Adam.

I spotted Larry and Hal standing watch on the roof and gave them a slight nod. Before I turned back to Adam, I cleared my throat and set my jaw. The intensity of the magnetism would diminish. It had to if this was going to work.

"Follow me." I headed for the dining hall at a quick pace, glancing back a hundred times to make sure he didn't disappear. I felt compelled to grab his hand but resisted. My thoughts fluttered about like leaves in the wind as we walked toward the glass building at the bottom of the hill.

When I pushed open the doors of the dining hall, a hundred teenagers turned to study us. If we had been in a movie, the music would have stopped, and my beating heart would have filled the silence. The moment lasted two seconds at best, but it felt like an eternity before everyone turned back to their friends, their phones, and their food. Conversation lit the air like a swarm of mosquitoes. I took a breath and stepped inside, doing a quick check for alternate exits.

The food line started to the right and snaked behind a wall, emerging through a doorway next to the big-screen television that hung above the fire alarm and endlessly looped a Campus News PowerPoint. The stench of fried food hung in the air and would probably cling to my clothes forever. When Adam's arm brushed mine, I remembered why we stood there, backs to the door, wide-eyed. Him because this was all new. Me because of the Conduit.

Anyone could hide in a crowd, but the Conduit wouldn't try anything with a hundred witnesses. He could be standing just outside the glass doors that reflected the lights or be buried in a book in the corner, biding his time until he could be alone with Adam. I surveyed the room. After a few moments, Larry and Hal entered through the back doors and stood at opposite ends of the dining hall, watching us closely.

Next to me, Adam placed a hand on top of a large brown garbage can filled to overflowing. I nudged him with my elbow. "You can't just go around touching things."

I scanned the crowd for Cassidy, my roommate. I only had a picture to go on, but I had memorized that picture. Blonde, straight hair, big white-toothed smile. Normally my memory didn't fail me, but twenty girls fit that exact profile. Adam stared at me, presumably wondering what to do next. It felt a little like training a puppy. The initial excitement of connecting with my first Initiate wore off when I reminded myself of the work that had to be done.

"Let's sit." I directed him to one of empty round tables off to the side, wondering if he wouldn't do better with a leash. "Are you hungry?"

"I don't know."

Of course he didn't. The body being new to him, he probably experienced all kinds of novel, inexplicable things. Things I didn't have time for. "Just stay here. I'll go get us some pizza or something. I assume you need to eat."

I made sure Larry saw me head toward the line so he could take over the watch. My stomach rumbled as I scanned the menu. They served fried everything. Mozzarella sticks, mushrooms, French fries. I ordered two slices of cheese pizza, not knowing whether someone like Adam would be vegetarian, and paid with the cash my mother had stuck in my pocket. At the table, I slid a plate of pizza over to Adam and sat down, marveling at the way he examined the food on his plate.

"You know what to do with it, right?" I said it half joking. This couldn't have been his first time eating. Larry and Hal must have fed him.

But it certainly seemed like his first time, judging by the way he raised the slice slowly toward his mouth and paused, as if he didn't know where to put it. He took a small bite, closed his eyes, and started to chew. I watched his whole body sink into the chair.

"It can't be that good." I started to laugh until an image of my mother, alone in the kitchen microwaving her frozen dinner, brought with it a stab of nausea. I missed her already, and I hadn't even been at Meryton for twenty-four hours. I pushed my own plate away, suddenly not very hungry.

"Hello again," I heard behind me.

Brandon stood there with his winning smile and expectant brown eyes, so comfortable in his own skin. I sat up straighter and buried my hands in my lap to stop from fidgeting.

"Hi," I whispered without meaning to. Adam stopped chewing and smiled. A big glop of sauce spilled down the front of his shirt, and I grimaced.

"Hope I'm not interrupting. Who's your friend?" Brandon dragged a chair over next to me and slid into it.

I hadn't counted on anyone joining us. I wouldn't have minded a hot boy at my table in any other circumstance. But this kind of distraction could ruin my concentration.

"Him? He's not my friend. I just met him. He's… um… he's an exchange student. From Iceland." *Iceland?* I don't know why that popped into my head, but I hoped it would explain whatever disaster happened next.

"Cool. Iceland has a soccer league, don't they?" Brandon braced his hands on the table and leaned forward. "I mean a football league? You guys call it football, right? Do you play?"

Adam shook his head. My knee bounced up and down under the table.

"You like Cristiano Ronaldo? Did you see his free kick? You have to see this." Brandon held up his phone. Of course Adam hadn't seen the free kick. From the look of awe on his face, Adam hadn't seen videos before at all. He came across like one of those kids from some impoverished village, raised in a ramshackle building without electricity. The Senders should have prepared him better.

Adam held up his empty plate when the video ended. "This was very good. It tastes beautiful."

Brandon gawked at me and raised his eyebrows in amusement. Speechless, I could only shrug.

"They don't have pizza in Iceland?" Brandon said to Adam, who looked to me.

"Things don't *taste* beautiful." I took a deep breath. "They *look* beautiful."

Adam stared at me with that glop of sauce on the front of his shirt. I couldn't imagine someone like him helping to save the world.

"Try a napkin." I handed him one, but he just looked at it.

Brandon waved at someone across the room who called his name. He bounded out of his chair, and I exhaled, happy to stop acting like everything was normal. But he stopped mid-stride and turned back with a smile. "See you around?"

I nodded and smiled for lack of anything witty to say. I couldn't help but stare after him as he sauntered away.

Once he was out of earshot, I turned to Adam. "You're not exactly trying hard to blend in. You have to at least pretend to know what people are talking about." I drummed my fingers on the table. My pizza sat untouched on my plate, burnt black around the edge of the crust. "And you have to work on your speech. You talk like you ate a mouthful of slugs."

People would notice him for that. I couldn't have people noticing him, though his good looks drew the curious gazes of most girls who passed our table. Even girls across the room stared at him, whispering to each other behind their hands.

From the article my mother showed me—one of the few clippings that had turned into a real lead—at least thirty miners had been lost in an accident. That meant Orientation had thirty bodies to choose from, and I assumed they weren't all as hot as Adam. We were supposed to blend in, but Adam stood out. Larry and Hal should have kept the distraction factor in mind when they stole him from the morgue. Men.

"Crap, I forgot." I pulled out my phone and texted my mother:

I'm with him. More later.

She sent back a row of exclamation points and:

Be careful.

"Can I get more pizza?" Adam said.

"No," I hissed. "You're not here for pizza."

His innocence irritated me. Maybe because I expected him to be different, to wake up in that body and take charge. Instead, he was asking for more burnt pizza.

When his mouth turned down, I immediately felt bad. I slid my plate across the table. "Here, have mine."

He didn't touch it.

"Aren't you going to eat it? You wouldn't want to waste a perfectly cold piece of overcooked dough."

He eyed me blankly. *It isn't his fault*, I reminded myself. He didn't choose this any more than I did. I had to cut him some slack, so I softened my tone.

"How does it feel? Being in a human body?"

He looked down at himself, at his forearms, his hands. When he looked back at me, he smiled. White teeth, one dimple, eyes crinkled at the corners. I attributed the fluttering in my stomach to hunger, and nothing more.

"It's not like training. The body is easy enough to operate." He raised an arm, made a fist. "I send a signal and it obeys. But the other part is unexpected." His pronunciation had evened out. He sounded more like a normal person, less *Icelandic*. My mother told me how quickly my father had adapted, but it surprised me, seeing it myself. It had only been a few minutes.

"What other part?"

From across the table, Adam's gaze grew serious. "The insides. Thoughts, I think. Feelings?"

I stopped it there, pushing out my chair. I didn't want to hear about his feelings. The body served only as a machine to him, a vessel. I had to keep that perspective, otherwise—my mother had warned me—the evacuation would be too difficult.

"We should go." I stuffed our plates on top of the trash, and he followed me wordlessly out the doors. Three girls in Meryton blazers filed past us, glared at me, stared at Adam, and huddled into themselves and giggled. I pushed my hair behind my ear, looked through the glass of the dining hall, and tried to spot Brandon. The wind picked up, rustling the thin branches of the pines lining the far edge of the crowd. Something drew my eye. Something, apart from the trees but entangled with them, something dark and fluid moving through them.

I shivered and pulled out my ID. "We should get back to the dorms. They take away points for stuff if you're late. You don't want to draw more attention to yourself."

Plus the housemother—Ms. Hendricks—wanted us back early for whatever fascinating event she had planned. Anyway, I didn't want to lose points. Not that it would matter. I wouldn't be here long enough to take advantage of any of the perks. But then again, looking around, buttoning up my sweater, maybe I would. Maybe things could be normal for just a little while. What would that feel like?

I leaned toward Adam. "What's your plan for tomorrow?" Larry and Hal headed toward the boys' dorm, and I knew Adam had to follow.

"English. Eight o'clock."

Not exactly what I meant, but I appreciated the effort.

"What is your plan for tomorrow?" Adam asked.

"Find the Conduit, of course," I said. "And get my father back."

Chapter Three

As soon as I opened my door the next morning, a stream of half-dressed girls with their plastic bins of high-end makeup, flat irons, and hair products ran past, vying for first dibs on the shower. I took a deep breath before I joined them, not really into the idea of a shared bathroom in the first place and definitely not into the idea of a jammed one. My anxiety about the Conduit, coupled with the lack of sleep, made everything more irritating. The girls' high-pitched giggles grated on my nerves. Their blaring pop music and their collective, carefree attitudes served as constant reminders that I'd never be so unencumbered.

I'd wanted to get started right away, to lead Adam to the pines, to draw out the enemy. But Larry and Hal had told me to wait, and I had to listen to them. They'd been through all of this before. They didn't care that waiting meant lying awake all night with jolts of nervous energy pounding through my veins.

"I forgot how much this blows," said the petite girl who stood in front of me in line for the shower.

"Is it like this every morning?" The start of a headache crept in around my temples. I tapped my foot on the tile.

"Nah, it'll die down in like a week. Once everyone finds out who's in their classes, they stop caring about what they look like." She smiled. Her teeth formed a perfect, straight line.

"I'll have to get up a half hour earlier tomorrow." I shuddered. "Mornings aren't exactly my thing."

She laughed. "Yeah, you and everyone else. I'm Betsy, by the way."

"Mira." I looked directly into her dark eyes. I would have offered my hand if I weren't struggling with the shampoo and conditioner, soap, toothbrush, and tube of toothpaste I cradled in my arms. Everyone else had cute little shower caddies.

"You're new here." Betsy flashed a sympathetic smile.

"You nailed it." I looked past her to my reflection.

"Starting a new school in your senior year? That's rough. Are you a fiver?"

"What?"

"A *fiver*. You know, students who don't board on weekends. A lot of the rich kids go home Friday after classes or sports. I'm sure you've seen their Miatas and Benzes in the parking lot."

"I'm not a rich kid." And I hadn't paid much attention to the cars.

"Scholarship?" She narrowed her eyes.

"Not exactly." I bit my lip, not knowing quite what to say. The network paid for everything. Every move, every school, my clothes, endless untraceable cell phones.

Betsy shook her head. She wore her hair in a neat, shiny black bob that swayed back and forth when she moved. "I'm not a rich kid either. But my parents still want me home some weekends. It's kind of nice in some ways. I don't have to do my laundry here. And I get two days without fried food. Though it's a bummer when your friends are all doing shit over the weekend, and you're home getting dragged to your stupid little brother's football game."

That Natasha girl from registration emerged from one of the shower stalls, pink towel wrapped around her lithe body. She glared at me. More bitch than evil, I decided.

"What do people usually do here over the weekend?" I shuffled forward about two inches in the never-ending line. "We're so far away from everything."

"Drink, mostly. Town is about five miles. Do you have a car?"

"No," I said. In the background, the constant barrage of girl chatter, blow dryers, and dropped things clattering to the tiles didn't help my headache.

"That's too bad. People with cars have it made here. Otherwise you're stuck sneaking off into the hills with a bottle and some smokes and hoping you make it in before curfew."

"Sounds better than your little brother's football game."

She laughed. A little balloon of joy threatened to lift off in my chest. This felt like a real conversation. This felt like making a friend. So bittersweet when I remembered what waited for me.

"Mira. That's a pretty name."

I beamed, that little bubble growing larger. "I'm named after a star."

She studied me for a little longer than necessary, and I thought I said something wrong.

"*Omicron Ceti.*"

She knew the scientific name of my star. I almost died right there. She must have read the disbelief on my face because she laughed again.

"It's weird that I know that, right? I'm not weird or anything. I just know my astronomy."

Trying hard to contain my excitement, I nodded. "It's just cool. You're the only person I've ever met that knows that. I mean besides my father. That was his favorite star. Hence my name."

"Really?" Betsy nodded toward my hair. "Because it's a red star, right?"

I shook my head. "No. He liked the fact that at certain parts of its cycle it disappears from sight entirely. Like it has some other life somewhere."

"That's something to live up to." Betsy shifted her pink shower caddy to her other arm. "But seriously, what are those girls doing in there that takes them so long? Time me. I'll be five minutes, tops."

"Thanks. Hey, do you know Cassidy Ellis?" The question escaped my mouth before I could think twice. Maybe I should have my own reality show: Mira Avery, Special Investigations Unit. An instant hit, I'm sure.

Betsy shook her head. "Does she go here?"

"She's supposed to be my roommate."

We moved forward again. A few of the girls smiled at me as they walked past. A few didn't.

"She hasn't shown up yet, but Hendricks said she was on campus." Now I could see the mirrors above the row of sinks. Between two girls vying for space, I caught a glimpse of myself. Stunned, tired, frizzy. Not perfectly kempt, like Betsy. Not naturally gorgeous or model thin, like Natasha. I looked away.

Betsy shrugged. "Probably decided to stay with a friend. Maybe you'll luck out. I would literally kill for a single."

Betsy had definite friend potential—if I made it out of this alive. She knew people, and she knew things…and she talked *a lot*, which took the pressure off me. In the span of about three minutes, she had covered which teachers had drinking problems, which boys to stay away from, how to get a free soda out of the downstairs machine, and how to sneak someone in or out through the basement window.

Added bonus: Betsy emerged from the shower in four minutes and thirty-nine seconds.

"Come by my room tonight before the Hendricks' show. Three-oh-six." She squeezed past me. "We'll compare schedules. Oh, and a few of us who stay on campus are going into town next Friday. Plan on going, if you can."

I didn't have time to stammer out a response before she disappeared out the door. My life could never be normal, so why even try? As long as the Conduit existed somewhere out there, I wouldn't be taking trips to town or hanging out all night in people's rooms.

When it was my turn, the hot water ran out within thirty seconds. I shivered through the rest of my shower.

Outside, torrents of kids headed to class on the cobblestone paths, new bags slung over their shoulders, hair coiffed, and clothes ironed. Girls wore funky barrettes or headbands or lined their ears with silver studs to express themselves. I had bright red hair. I didn't need to do anything to stand out.

In calculus, I chose a seat in the third row and watched as people filed into class. Since I doubted the Conduit wanted to explore sines and cosines, I should have felt safe. But I never felt safe. My mother had instilled that in me, and what happened to my father justified her paranoia.

Seconds before the bell, Brandon strolled in. He caught my eye, and I inhaled quickly and busied myself with the syllabus on my desk, hoping he wouldn't see the stupid red face that gave me away every time.

"Well, this doesn't seem right." He slid into the desk next to me. "I don't even have to dive in front of you." He wore his white shirt tucked in at the front and a navy blue woven belt with a metal-tipped end that dangled down past his pocket. He didn't wear his baseball cap since Meryton didn't allow hats in class. He pushed his hair to the side when it fell over his eye, put his hands in his pockets, and tipped the chair back.

"Are you sure you're in the right place? Remedial math is down the hall."

He laughed. "Is that a dumb jock joke? I'll have you know I was top of the class last year."

"Overachiever?" I smiled down at my desk.

"Blame my parents."

The only thing I could think to blame his parents for were his stunning smile and bedroom eyes. I dug my fingernail into a deep groove in the desk and pulled out my phone.

Brandon leaned over. "Hey, not to be annoying, but I would put that away. Dolby's a hardass."

Number 17: Cell phones are forbidden during class hours. A stupid rule that could not apply to me. My phone was my lifeline. Mr. Dolby bent over the array of papers on his desk at the front of the room. My mother had texted fourteen times. Most of them—

"Hand it over."

I looked up directly into Dolby's enormous mustache.

"Sorry," I said, aware that everyone was looking at me.

"Sir, that was my fault." Brandon sat up straight and folded his hands on his desk. "This is her second day. She didn't know. I was just telling her to turn off her phone, and you walked up right when she was about to do just that." He smiled and crossed his ankles, the perfect teacher's pet.

He could charm almost any living human being, but he couldn't charm Dolby.

"Thanks for that input, Mr. Tate." Mr. Dolby turned back to me. "That's five points. You'll get it back at the end of the week."

"End of the week? That's not going to work. I need—"

Dolby held his hand out. He must have done a lot of frowning over the years to form that deep groove between his eyebrows.

"Super." I placed the phone across his palm and watched him pocket it, cursing under my breath.

Behind him, Brandon mouthed an apology at me. My face burned, my eyes stung, and the whole room went quiet. By the end of class, I hated Dolby, and I hated calculus. When the bell rang and kids threw their books in their bags, Dolby kept talking. As if he did it all for the *math*. I closed my book hard and stuck my pen in my bag. Mr. Dolby droned on and on, and I thought *are you kidding me with the mustache?* How could he even eat with that thing?

That was the one good thing about my situation: my stint at Meryton would be short, if all went as it was supposed to.

Finally, Dolby sighed and thumped a fist on his desk. "That's it for today. See you all tomorrow."

In the rush of students crowding for the door, I thought maybe Brandon would wait for me, try and talk to me, but why would he? He had a thousand friends. He disappeared into the crowd with a quick look back while I made a big to-do about trying to fit the giant calculus book in my bag. Without my phone, I felt naked and anxious. I hoped Mr. Dolby would take pity on me and make an exception just this once. He didn't look up when I approached his desk.

"Mr. Dolby?"

"Hmm?" He scribbled something in the margins of the textbook.

"I'm new here, and I wasn't really aware of the cell phone rule. I promise I won't let it happen again."

"Mmmm," he said.

"See, the thing is, I really need to text my mother. This is my first time away from home, and she's a worrier." I clasped my hands behind my back to keep from biting at my nails. The wall clock ticked away the seconds.

Dolby finally looked up, raising one eyebrow. "If I make an exception for you, I have to make an exception for everyone."

"Actually, no you don't."

"Friday, Ms. Avery. You'll get your phone back Friday. Imagine what people your age did before cell phones. Amazing they survived at all."

I headed for the door with my head down, lacking a phone, and loaded with a pile of calculus homework so thick I should have started it last year. I wished Dolby was the Conduit so I could banish him and his ridiculous facial hair from this earth entirely.

In the hallway, Adam leaned against the radiator, hands shoved deep in his pockets, his eyes trained on me.

"Hello, Mira." He tipped his head in that awkward, formal way he had. Hearing him say my name felt intimate, an invasion, and I had to turn so he wouldn't see me blush. The windows to my right revealed a bright blue sky.

"What are you doing out in the hall? Where's Larry?" They weren't supposed to leave him alone.

"They're both around. Can I walk with you?" He didn't carry a bag or hold any books, and he wore the same clothes he had on last night, complete with the sauce stain. He stood so close to me I could make out traces of golden-yellow in the blue of his eyes.

"Yeah, fine." I sped in front of him. "But listen. You have to go to class too. You can't just loiter around looking lost. People will get suspicious. They'll ask for your ID or something."

We passed a few classrooms. The acrid smell of cleaning products and new sneakers permeated the air.

"I have an ID. Orientation saw to it." Of course they did. They saw to everything. They called themselves Orientation for a reason.

"I saw Brandon this morning," he said out of the blue.

"Me too. He was in my class." I rifled through my bag to try and locate my schedule. In previous high schools, classrooms were down the hall from each other. Here, I had to switch buildings.

"Yes, I know." Adam walked easily next to me.

Students passed by us. I waved to Betsy, and she grinned at me and eyeballed Adam. I wanted to say, "No, this isn't…" but it didn't matter. The moment had passed, and the wave of bodies had carried her off.

Adam glanced around before lowering his head to speak. "Do you wonder why it is that Brandon approached you?"

My guard went up immediately. "What do you mean?"

"I found it odd that he was so friendly, and you said you had only just met him."

"Brandon's a friendly person. What are you trying to say?" I looked around for Larry or Hal so I could offload Adam, but only because his suspicion hit too close to the mark. Apparently it was strange that any boy would want to talk to me. I didn't need an alien to point that out.

We turned the corner and came to an impossibly long hall empty of students. *Know your exits.* Stairwell halfway down, ladies' room on the left. Plate glass windows, breakable with metal chairs with the right kind of impact.

"They said the Conduit would blend in. They warned he would try and befriend me. And you." Now gray flecked the blue of Adam's eyes. In every light, they looked different. I kept walking.

Anyone that overheard this conversation might seriously question our sanity. Fortunately, the two of us stood alone in the hallway.

"Brandon is not the Conduit." I knew I sounded defensive, but I resented him for even suggesting such a thing. "He's about as evil as a baby bunny. You have to trust me. I'll know the Conduit when I see him. I'll be able to feel it. It's in my blood."

I took a deep breath. Fluorescent lights flickered overhead and went out. In just a few short minutes, the blue sky had darkened to slate gray. Distant thunder rumbled.

"Anyway, your accent sounds better. What did you do, practice talking to yourself all night?"

"No, I tried to sleep." He watched the sky out the window. His hair stuck up in the back. I refrained from smoothing it down, though I imagined how it would feel under my fingertips.

"I saw things against the eyelids," he said.

"It's called dreaming. Look, whenever you have a question about something, you should just ask me, okay? Or Larry. Or Hal, I guess, if you can stand talking to him."

Adam nodded. "You don't want anyone getting suspicious."

"Well, not exactly." I waved him down the hall as I checked room numbers. "It's not like the whole world is aware of the Senders. Only a handful, maybe more." God, I was going to be late. "I just don't want you to draw attention to yourself. Or to me. I like to try and blend in. The Conduit would love to get his hands on me too."

The second bell rang, and I had to pretty much accept my fate. I'd lose five more points—one point for each minute late—and it was only my second day. So much for saving up enough to earn a free lunch, or whatever rewards there were for obeying the rules. Rain pelted the windows, leaving streaks.

"That's what you call us? Senders? I'm not familiar with that word." Adam drew his finger along the glass as he walked.

"Senders, yes. Your kind is on the brink of extinction, so they *send* their members into dead human bodies in order to survive. Anyway, it's good you're not familiar with the word. We've made it as seamless as possible for your kind—for Senders—to blend in. No one has ever found out, and no one ever will."

Shit. Right there. English Lit. Room two-thirty-seven, my door. Already closed.

"I'm late." I threw my hands up. "I'm going to be the only student in Meryton history to start out with negative points."

"You can't leave me yet." He took my arm.

Under his touch, my skin burned. I forgot about English Lit, forgot about the Conduit. Laughter bubbled up from somewhere deep and bright inside me, and I lost myself in the warm current that coursed through my body. Not just as if Adam had simply touched my arm, but as if he had enveloped me.

A random, slamming door, somewhere down the hall, snapped me out of my trance.

I used all my strength and willpower to pull away. "You can't just grab random people." I took a moment to gather my wits, chastising myself for losing them in the first place.

"But Mira, you're not random."

Missiles fired in all directions from my heart. Thank God Larry and Hal appeared at the end of the hallway before I said or did something stupid. "Orientation is here." I nodded in their direction. "I have to go to class. I would like to pass high school."

As I took my seat, I could still feel his hand on my forearm. I kept looking down at the spot as if he'd left fingerprints behind. Thunder rattled the windows of the classroom as the storm drew closer.

Chapter Four

I could have sworn I locked the door to my room when I left. But as I approached, I noticed it was open an inch. An electric current of fear raised the hair on my neck. My backpack slipped down my arm and fell to the floor. Before continuing, I flattened myself against the wall a foot from my door, listening.

Air blew through the vents. Every new noise in this old building suggested a mystery; every creak and shift brought new images of terror. My first instinct told me Cassidy had finally decided to show. My second instinct told me to question my first. Knowing what I knew, I should have backed out of there and found Larry and Hal and let them investigate.

But I didn't. I took a breath and pushed the door wide open.

A girl my age glanced up and regarded me with wide, green eyes. At the top of her head, her dyed black hair formed two buns that resembled cat ears, and she wore a faded Nine Inch Nails shirt and cutoff shorts with ripped black fishnets underneath.

I flinched. "You're not Cassidy."

"I'm Decklin!" Her voice was two octaves higher than mine. "I was surprised too. They switched my room last minute. Don't ask me why. Come in, come in!" She pulled me into our room. Her army surplus duffel bag lay open on the floor spewing its contents. Wadded up clothes spread across the floor, and her books littered the second desk. The room had a different energy with her stuff in there. With her in there. An infectious, pulsing energy.

"Is this all you brought?" Suddenly my ratty suitcase didn't seem so inadequate. She'd brought a duffel bag, a backpack, and a dark purple throw—on the bed, still in plastic.

"I travel light. Never know when I'll need to make a quick getaway." She winked. I knew something about quick getaways myself, but I held my tongue.

"You're a transfer too?" she said. "What brought you to Meryton?"

"Fate, I guess." I stepped past her. She smelled like coffee and cigarettes, like my old piano teacher.

"We have a lot in common then. Except for taste in books, apparently." She nodded toward my shelf, to the dog-eared, highlighted, coffee-stained remnants of my father: *Advanced Celestial Photography*, *Atlas of Astronomical Discoveries*, *Decoding the Universe*. They had taken up most of the room in my suitcase.

"They were my dad's." I knew how it would come across, what question would come next, and I clenched my teeth to brace myself for it.

"Oh. Did he die?" She smacked her gum and sat cross-legged on my bed.

"He had cancer." I cast my eyes down to let her know I didn't want to talk about it.

"Oh, I'm sorry," she said in that way most people did when they didn't know what else to say. "Cancer's a bitch."

"So what happened to Cassidy?" I sat on the edge of my bed and watched the girl in front of me: tall, gorgeous, outgoing. Everything I wasn't. She moved soundlessly to the desk chair, her long limbs stretched out in front of her.

"Who?" she asked. Apart from the fact that someone had constructed the perfect high school rebel, dressed her in torn fishnets and heavy black mascara and set her down on campus, nothing seemed off about Decklin. I would have felt it. Evil was not a disguisable trait.

"Cassidy was supposed to be my roommate. Never mind." I focused on relaxing all the muscles that had tensed when I walked into the room. I didn't want to appear like some paranoid freak. "I'm glad you're here. It was creepy being alone in here last night."

"I like creepy," she said. "And thanks for leaving me the top bunk. I like looking down on everything."

I liked looking down on everything too. Part of the reason I had ended up on top of the Math and Science building yesterday. I couldn't remember seeing Decklin though. Someone like her would stick out. "You just got here? Did you miss morning classes?"

"Yeah. That's a shitload of points, right? I already got the lecture. I blame my parents. They got lost, and we had to stay at some motel in the boonies. Then this morning, they overslept." She lined up the pencils on her desk as she spoke. "And of course they had to spend an hour saying goodbye and hugging me to death. What about you? Did your mom totally freak out on you?"

"She didn't come. She doesn't leave the house much," I said. *Or at all.* I picked a piece of fuzz from my sweater. The bed creaked every time I moved. Every time I breathed.

"Is she sick?" She leapt out of the chair, seized an armful of clothes out of the duffel bag, and shoved them in the top drawer of her dresser.

"No. She's just kind of… paranoid. About stuff." I'd already said too much. Decklin stopped what she was doing and glared at me, waiting for more.

"That's vague," she said when I didn't continue. "Don't feel like sharing? Don't worry. My mother smokes pot in the bathroom and listens to Peter Frampton. Anyway, I'm starving. Are you starving? Let's go get something to eat. Mingle with our peers." She adjusted her shirt in the mirror, turned, and looked at herself over her shoulder.

"I think we have to wait until lunch block. I'm not sure—"

"Don't be dumb. They're not going to turn away two hungry, hormonal females. You have a free period, right?"

"I was dropping my books. I'm supposed to be at study hall."

Decklin rolled her eyes. "Live a little." She talked to me from the perspective of experience, I could tell. She was the kind of girl I fantasized about trading lives with, the kind I'd seen on television or walking down the street. Such promise of lightness, of adventure, of not caring about what's beyond the next moment.

I shook my head, sorry to let her down already. "I'm already out a bunch of points. And the calc teacher has my cell phone."

She eyed me carefully, disappointment creasing the smooth skin around her eyes. "All right, fine. I'll walk you to study hall." She tucked her phone into her bra. "I have no idea how to get around this place. And I'm trying to avoid Hendricks. She has it out for me already."

I could only imagine. "Are you going to change?"

"Are you?"

I contemplated my bland outfit, a cookie cutter of every other white shirt, blue skirt Meryton girl. "We have to wear this."

"Oh bullshit. What are they going to do? Kick me out?"

"Possibly?"

She laughed—this high, tinkling sound—and produced a wrinkled white blouse from her dresser. I dropped my books on my desk and rummaged through my bag while she shed her shorts and peeled off her fishnets, dropping them in a pile by the closet.

"What made you choose Meryton?" I grabbed a blank notebook and a pen.

"I like to go where the action is, obviously."

We both laughed. Decklin wrestled on a tight blue skirt and laced up her boots. "No, seriously though. Some unseen force pulled me here. What about you?"

"That about sums it up for me too." I shoved my hands in my pockets so I wouldn't keep fiddling with everything. I hated to lie, but what else could I tell her? That two old guys from Orientation had tracked the Conduit to this area and purposely initiated Adam to lure the Conduit in? I would have had to create flashcards or something just so she could follow.

"Let me guess." She batted her long eyelashes. "Your boyfriend goes here?"

"If I'm lucky." I thought of Brandon's chestnut eyes. Then, for some reason, I thought of Adam.

Decklin stood in front of the closet mirror and took her hair out of the elastics. It tumbled down her back like those women in the shampoo ads. "How do I look?"

"Obscenely normal." I regarded her in her blue and white Meryton regimentals. "A walking paradox."

"I feel like a lion in a business suit." She unbuttoned her top button and flashed a devious smile. "Ready?" She didn't put her hair back up, much to my disappointment.

I started heading for the door when it swung open.

"Oh." Betsy hugged her books to her chest, her eyes darting from me to Decklin. "Mira, I just dropped by to see if you wanted to walk with me. I see your roommate showed up."

"Decklin, this is Betsy."

Decklin issued an exuberant hello. Betsy didn't make a move, just flashed a quick smile and hugged her books tighter.

"Not Cassidy?" She stood in the doorway, addressing only me. She wore the navy blue Meryton issue skirt and dark socks that came up to her knees, a look I could never pull off. She had buttoned her white blouse up to her neck and pinned a bright pink rose to her collar. For some reason, I imagined Decklin sizing her up and judging her, but maybe I was the one doing that.

"There was a mix up or something. We were just getting to know each other." The three of us stood there staring at each other. I tugged at my too-tight collar and tried to think of a polite way to dismiss Betsy. "Maybe I'll catch you later?"

Betsy stared at me, then flashed a quick grin. "Sure." She gave Decklin a final once-over before turning and disappearing into the hall. I had to stop myself from calling after her.

"Look at you making friends left and right. I never had a knack for that at all." Decklin pushed ahead of me through the door and waited while I pulled it shut.

Somehow I found it hard to believe that Decklin had any trouble attracting people.

We walked to the library together, through the quad and past a bunch of boys who gawked at Decklin like they wanted to eat her up. I practically disappeared next to her.

"This is me." I nodded toward the library, an immense and foreboding stone building with a high-arched entryway and a bell tower.

"So you're deserting me. I'll let it go, but just this once." She glanced around the small campus. "Can you at least point me toward the dining hall?"

"It's the only one-story building, there." I pointed down the hill toward the glass structure.

"Thanks," Decklin said. "And hey, I'm excited about this year. We're going to have a lot of adventures." She smiled, revealing dazzling white teeth.

As I walked away, I caught sight of Betsy standing alone against the brick of the Math and Science building. I raised my hand in a wave, but she must not have seen me because she didn't wave back.

Chapter Five

I waited until I heard Decklin's slow, steady breathing above me before I slipped from my bed, pulled a sweatshirt over my head, and unlocked the door. I left my ID on the desk, since I didn't plan on going out the front door. The system tracked each time I came in or out, and I didn't want to leave a trace.

Tiptoeing past the closed doors of the sleeping girls on my floor, I expected to run smack into purse-lipped Hendricks at any moment. I couldn't imagine how many points this would cost me.

I inched past the common room, peeking behind me once to make sure no one had followed me, and headed for the basement. The nightlight in the corner cast a long shadow across the ceiling. Water dripped from the faucet next to the dryer. At the back of the room, in the faint light, I could barely make out the supply closet door. The door clicked open when I turned the knob. I closed it behind me and made my way over to the window, which was little smaller and a little higher than I had imagined.

I boosted myself up to the second shelf so I could peer outside. There was a three-foot drop, but nothing I couldn't handle. I launched myself through headfirst into the night, landing on the wet grass and rolling to an awkward stop.

The stars Polaris and Arcturus hung above me in the night sky. If I waited long enough, I might have seen Cetus rise. I looked for it, low hanging in the sky, remembering the feel of my father's heavy astronomy book resting on my lap and the smell of the thick, illustrated pages. I would turn to the page dedicated to Cetus the Whale—the constellation containing my star. My father would read the words aloud, and I would follow them with my finger. *Mira travels along at 291,000 miles per hour, three-hundred and fifty light-years from Earth.* I remember closing my eyes, almost able to feel the fiery tail trailing behind me. That's the way my father had made me feel. Significant.

A twig snapped under my feet, jolting me back to the present. I stuffed my hands in my pockets and walked in shadow toward the Math and Science building.

By the time I approached the building, the wet grass had soaked through my socks. A slight wind blew through the trees. The scent of pine sap filled the air, and tree frogs called to each other across the field. Nothing moved. Nothing dark and malicious interrupted my journey into the calm of the night. I stood alone, deep in a field, way past curfew, yearning for something to happen. If the Conduit were here, now would be the perfect time. He could take advantage of me wandering campus alone at night, and I could finally stand and face him. When nothing happened, disappointment flooded through me.

The heavy wood and cast iron doors to the Math and Science building creaked open as I pushed them, revealing a dimly lit hallway with exit signs glowing red. I took the stairs to the second floor and felt my way along the wall, aware of every sound echoing in this ancient hallway. My wet footsteps broke the eerie silence of the building. I sped up until I stood before Dolby's locked door.

I took the hairpin from my loose bun, wiggled it around in the lock a bit until it clicked into place, and turned the knob. A thrill ran through me. Old doors, old locks. Meryton wasn't exactly high security. I'm sure they didn't expect this kind of thing.

The hairpin dropped to the tile as I eased the door open. Dropping to my knees, I felt around for it but finally gave up. Girls dropped those things all the time. I made it to the desk and opened a few drawers before I found it: a cell phone goldmine. How many kids had to place their phones in his meaty palm today? I dug through the drawer looking for mine—a simple black case amid striped and bedazzled cases, not too hard to locate. I headed for the door, phone in hand, already feeling better.

As soon as I stepped outside, a figure emerged from the shadows. I jumped back and gasped, clutching my phone to my chest. When I saw who it was, I let out a huge exhale.

"A little late, aren't you?" I approached Larry, sliding my phone into my pocket.

"I was here the whole time. I'm just better at not getting caught." Larry smirked, but his face wrinkled with concern.

"Where's Adam?" The late summer night had turned so cool I could see my breath.

"In his room. Like you should be."

"I should be in Adam's room? You know that's against the rules."

Larry raised an eyebrow.

I shrugged. "I needed my phone."

He put his hands on his hips. "You should have let us handle it, Mira. I don't like it, you all alone out here."

"You have to let me do some of the fun stuff." I patted my pocket and headed toward the dorms. "Otherwise I get bored."

"Hurry back now," Larry called behind me. "I'll be watching."

"That's not creepy at all," I muttered and started across the field. For a moment, the constant sense of urgency inside me quieted, and I let myself enjoy the chorus of late summer bugs whirring in the trees, the cool, wet grass, the smell of fresh air. *If only this moment could stretch to last forever.* That way, I wouldn't have to deal with banishing the Conduit or saving the world.

But nothing lasted forever. That was a plus when it came to math class or the flu. When it came to people though, it was heart wrenching. I'd lost my father, and I didn't plan on losing anyone else. I needed laser focus to avoid making the same mistake he had.

Something shiny in the grass caught my attention.

At first, I thought someone had dropped a pack of gum. Or cigarettes maybe. But when I walked closer, I froze.

"Hey!" Someone rested their hands on my shoulders. I knew at once it wasn't Hal because I didn't recognize the voice. I swung my fist around, hoping to connect at a meaningful place. My fist met the hard angle of a collarbone, and I recoiled in pain. It took a second for my brain to catch up with my body.

"Ow!" Brandon clutched his collarbone, feigning injury.

"You asshole! You surprised me." My knuckles throbbed. I hid my hand behind my back. "What are you doing out here?"

It was the middle of the night. Had he been watching me? *Following me?* Maybe Adam was right. I took a step back and braced myself, ready to run if I needed to.

"Well, at least we know you can defend yourself. I'm impressed." He shook his head and smiled. That smile lit a firecracker in the pit of my stomach. No way Brandon was the Conduit.

"One of my boys got us a twelve pack. There's a spot right over there." He pointed toward the pine trees. "Where the cameras can't see you."

"There are cameras?" Larry never said anything about cameras. I ducked, shielding myself with my arms, and backed into the shadows to have a look. There, mounted on the corner of the building, obvious even in the dark, a surveillance camera pointed toward the quad. I had never even noticed.

I straightened up while Brandon watched me, grinning broadly. "You look like you're on some sort of a secret mission."

"I'm a night owl." I opened and shut my hand to make sure it wasn't broken. It wasn't. "Couldn't sleep. It's kind of claustrophobic in my room, especially with someone else in there. Someone I barely know."

"I've got a single." Brandon raised an eyebrow. An invitation? "And even I get claustrophobic."

"Why wouldn't you just drink in your room?"

"Not worth the risk. Plus, what a night, right?"

I nodded. Yes, what a night. Any other girl would have called it romantic, but I wasn't any other girl. To me, the night hid terrors just out of sight. Although standing there with Brandon, it was too easy to let down my guard, to let myself relax. To become that *other girl*.

A whistle floated between the pines, along with the distinct sound of someone clearing his throat. Brandon ignored it, focusing his attention on me instead.

"Come with me." He offered his hand.

I shook my head. "I can't. You better get back. Your beer is waiting."

"Beer is amazingly patient."

"Well, it's chilly." I wrapped my arms around myself and feigned a shiver, though I was burning up.

"Okay, I can take a hint." He looked down. "Hey, you dropped your ID."

I followed his gaze to the ground, and my mouth fell open. I had totally forgotten about the card. I scooped it up and slipped it into the back pocket of my jeans. An icy coldness spread through me. I didn't even have to look at it. A fleeting glance at the smiling blonde in the small, square picture, and I knew who it belonged to. Cassidy Ellis, my mysteriously-absent roommate.

"You're really pretty, Mira Avery."

My head snapped up. I hadn't noticed how tall Brandon was until now, as he towered over me. "And you're very bold."

His eyes lingered. "Life's too short for anything else. Have breakfast with me tomorrow."

I struggled to keep my voice steady. "Don't we all eat at the same time?"

"I mean find me. Sit next to me. Or across from me. Anything."

When I hesitated, he tilted his head. "Come on. I practically saved your life yesterday. That ball could have hit you in the temple, knocked you flat dead."

My heart continued to race. The card practically burned a hole in my back pocket. As much as I wanted to stand there with Brandon all night, I had to get back to my room. I had to think.

I relented. "Okay. Okay. But I have to go now."

He stood a moment longer. His gaze moved to my lips, and I froze in place, thinking at any moment he was going to pull me to him and kiss me. Thinking of the way his lips might feel on mine.

"Be careful." He pointed to the camera before he melted into the darkness. "They're everywhere."

❀ ❀ ❀

I scraped my legs when I launched myself back through the window, but thanks to my father's alien blood, I'd heal by morning. It came in handy with papercuts and cat scratches, but I'd never really tested it on major wounds. The whole super healing thing seemed kind of worthless to me. It would have been cooler if I could become invisible or read people's thoughts. Then I might have known what Brandon really thought of me and why he looked at me like he did. I felt like an idiot standing there, thinking he was going to kiss me. Wanting him to.

I entered my room as stealthily as possible, but I slipped on a rogue pencil and hit my elbow on the corner of my dresser. Decklin breathed loudly in her bunk. A soft breeze fluttered the pages of the notebook on my desk.

"He was looking for you."

Already on edge, I jumped at the sound of Decklin's voice.

"Did I wake you up?" Adrenaline raced through my veins. I focused on plugging in my phone so she couldn't see my face.

"No." Decklin rose to her elbows and clicked on her lamp. Even in the dead of night, she looked amazing. "Brandon did."

My heart gave a whack against the inside of my chest. "Brandon was here? In our room?" So much for coincidence.

"He saw me in my underwear." Her voice sounded bored, as if guys seeing her in her underwear occurred nightly. Maybe it did.

"No doubt the thrill of his high school career." If he saw Decklin in her underwear, what chance did I have? My heart sank. No wonder he didn't kiss me. She was the swan, and I was the ugly duckling.

"And where were you, Miss Avery?"

I held up my phone in mock triumph, wishing she would just go back to sleep.

"No you didn't." Decklin slapped the side of the bed with both hands and let out a whoop. "You are a badass!"

"Sure did." I slipped my wet sneakers off all casually, reveling in satisfaction. "You think I was going to wait around until the end of the week?" When I threw my jeans over the back of the chair, the ID fell out onto the floor.

My heart stopped. I stared at it. Thin and rectangular and real. "This is so strange."

"What?" Decklin bent over the side of the bed to see what held my attention.

Blonde as everything, the girl smiled at me from behind the clear laminate. *Cassidy M. Ellis. Senior, Meryton Preparatory Academy.* The hair on the back of my neck stood on end.

"What is it?" Decklin asked.

"It's Cassidy's ID." I held it up for her to see. "I found it on the ground in the quad. That means Cassidy is here. Or was." I gnawed on my thumbnail.

Decklin yawned and stretched. "She must have been assigned to a different room."

"Yeah, maybe. But don't you think it's a coincidence that I found this?"

"I don't believe in coincidences." Decklin flopped onto her back and out of view. "Anyway, too bad for her. Lost IDs are a ten dollar processing fee."

Chapter Six

In my foggy, half dream state, I heard Decklin's alarm go off. I heard her rustle through her drawers for clothes, followed by the silent concentration of her zipping, tucking, and tying her shoes. I heard her close the door behind her and knew I was late, but I couldn't command my exhausted body to get up. When I finally did open my eyes, the light streaming through the shades told me it was later than I'd hoped, and a glance at my phone confirmed that suspicion. I texted my mother as I ran for the dining hall:

Still nothing.

That wasn't entirely true, but I couldn't exactly explain everything mid-stride. Cassidy's ID rode along in the zipped inside pocket of my backpack. I'd give it to her if I saw her.

I finished dropping a scoop of pale yellow powdered eggs onto my plate and scanned the cafeteria. At a small table near the back doors, I spotted Brandon and began to move in his direction. I yanked my hair into place with one hand and balanced my tray with the other. Halfway there, I stopped.

Decklin sat across from him, engaged in a hearty, open-mouthed laugh that showed her perfect teeth. I almost dropped my tray. I thought the two of us were supposed to have breakfast together. Alone. Now I would have to plaster on a smile and pretend my insides weren't roiling with jealousy. I loosened my grip on the tray and reminded myself I wasn't there to find a boyfriend.

"Maybe I'm not looking for a fulfilling relationship," Decklin was saying as I slid into the empty seat between her and Brandon. She wore her hair down and parted to the side, which took away some of that high school rebel thing she had going on but didn't make her any less striking.

"Did I miss something?" I attempted to sound upbeat, but my voice came out flat.

Brandon leaned toward me and whispered in my ear, "*Omicron ceti.*" I broke out in goosebumps. He straightened up, his eyes sparkling with the secret of how he knew the scientific name of *Mira*. He must have Googled it. Must have read that it went by *Mira the Wonderful*, a red giant shedding debris from its tail as it rocketed through space.

Maybe I did stand a chance. I looked him right in the eyes and tried to dazzle him with my smile. He smiled back.

"What were you guys talking about?" I ripped open a packet of salt and sprinkled it on the pale yellow eggs, suddenly ravenous.

"Decklin is on the prowl. I told her she had her pick." Of course Brandon meant boys. She had her pick of a hundred boys. Boys talking with their mouths full, quiet boys bent over books or laptops, skaters, hipsters, preps. I recognized some of their faces now from class, from the hallways. None of them meant anything to me.

"I'll take *him*."

I heard the awe in Decklin's voice and looked up. My fork didn't quite make it to my mouth. There in the doorway, looking as lost as ever, stood Adam. He wore the same white shirt, the same wrinkled blue pants, the same dope-eyed grin that, for whatever reason, made my blood rush. If he saw me, he didn't let on. He lowered his head and rounded the corner. Larry trailed him, not far behind, his bulk taking up half the hallway.

"My God." Decklin fanned herself. "I am in love. Did you see that boy?"

I stammered out an answer. "He's not that great. Kind of...tall." I should have kept my mouth shut. I didn't want Decklin anywhere near Adam. The water from my eggs ran into a lump of undercooked potatoes.

Brandon leaned back in his chair and rubbed his hands together. "That's Adam. You two would be perfect together."

I feigned disinterest despite the twist in my stomach. At least Brandon hadn't fallen for Decklin, but I knew what he meant, and why Decklin and Adam were perfect together. They would make a stunning couple, have beautiful perfect children together, and we'd all bow in reverence. Since crawling under the table to hide would have gotten me pegged as the *weird girl*, I refrained.

The giant clock on the wall showed nine minutes until calculus. I willed time to move faster. I longed for the sight of Dolby's mustache, for the feel of the pencil in my hand as I struggled through the chain rule.

With dexterous fingers, Decklin braided the hair that fell over her shoulder. "Do you think he's my type?"

"What, two legs and breathing?" Brandon clicked his teeth and winked.

"Two legs, one leg. I don't discriminate."

They went back and forth as if they'd known each other for years. I wanted to pound my fists on the table. I could never carry on so smooth a conversation with someone I'd just met. Decklin told me she'd had so many boyfriends she lost count. Her father had been in the military, so they'd moved around a lot. Each city, each town, each base brought a new boy, and each time they moved was an easy out. I felt out of my league sitting between them, like a watercolor on a motel room wall, boring and unassuming and hardly worth a look.

"Adam's kind of dim," I interrupted. "And anyway, he's an exchange student. He won't be around for long."

"Even better. And brains don't matter when you're that hot." Decklin smirked. She rested her hand on mine and squeezed. "Mira, there's nothing wrong with having a little fun. Isn't that what you were after last night? Breaking curfew and sneaking around. Admit you were after a thrill." She picked away at her nail polish and watched each student emerge from the food line.

Five minutes to calc.

"Decklin, we have to go." I hadn't eaten a thing, and the orange juice sat heavy in my stomach.

"We've got four minutes." Brandon held up four fingers and started to count down. "Thirty seconds to drop our trays, a minute to sprint across the quad, and thirty more seconds to find the classroom and slide into our seats. That gives me exactly two minutes to tell you my idea." Brandon pushed back from the table, slapping down both hands at once, a big grin on his face. "Let's go camping. The four of us."

"What four of us?" I asked, alarm bells going off in my head.

"Camping?" Decklin scratched her head. "You mean like in the woods? In a tent?"

Brandon nodded. "City girls are fun to take in the woods."

"What four of us?" I asked again. Decklin, with her sculpted eyebrows and black eyeliner, bedding down in a sleeping bag next to Adam? No way.

"My mom would never let me." I crossed my arms over my chest.

"Mira." Brandon tipped his chair toward me and took both of my hands in his own. His touch sent a shockwave down into the pit of my stomach. How could anyone resist his smooth hands, his pleading eyes, his crooked smile? A small burst of fireworks exploded inside me.

"You don't have to tell your mom. Think of it—nature, isolation, a cramped tent, and a chilly night. We can spend some time together away from all this pressure." He must have noticed my sweaty hands. But his were sweaty too.

"I'm up for anything." Decklin shrugged. "My parents don't care what the hell I do."

The sounds of banging trays and pushed out chairs filled the cafeteria. Students began to file out of the doors before first bell.

"It's settled then. Next weekend," Brandon said.

"Why not this weekend?" Decklin asked.

"I've got a game. Next weekend works better."

Even though I hadn't agreed, I knew it was inevitable. I pictured driving stakes into the ground, gathering sticks, roasting marshmallows, and sleeping next to a boy who liked me enough to Google my name. Never mind Adam and Decklin. Imagining Larry and Hal squatting just at the edge of the darkness, cursing the mosquitoes, gave me kind of a kick. I mean, they could have told me there were cameras last night.

"We'll leave next Friday after study hall." Brandon drummed his fingers on the table, a gleam in his eyes. "I'll hook us up with some beverages. God, it will be good to get out of here, to breathe for a second."

"Yeah, okay. It will be fun." It seemed like a normal teenage thing to do, and that's what I wanted. And at least it would keep Adam close. Maybe it was just the thing to lure the Conduit out of hiding. I ignored the pit in my stomach and resigned myself to the idea.

"Mira, can you ask Adam if he'll go? Bait him with Decklin. Really play her up."

Decklin tossed her hair. "I need playing up?"

"Play her up a bit." Brandon slid out of his seat and hiked his bag over his shoulder. He offered me his hand, and I took it as natural as anything, though I wanted to spin cartwheels across the floor.

"I'm gonna use the facilities first. Save me a seat." Before he left us to go the opposite direction, he kissed my knuckles. I almost walked straight into the door.

"Smile much?" Decklin raised her eyebrows at me. "You know, I really don't see the appeal of sleeping outside." We blended into the current of students streaming out of the building. If Adam lingered behind us somewhere, I couldn't tell. I held my bag carefully so as not to brush Brandon's kiss away.

"Technically, you're in a tent."

Clouds blotted out the sun entirely, and the breeze felt crisp through my cotton blouse. The bell at the top of the library began to chime the hour, which meant I had half a minute, maybe. Dozens of students flooded into the Math and Science building in their Meryton blue and white.

"A thin layer of nylon separating me from whatever is creeping around out there? It gives me the shivers."

"I thought you liked creepy," I reminded her.

"Creepy, yes. Bears, no."

"Don't worry. I spent a lot of summers camping when I was little. Never saw a bear." It was technically true. I heard a bear once, when I was nine. My father unzipped the tent to look, and it ran away. I hadn't been camping since.

"Don't you think Brandon's moving too fast?" I asked as we ascended the concrete steps and walked through the large open doors.

"Only because he knows what he wants." Decklin grinned. "We should all be so lucky."

I had zero experience with boys, so I took what she said as fact. "But he doesn't even know me."

Decklin shook her head, like she knew some big secret about life that I didn't. "Doesn't matter. You don't have to know each other at all. Ever heard of love at first sight? One glance, and something inside both of you just... clicks. Then *boom*. Resistance is futile."

"No way. That only happens in movies."

"Really? Then how do you explain Adam?"

Without thinking, I blurted, "That click I felt with Adam wasn't love. It was..."

Decklin frowned at me. "I was talking about me."

I cleared my throat. "Yeah, I know."

The last bell rang before I could dig myself any deeper. "I have to go."

I could see the numbers on the door. I could practically smell the wax on Mr. Dolby's mustache. But Decklin slipped her hand around my arm and stopped me. The color drained from her face as if she had sprung a leak, and then the color returned, starting at her chest and working its way up to her neck and her cheeks. I recognized that shade of cheek-flush red. I knew it intimately.

"Oh my God, there he is." Her voice had dropped an octave.

Adam strode toward us, his eyes moving between Decklin and me, his hands dangling at his sides in that awkward, not-quite-right manner of his. The three of us were the only ones left in the hall. I rubbed my forehead and forced myself to breathe.

"Adam, right?" Decklin said when he approached, before I had a chance to intervene. "I'm Decklin."

Adam said nothing, even as I urged him under my breath to act normal.

"Do you speak English?" Decklin said.

Adam nodded and smiled. "Yes."

"Feel like going camping next weekend?" Decklin's boldness had no bounds.

Adam shifted his weight from one foot to the other and looked sidelong at me, no doubt waiting for some kind of cue. I nodded, eyeing my classroom.

"I'll have physics and calculus to study," he said, obviously not picking up on the hint.

"Sounds boring." Decklin twisted a ringlet around her finger. I wanted to barf. "Come with us instead. Physics and calculus aren't going anywhere. I mean they've been here for hundreds of years."

"Thousands." I tried to calm my nerves with deep, slow breaths. He had to say yes. I willed him to say yes. He couldn't stay here while I traipsed into the woods for a weekend.

"Listen, camping's not really my thing either. It was Brandon's idea. Do you remember Brandon?" She spoke to him like she would speak to a child. It annoyed me, but I probably did the same thing. "But it's better than hanging around this dump. We'll build a campfire and do a bunch of other campy things that people supposedly do. Maybe roast some marsh—"

"Okay." Adam caught my eye. "I'll go."

"Great," both Decklin and I said at the same time.

I breathed a sigh of relief and brushed past them to open the door. Everyone in the class turned to look at me, including the dour-faced Mr. Dolby. I took an empty seat near the front. Heads turned once again as Adam walked in and chose the desk next to me. Larry must have gotten him into this class so I could keep an eye on him. I didn't know why my hands shook. I barely looked up when Brandon squeezed through the door.

"Nice of you three to join us." Mr. Dolby wrote something in a book on his desk and went back to droning on about... honestly I had no idea. I did not hear a word. The clock ticked, and time moved forward as it always did, no matter how much I wanted it to just stop for a minute so I could exhale.

Camping. Out in the middle of the woods, in one tent, the four of us. Adam's presence beside me was as tangible as my knuckles on the wood desk... the knuckles that Brandon had kissed. I commanded the two halves of me to stop battling it out, stop knocking around my guts.

"Camping wasn't my idea," I whispered out of the side of my mouth when Dolby had his back to everyone. "But you have to go. It might draw the Conduit out."

"I know." Adam spoke loud enough to attract Dolby's attention. I sunk down in my seat and tried to become invisible. After class, Dolby called me to the front of the room and slapped something down on his desk. A bobby pin. My bobby pin.

"This belong to you?" He tapped his fingernail on the hair accessory in question.

"Nope."

He stared at me for a long time. The next bell rang. He raised his eyebrows, and I raised mine.

"See you Thursday," he said. I was the last one out of the classroom, but thankfully, no one had waited for me.

❖ ❖ ❖

I dialed my mother's number and reclined on my bed. I pictured her sitting on the floor of the living room with her scissors, looking for whatever article or obituary would determine our next town, our next state.

She answered on the first ring. "Mira, thank god." Relief saturated her voice. "Any sign of the Conduit?"

I sighed. "It's great to hear from you too. School is going fine. Thanks for asking."

"Sorry. You don't know what it's like, sitting here all day waiting for the phone to ring."

She had me there. My mother wasn't used to being alone, and she wasn't used to being left out of the details. I had to cut to the chase anyway because Decklin would be back any second.

"We haven't seen the Conduit. Shouldn't he have made an appearance by now? The others, you said they were all evacuated within minutes of initiation. It's been days." The random sounds of the dorm floated through my open door: girls' footsteps in the hall, closing doors, a distant flushing toilet. The metal springs in my mattress pressed against my back.

"I don't know any more than you do." Her voice echoed faintly through the phone, a reminder of the distance between us. "The Conduit must have been there waiting when each Initiate woke. Maybe he was tipped off somehow."

"Someone on the inside. Someone in Orientation." Hal's tight frown flashed in my mind. But Larry trusted Hal, and my mother and I trusted Larry. I wouldn't even think of suggesting such a betrayal.

"So if the Conduit doesn't show up, what next?" I leaned over and peeked through the slats of my blinds. "How will we get Dad back?" My voice cracked at the end of the sentence.

Last summer, they thought they had the Conduit. Orientation had performed three initiations around Thibodeaux. After all three Initiates disappeared, they called us in. We'd squatted in a trailer in the middle of a swamp for a month waiting him out, but he evaded us once again. That's when my mother started thinking someone tipped him off. It was too convenient. Each time we started closing in, things would suddenly go quiet.

That's why we needed bait.

"He will come for this one." My mother's confidence both inspired and frustrated me. Everything seemed like such a waste, a dead end. From time to time, I secretly wondered if it was all worth it. No one had ever seen the Conduit. So how did we know he wasn't among us already?

"Or we'll just keep doing this." If it didn't work out with Adam, they would send me somewhere else. I was so tired of moving. Across the room, I looked at the pictures Decklin had tacked to the wall: a Hubble photo of Earth, a creepy character from some zombie movie, a few inspirational quotes from magazines. She was settled in already. I would never dream of putting up pictures, only because I dreaded the act of taking them down again.

My mother stated, "Yes, we will keep doing this." The sound of running water drowned out the rest of her sentence.

"Are you in the shower or something?"

"I'm doing dishes."

"Can you do them after we get off the phone? I have limited time. The cell phone rules here are ridiculous."

"I'm trying to keep busy." She turned off the faucet. "Otherwise, I worry too much."

We hadn't been apart this long, ever. I had homework and class and hardly a minute to myself. Being so busy kept my homesickness at bay, for the most part. My mother had the four walls of our tiny home. The thought squeezed my insides like someone had just tightened a belt around me.

"You should take advantage of being alone. Watch those movies you like, read some books, boondoggle, bake cookies."

"Boondoggle," she laughed. I seldom heard my mother laugh. It had disappeared with my father. I closed my eyes and tried to remember her smile. Her real smile. "And for your information, I did make cookies. That's why I was doing dishes."

"You made cookies? You never make cookies. Can you send me some? The food here is crap."

"You'll survive."

"That's the plan."

In the silence that followed, I pulled out Cassidy's ID and ran it over my knuckles, the same thing magicians did with cards. I'd learned it as a little girl and had never forgotten it.

"There is a possibility." I told her about Brandon, that Adam suspected he was the Conduit. I left out how Brandon's muscles strained against his shirt, how his deep brown eyes looked straight into me, how his lips felt brushing against my skin.

"He doesn't sound like a Conduit," my mother said.

"He doesn't act like one. He has a ton of friends; he cracks jokes all the time." And he likes me. He *likes* me.

"Go with your gut. And be patient, Mira. The Conduit will show up. He has to. If he leaves one Initiate—just one—it would be a total failure. He wouldn't be that careless."

Thank God my mother had no radar for impending romance. I switched the phone to my other ear and thought a moment before I spoke, tracing a crack in the wall with the tip of my finger. Meryton gave a nice impression from far away, but when I got real close up, I realized the whole place was falling apart.

"I've made a couple friends." I was careful to temper the excitement in my voice as I told her about Decklin and Betsy.

"Good for you."

I silently thanked her for not warning me about getting too attached.

"Hey, who are you talking to?"

I jerked my head around to see Decklin standing over me. I hadn't even heard the door open. I cursed myself for my lack of vigilance.

"Mom, I have to go. I'll call you later." I hung up before my mother could protest.

I sat up and glared at Decklin. "Were you a cat in your previous life?"

"I hope not. I hate cats. And I hate these goddamn uniforms." Decklin unbuttoned her shirt, took it off, and climbed up onto her bed in a white tank top, the tip of a tattoo visible above her shirt.

"Anyway, I don't believe in previous lives. It's the here and now, baby." She draped herself over the side of the bed so her hair made a wavy curtain as it hung toward the floor. "Now who are you texting?"

"Cassidy. I haven't seen her around at all, and no one seems to know her. She's not answering my texts, and I still have her ID. It's kind of a mystery."

"Ease up, Sherlock. We have more important things to discuss."

She sprung from the bed and landed on the floor in bare feet. Out the window, I heard the cadence of short whistle blasts coming from the fields, and I got up to look. Mid-morning drills. Thank God I didn't have gym until second quarter. If I was here that long.

Decklin straddled her desk chair, gazed levelly at me, and demanded, "Tell me about Adam."

My face grew hot. "Now? I have to go to class."

"You have time," Decklin said. "Come on. Give me something to hold me over."

I sighed, knowing I'd have to give her something or she'd never let it drop. "What do you want to know?"

"Everything."

Where did I begin? The part where Orientation aided in the transfer of Adam from his other body—somewhere *out there*—to the one he's in now, which happens to be the husk of a former miner killed in a mine collapse and stolen from the morgue?

"He's from Iceland, and he likes pizza."

Her eyes lit up. "Iceland, right. What else?"

"That's about it. I've known him for a few days."

Decklin stared at me with such intensity she might have been better off drilling a hole into my forehead and peering inside with a headlamp.

"Do you have a thing for him?"

The words punched me in the gut, but I couldn't show it. I wished she would stop looking at me like that. Like she knew everything I said was some stretched version of the truth.

"No. What makes you say that?"

"I saw the way you two eyeballed each other." Her green eyes blazed.

"You're reading into things." I struggled to meet her eyes, too afraid of giving everything away. "Anyway, I like Brandon."

"All right. Don't get your panties in a bunch." Decklin yawned. "Brandon's kind of white bread, but that's fine if it's what you're into. Oh, and I ran into your friend in the hallway."

"Betsy?" I'd been trying to keep Betsy away from Decklin. The two of them were polar opposites, and I could only navigate one friendship at a time.

"She totally avoided me. So of course I went right up to her and said hello. I told her we should all hang out. But not next weekend, because we're camping."

"You told her we were going camping?" I put my palm to my forehead.

"Did I do something wrong?" Decklin batted her long eyelashes at me.

"No. It's just that she asked me to go into town next weekend."

"Ouch," Decklin said. "Sorry."

My stomach sank, but at the same time, my heart raced. These were real teenage problems. My phone buzzed in my pocket.

"Miss Popularity," Decklin said without a hint of sarcasm.

I looked down at my phone. The text from Larry read:

Midnight. Meet at the clearing.

Thank God. Because things here were starting to get too complicated.

Chapter Seven

I slipped out unseen just before midnight, bundled in my Michigan State sweatshirt, and made my way across the parking lot. A crooked sign at the edge of the grass marked the entrance to the trail. I jammed my hands into my pockets and crept forward, leaving the lit campus behind. After a few steps, the darkness of the woods swallowed me. The trees blocked out the moonlight, and I could barely see a foot in front of me.

"Larry?" I whispered, turning a full circle. Something rustled in the bushes to my right. A mosquito buzzed near my ear.

"Up here." Just as I began to lose my nerve, Larry's voice floated down from somewhere above. I headed up the trail toward his voice, using my phone to light the way. From the look of it, no one had used this path in a long time. I schlepped through the damp undergrowth, where I knew crawly things oozed and tickled and slithered. I imagined their carapaces and antennae, their slimy segmented bodies. Every so often, interrupting the unnerving quiet, I heard the snapping of twigs in the distance. Alone in the woods at night with no visible sky, just the outlines of trees, I felt things I couldn't fathom staring out from eyes I couldn't see. My leg muscles tightened, preparing my body to run.

I turned the corner at the top of the hill and let out a sigh of relief. Larry, Hal, and Adam stood silhouetted against the slate gray night sky. The yellow half-moon hung in the background, propped up by the peak of a distant mountain. The view served a welcome contrast to the deep woods I had just stumbled out of. Night birds called from the trees as I rounded the crest. Adam stood with his hands in his pockets, Larry's round figure next to him, and Hal in back, as thin and angular as a tree himself.

"I hope you guys brought bug spray." My teeth chattered as I approached them. "I'm getting eaten alive."

Larry stepped forward into the moonlight. "The plan is to wait in the trees. Leave Adam here and see if the Conduit takes the bait."

I watched Adam and thought of that poor goat in *Jurassic Park*, the one they used to coax the T-Rex into the open. Adam didn't look scared. His face betrayed no emotion. I wondered if he felt anything at all.

"It's been too long." He spoke like the rest of us. No trace of an accent. The ability to adapt quickly was necessary for his survival, like a foal that gets to its feet right after it's born. "You'd think the Conduit would be here by now. Unless he's moved on?"

Larry itched his scalp and stared down at the ground. "Nah. He hasn't moved on. I've heard from the others. There hasn't been another evacuation since you initiated."

We were silent for a second as this news sank in.

"You mean the Conduit has evacuated all the rest of them?" I asked under my breath.

Larry nodded.

"That's impossible. Hundreds were sent down into bodies over the years." I looked around, desperate, as if I'd suddenly catch a glimpse of our mortal enemy darting behind a tree or something.

Hal had stayed quiet the whole time, his giant lanky figure a prop in the background just taking up space. He stepped forward. "Think about it. They're supposed to keep coming until their species has completely deserted wherever they live... up there. But if the Senders feel they're in danger here as well, they're gonna stop sending Initiates, Mira."

Which meant Adam was the last one. And if Adam was the last one, we couldn't fail.

Larry offered nothing else, but he probably knew plenty. They probably both did, as members of Orientation. According to my mother, the more I knew, the more I was in danger. If word leaked out about this little operation, all manner of government operatives would swoop down on us. Unmarked white vans. Hazmat suits. *Probes.* Just thinking about it made me tremble.

"Maybe the Conduit died." I took a deep breath of the night air to try and steady myself. "Or maybe he realized the error of his ways." Of course, this would be very bad for me, my father, and the countless Senders that had been evacuated from the bodies they inhabited. Without the Conduit, I had no hope of finding any of them, no hope of bringing them back.

Everyone knew that, and though no one said it out loud, it floated in the air around us.

"We'll try this," Hal said. "And if it doesn't work, we'll make a different plan."

Adam nodded, and the three of us headed for the woods, leaving him alone in the clearing on the hilltop like the goat tethered to the iron ring, *sans* the iron ring. Larry and Hal took their positions behind thick, knotty pines, and I crouched in a thicket that buzzed with tiny biting things.

We waited. We had nothing to do but wait. But as the minutes ticked by, each as uneventful as the last, restlessness overcame me. I had to move. I had to do something. *But what?*

Adam cast a shadow down the hill, a dark figure alone in the moonlight. I couldn't make out the features of his face, though I tried. I thought of him at initiation, what he must have experienced, how he must have acted. I wondered what his first moments in a human body felt like. My mother told me a little about how my father initiated. How he'd suddenly opened his eyes and they'd brimmed with life, how he'd watched his fingers move for a full minute before realizing he controlled them. Like an infant.

Adam removed his hands from his pockets, sat on the ground, and leaned back, lifting his face to the sky. Hard to imagine, looking at his peaceful profile, that his kind had brought about the destruction of an entire species. According to my father, his ancient ancestors had ravaged their native planet past the point of no return. They'd needed a new place to live, so they'd sent scouts into the universe in search of a new home and new bodies.

They'd found what they were looking for. A bright place where a species similar to their own thrived.

Only instead of inhabiting the dead of that species, they inhabited the living. Kicked the occupants right out of their bodies and settled in, leaving a whole mess of bodiless souls wallowing in the Dark Eternal.

My father said that's what the Conduit was: one of those souls, bent on revenge. And he somehow found his way down to Earth.

But Adam's kind—the ones we called Senders—learned from it. They evolved. They wouldn't make the same mistake again, not with humans. Hence the dead bodies. It was gross, but it was better than the alternative. Too bad the Conduit didn't see it that way.

I could smell my mother's fabric softener in the hoodie I wore, and I wondered what she was doing at home right then. Probably not battling mosquitoes. I brought the hood up over my head and swatted at the swarm of dive-bombing bugs. Every once and a while, I glanced back toward the path, thinking at any moment the Conduit's head would appear. I couldn't help but imagine Brandon, wearing his favorite cap and his tie-dyed shirt, emerging over the crest.

A large bug crashed into my forehead with a thunk.

"That's it." I stood, flailing my arms, and marched to the top of the hill where Adam sat. Larry and Hal shouted at me from their hiding spots. Hal's white hair reflected the moonlight. Some hiding spot.

"It's not going to work." I squatted next to Adam on the damp grass. "Larry and Hal are desperate. But the Conduit isn't stupid. It's obviously a trap. I'm starting to think my mother was right. There's a rat in Orientation."

"Wait." Adam looked back at the two men. "Let them hope for a little longer. Everyone is in such a hurry. But look at the view." He swept his hand across the landscape as if presenting it to me as a gift. I was surprised he would even care about such a thing.

"You want me to look at the view? What will that accomplish?" I did look though. I couldn't help it. Orion hung in the sky in front of us, the big dipper to the left. Constellations didn't change. They moved across the sky in the same predictable pattern year after year, decade after decade. These, the same stars my father had shown me through the lenses of his collected telescopes. I remembered how Saturn looked through their powerful lenses, like a tiny silhouette cut out of white construction paper.

To the right of us, Larry settled back down behind his thick tree, masked in darkness. Adam's breathing filled the gaps in the rising and falling symphony of night bugs. On the other side of the valley, a dim, orange light signified someone else's existence. An existence so far from my own it seemed otherworldly.

Next to me, Adam shifted. "I don't sleep, you know. Haven't quite figured it out. I close my eyes, lie down, and wait for sleep. But all that comes are thoughts and images. So I sit up. Then I stand up. Then I pace the room. I can't go anywhere. Sometimes I look out the window."

I thought of the boys' dorms. That one light in the window I saw night after night. I wondered if he saw me, sitting at my own window, looking out. My face burned as the blood rushed to my cheeks.

"Why are you telling me this?" It seemed too personal, like an invasion of privacy. He didn't need to share things like that, and I didn't want to hear about what he did up in his room.

A pair of bats swooped low in the clearing.

"What will you do," I said, "if the Conduit doesn't come?"

"The same thing the rest of them did before me. Live my new life."

It seemed strange to hear him refer to his life that way. "But unless he's destroyed, he'll always be a threat. Believe me, you don't want to live your life knowing something out there wants to hunt you down and extinguish you. That sums up the last seven years of my life. Constantly on the move, constantly paranoid, always vigilant. Always lying. Even to the people I want to be close to." I was referring to Betsy, Decklin, and Brandon. At least I didn't have to lie to Adam. The thought didn't bring me much comfort.

"You let your guard down once, and that could be it," I added.

A chorus of crickets increased in volume then died down just as abruptly. I picked a lone dandelion that had gone to seed and fiddled with it.

"I just want it to be over, but I'm afraid it never will be." At night, in the cover of darkness, my emotions clawed to just under the surface of my skin.

"I want it to be over too." Adam said it so softly I barely heard him. He stared straight up at the half moon. In that light, he could have been created in some kind of Orwellian factory and placed here on Earth right next to me. He was that beautiful. Too bad he was just a shell.

"You're the first one I've been this close to since my father, you know." I regarded him like I might a planet through a telescope. He didn't seem real, and that made it okay to study him. Everything about him screamed teenage boy. Yet I had sensed his true identity. In the middle of a crowd, I had picked him out. The human half of me didn't control everything after all.

"They told you not to get close to me, right?" he said. "Orientation?"

I shook my head. "It's more of an unspoken understanding. I can't get emotionally involved. We have to stand back and watch while the Conduit evacuates you, so we can follow him to wherever he's keeping all the Senders."

Did I just say emotionally involved? The stars, the fresh air, screwed with my sense of purpose. "I mean I have to keep a clear head about things."

Adam took the dandelion from me and traced it along his forearm, transfixed with everything. When had I lost that innocent curiosity?

"And what happens after that?" he asked.

"Then I'll destroy the Conduit and bring you all back."

"Mira. There were so many of us. Hundreds evacuated. You're only one person."

"The Conduit evacuated hundreds by himself because that's his mission. I can bring back hundreds by myself because that's mine. And when I find my father, he can help. He has the same ability I do." *When I find my father*, I'd said. I meant *if* I found him. That emptiness in my heart—a cut-out in the shape of my dad—tainted everything I did, everything I thought.

"And if something goes wrong?" Adam said.

"It won't." What I really meant was, *it can't*.

He tossed the weed aside. "It might. And if it does, I'll be stuck in the Dark Eternal forever."

I flinched at his mention of the one thing I had no understanding of. The Dark Eternal: the place bodiless souls wallowed. The place where the Conduit had sent my father.

I swallowed hard, steeling myself for what I knew was nothing more than groundless hope, but I wanted to comfort him. "We have it under control."

Adam turned to look at me, imploring me with the kind of eyes I had only seen in movies. "Is that what you think? Then why am I sitting on top of a hill right now, no Conduit in sight?"

Though he may have been right, he didn't call the shots here. I stood and brushed off the backs of my legs. "How about this: Enjoy it for a while. Being a normal person. Being in a body. Make the most of it because you don't know how long it will last. None of us do."

Adam gazed up at me.

"Is that what you're doing? Making the most of it?"

I wanted to kick him in the forehead.

"You're seriously asking me that when I'm trying to keep your species alive? I'm going back to my room. I've got class in the morning. And then I'm going to risk my life a little bit more to try and save yours." I turned from him and stormed down the hill. I felt him watch me disappear into the darkness.

Chapter Eight

On the way to our camping trip the next weekend, Adam's knees dug into the back of my seat for the entire drive. Decklin sat in the back with him, nestled among the backpacks, blankets, pillows, and everything else we'd thrown in last minute: toilet paper and ramen noodles and the giant cooler of beer Brandon managed to squeeze between the two of them. Adam wore a light cotton t-shirt and fitted jeans, something I'd never seen him wear. I made a mental note to thank Larry and Hal. They trailed a few miles behind us, linked in to my GPS and most likely griping about this whole trip.

The last two weeks had been so quiet, it made me wonder if the Conduit hadn't disappeared into thin air. The Meryton routine had become familiar to me. Calc got easier because Betsy had a real knack for it, and even after I stumbled through some lame excuse about not being able to hang out over the weekend, she still agreed to help me with my homework. The food started to taste better once I knew to avoid anything that formerly breathed. Somebody had a crush on me. At least, I thought he did. Life approached normal for the first time in years.

It made me nervous.

"Will you either find something and settle on it or turn the radio off?" Decklin crawled forward and perched between the front seats. "How much farther is this place?"

Brandon flipped off the radio. "Not far. Anyone want to play license plate bingo?"

Decklin sat back in a huff. "Adam, please kill me right now."

She would have rested her head against his shoulder if the cooler hadn't been propped between them. I tried not to look back there. I tried. By then I had become used to the way she coddled him—the boy from Iceland. Every morning at breakfast, I had endured the way she pointed out every little thing to him, as if he didn't have a mind of his own.

Which, technically, he didn't.

Taste this French toast! Look at the way the froth swirls on the top of the hot chocolate! Feel my hair; isn't it soft? Adam followed her around like she had him on an invisible leash. I had bitten my nails ragged trying to figure it out and then bit them more wondering why I cared.

"Why do you like her?" I had asked him in a rare moment of privacy.

"Why wouldn't I? She's nice to me."

Maybe it was that simple for him. I couldn't imagine it being that simple for anyone.

"I'm nice to you," I had said.

He hadn't responded. I knew it wasn't true. I had a hard time being nice to Adam because being nice to him hurt. It physically hurt, and I couldn't lasso those human emotions, pull them to the ground, and wrestle them into submission. Despite the otherworldly attraction between us, despite the whimper of my alien soul every time he left my side, if things went the way they were supposed to, Adam might soon be gone. Then where would that leave me?

It would leave me with Brandon.

And Brandon wasn't going anywhere. He drove to the store in town to buy bread and peanut butter and jelly because I told him it was my favorite. He arrived late to soccer practice because he'd been talking to me, his face covered with a fine mist, his brown eyes shining down at me. And now, his hands rested in his lap, and he drove with his knee, the picture of cool.

Brandon made my heart speed up. An entirely human reaction, but one I welcomed. When he looked at me and smiled, those parts of me I allowed to went soft.

"There," I said. Finally. The sign for Gorham Bridge.

"Are we here?" Decklin asked from the back, sleepy-voiced and possibly more impatient than me.

"Well. This doesn't look promising." Brandon slowed down. A thick yellow rope hung across the park entrance. The sign said *Closed for the Season*. He brought the car to a stop.

My heart sunk. I'd actually been looking forward to this trip.

Decklin poked her head between the front seats. "Should we turn around?"

"I guess." Brandon put the car in reverse and looked over at me. "I don't know of anywhere else near here."

"Well shit." Decklin collapsed back into her seat.

"No. No way." I thought those words so hard they actually came out of my mouth. "Brandon, how well does your car do on grass?"

He raised his eyebrows. I swung my leg over the stick shift, pressed his foot to the gas, and yanked the wheel to steer the car around the cones. Decklin whooped from the backseat.

"What are you doing?" Brandon threw his hands in the air to let me take control, his eyes wide. I jerked the wheel again, and we went up and over the grass and back onto the entrance. We wobbled a few times before straightening out.

"I got it; I got it." Brandon took back the wheel, looking sideways at me with a giant grin. He clearly liked the impetuous, unpredictable side of me.

"Mira, I am impressed." Decklin slapped me on the back. "That's my girl. So wait. We're alone here? Does this mean we have free rein? No country folk with their giant campers and yappy dogs? This is going to be better than I thought."

When I glanced into the backseat, I saw the cooler had dumped its contents onto Adam's lap. He picked off chunks of ice and threw them out his open window.

"You're all wet." Decklin didn't pass up the opportunity to dig her hands into his lap and help him out. The more she giggled and teased him, the tighter I clenched my jaw. I tried to ignore them, focusing on the view out the window instead. Oaks and pines and pockets of white spruce lined the winding road. The forest floor became a carpet of orange, brown, and yellow. Fresh air filled the car, and a buoyancy filled my chest. Hopefully this would all be over soon. I would have my father back, everyone would leave me alone, and a trip like this could consist of camping and nothing more. Once I evacuated the Conduit.

"Ahhh," Decklin sighed from the backseat. "Check out all those trees and stuff. I feel one with nature already."

❊ ❊ ❊

I stood, hands on my hips, in front of the entrance to the tent we'd just put up—a tent so small it must have been designed for Barbie and a few of her friends.

"We're not all going to fit."

"Mira's right. We'll have to stack up. Smallest on top, biggest on the bottom." Brandon looked right at me, and I blushed.

"Do we have any hand sanitizer?" Decklin wiped her hands down the front of her very short shorts, backing away from the moss-covered picnic table where she'd left the cooler. "I think I touched a slug."

"Spit and a paper towel." Brandon tossed her a roll and turned to me. "Mira, do you want to gather sticks? We should get a fire going. It's getting dark really fast."

The sun disappeared behind the hills in the distance, leaving behind a swath of yellow-orange. Nighttime was approaching, which meant in a couple hours we would pile, slide, and squeeze into Brandon's backpacking tent, probably busting its seams. God only knew what Adam wore to bed, and God only knew where Decklin's hands might end up in the pitch black.

Not that it mattered.

I busied myself with the task at hand—the Conduit. Larry and Hal thought this might be our last chance. If the seclusion of a deserted campsite didn't lure him in, nothing would. The only impediments out here were the bugs. I pictured Larry and Hal ducked behind a tree somewhere out there: swatting mosquitoes, trying hard not to snap twigs, battling poison ivy and woodland creatures. I felt sorry for them. Sort of. They stayed well hidden, at least. I saw no trace of them, and I'd scoured those woods.

"All right, campers. I've been putting off asking this, but where, pray tell, is the bathroom?" Decklin squeezed her eyes shut and crossed her fingers.

"I went in the woods," Brandon said.

Decklin winced. "I'm not going in the woods."

"Real campers go in the woods."

Adam met my glance across the top of the car as he pulled out two chairs and a blanket. He didn't have to say what I already knew. We couldn't have Decklin traipsing all over the woods. If she came upon Larry and Hal—two old men watching us in the woods—she might get the wrong idea.

"We passed one on the way in." I pointed back the way we came. "It's probably faster to cut through the field."

"Adam, come with." Decklin headed across the campsite, drawing her sweater around her.

Adam dropped the armload of sticks he had gathered and smiled at her. "Okay."

I tried to shrug it off, but I watched Adam and Decklin out of the corner of my eye as I hunted for sticks.

"Maybe we all should have gone." Our shadows grew shorter, and soon, I couldn't see well enough to find any more twigs on the ground.

"A little alone time isn't such a bad thing, is it?" Brandon poked the fire with a large forked branch, arranging the tent of wood just so. "Between Decklin and Adam, I hardly ever get you to myself." He opened the cooler and cracked the tab on his beer.

"Want one?"

"Yes." I knew I should have said no, but maybe one beer would relax me. The fire roared to life.

"We used to come up here when I was a kid." Brandon set his chair next to mine. "My dad was a big camper. Taught me how to build a fire."

Mine too, I wanted to say. But I couldn't reveal anything. No personal details. No mention of my father.

"There's a huge playground just beyond that field." Brandon pointed into the darkness. "It's not your average playground. They brought in some designer who specializes in kid psychology. So there are all these cool structures. These spinny things. And a giant rope spider web. At least that's how I remember it."

"Maybe we can go there tomorrow," I said.

"No, I don't think so." Brandon rubbed the back of his neck.

I wished Decklin and Adam would come back just then and fill in the silence.

"You don't say much, do you?" Brandon studied me in the darkness. "I know nothing about you." Normally when people accuse me of being too quiet, too shy, I take offense. But not with Brandon.

"I talk when I have something to say." That sounded so, so dumb.

"I respect that," he said. "I've always hated silence because I feel like it means something is wrong." He took a long swig of his beer. I took a long swig of mine and tried not to gag. The fire crackled and jumped, and we both stared into it. He reached over and took my hand from my lap.

"This okay?" he asked.

The beer can had left his hand cold and wet. My pulse skyrocketed.

"Yes." I stared ahead, trying not to squeeze his hand too hard or hold it too loose.

He rubbed his thumb lightly over the backs of my fingers. "I know you don't take me seriously, but I really like you."

He rested my hand palm-down on his thigh, just above his knee. His muscle underneath felt as hard as a steel cable. He played with my fingers with both of his hands.

"It's hard to take you seriously. Betsy said you only date cheerleaders." My heart fluttered in my chest like a caged bird.

"I think Betsy only wants you to herself. But yeah. I've dated a lot of cheerleaders." He laughed. I almost pulled my hand away. "They were exact replicas of each other. I noticed you from far away. All I saw was this enormous head of bright red hair on this petite little girl. I wanted to know who you were. You're so different than anyone else I've ever met. You have this, like, glow. You don't care about what anyone thinks. Do you know how refreshing that is?"

I had to chuckle. "I care what everyone thinks. It's constant. That's why I don't understand why you like me. You're this superstar athlete, Mr. Popularity. Everyone knows you, and everyone loves you. You make people feel… calm. You make me feel calm."

He took his hand back, and I sucked in a breath. "Did I say something wrong?" *God, I'd blown it already.*

"That's exactly the way I want people to see me. So kudos to you. But that doesn't mean that's who I am." He stared at the fire for a long time. The beer tasted bad, but it sat in my stomach, warm and welcoming. If Larry saw me sitting near a campfire, holding hands with a boy, drinking beer…

"I had a sister." Brandon interrupted the peaceful silence. My hand still rested on his knee, but now it felt like an intruder. I held myself so still I could have been a statue.

"She was three years younger than me. Annabelle. Apple of my parents' eye." He sniffed, rubbed at his chin, and took a sip of beer. "We came here every summer. She used to wear her hair in two braids. Her ears stuck out." He laughed again, but not in a way that meant anything was funny at all. "She fell riding her bike, right at the end of our driveway. Carotid aneurysm. They said she died before she even hit the pavement."

Heaviness soaked the air. I sat paralyzed, watching his face, the twitch in his eye, as he stared ahead. He flexed and unflexed his hands. "Anyway, my parents were devastated. I was sad too. Wrecked." He swallowed and waited a moment before going on. "But I had to push that way down. I tried to become the best kid possible. Do all the right things. Distract them with my jokes, my accomplishments. I needed to make sure nothing else bad happened. Because they would just unravel. You know? If parents unravel, what do you have left?"

Suddenly I understood him, like a dark corner had been illuminated. I understood why people flocked around him, why the sun shone brighter, why people looked to him for answers.

Because he held the world together with his own bare hands.

He turned to me, and in an instant, his face lightened. "I've never told anyone that." He shrugged. Though I'd heard that line before, at least in movies, I believed him. He had cracks. We all did. I started to speak, but he moved his hand to my cheek and drew my chin toward him. His eyes had *kiss* written all over them; his lips parted. When he pulled me toward him, I braced my hand on his chair to keep my balance and knocked his beer over. He didn't seem to care, so I closed my eyes and let him kiss me. I felt the warmth of the fire and his lips on mine, and for a moment, I forgot the universe.

For a moment, I became the universe.

When I opened my eyes from so far, far away, Brandon gazed at me with a half smile. "I've been wanting to do that since I met you."

"I think I need another beer," I whispered, because all my strength had seeped into the cold dirt that held us up.

Behind me, Decklin cleared her throat, and I knew she had been standing there for a while.

"There they are." I straightened up quickly, my heart thundering in my chest. Brandon's beer lay on its side on the ground, steadily streaming liquid into the dirt. Decklin and Adam appeared as two moving shadows in the darkness, masked behind the yellow spotlight of the flashlight on the grass. As they drew closer, I saw their arms were linked, and though I had just kissed a very good looking boy, the sight sent my stomach to my shoes.

Brandon fished a beer out of the cooler next to him and handed it to me, wet and ice cold.

"To be continued," he said under his breath. With a grin, he scooped his spilled beer off the ground to salvage whatever remained, kind of like what I was trying to do with my heart. The whole rest of the weekend, he would be trying to get me alone. I took a giant gulp of beer. It went down too easily.

"Sorry to interrupt," Decklin panted. "But I just have to say, that does not qualify as a bathroom. Secondly, I can't believe you started the party without me. I'll take one of those, please."

She spread a blanket on the ground next to the fire pit and lay on her side. Adam reclined next to her, propped up on his elbows, staring at the fire like he had never seen one before.

"Don't they have fire in Iceland?" I didn't intend for it to come out so snarky. I had to pull it together. It wasn't easy with him gazing at me, his eyes the lightest shade of blue even in the dark. Had he seen Brandon kiss me? Did Adam know what kissing was? A wave of nausea rolled through me thinking he might have done the same thing with Decklin.

"They only have fjords." Decklin pushed Adam with her foot, and they smiled at each other. Inside joke, apparently. Which meant they had spent more time together than I thought. Jealousy hammered through my veins, leaving me no choice but to drown the feeling in lukewarm beer.

At that point, I'd drunk exactly one time in my life—with a friend in the woods behind her house. A bottle of peppermint Schnapps, the first sip of which had made my eyes water. After the world had spun out of control, I'd thrown up behind a tree and gone home with the knees of my white pants covered in mud. I'd been fifteen at the time.

I finished my can in record time. The fire spit and sparked.

"What was that?" Brandon sat bolt upright. I sat at attention too. If Larry and Hal had given themselves away, they'd have a lot of explaining to do.

"What was what?" Decklin craned her neck to see what might materialize out of the darkness behind her. Jumpy, always. She moved closer to Adam. I moved closer to Brandon.

"I swear, I heard something." Brandon stood up and threw a log on the fire before walking to the edge of the darkness and peering out. "Something's out there."

"If we get attacked by a bear, I swear to God I will kill each and every one of you," Decklin said.

"Not if the bear kills you first." My voice trembled. "Anyway, it was probably just a—"

"Shh. Listen." Brandon stood completely still, listening.

"Wait, I hear it too." I cracked the tab on my second beer, and everyone laughed, even Adam. That smile was more dizzying than the buzz I had. Adam stared at me so intensely I choked on my next sip. I coughed and sputtered like an idiot while he kept his gaze locked on mine.

"Maybe the woods are haunted." Brandon eased into his seat next to me. Decklin sat with her arms wrapped around her knees, the same way she sat on the top bunk while she waited to walk with me to class.

"Shut up." Despite the beer, my mouth went suddenly dry. It occurred to me maybe Larry and Hal weren't responsible for the noise after all. Maybe the Conduit had tracked us here—had slit their throats in the darkness without a sound and now stood just outside my line of sight, waiting to make his move.

"No really. Don't you feel it?" Brandon leaned forward and concentrated. "Something's out there."

The dusky light streamed through the gaps in the tall trees, casting an eerie glow. I had seen too many horror movies: teens disrupt nature, teens sin and drink beer, teens engage in pre-marital sex, teens are dismembered one by one.

"It's probably a raccoon sniffing around to see if we have food." I set down the beer, blinking hard to stop the spinning.

"Speaking of food, I'm hungry." Decklin patted her flat stomach.

Brandon got up and opened the cooler. "I've got beer. I've got hot dogs. I've got ramen. The three staples of camping."

"Hot dog me," Decklin said.

And just like that, they forgot. Except for me and Adam, who watched each other across the fire with knowing looks. Even the beer couldn't numb the impending sense that something was about to happen. Every nerve in my body stood at attention. Above the crackle of the fire and the bugs, I strained to hear something else. Someone else.

Brandon threw Decklin the pack of hot dogs.

"Do we have a pot for the ramen?" My voice cracked, and I cursed my decision to come camping, to drink, even my mother for bringing me into this situation.

"Do you doubt my outdoorsmanship?" Brandon jumped from his chair, popped open the trunk, and produced a cardboard box filled with cookware, utensils, propane, and a compact camping stove.

"You came prepared." Decklin slid the hot dog over the end of a stick and held it to the fire. My stomach rumbled, but I couldn't have taken one bite of anything.

"I always come prepared." Brandon slid the stove out of the box. "Been camping since I can remember. Just listen to the sounds. It's like a symphony. Tree frogs, crickets, cicadas, the crackling fire."

For a time, we remained quiet, watching Decklin cook her dinner over the flame. As I continued to sip my beverage, despite the warnings deep in my entire being, I came to the conclusion that beer was disgusting. I couldn't imagine the guy who invented it taking a sip and saying, *Oh by golly! This is delicious! Let's drink a lot of it.* It tasted bitter, it made me gag, and by the time I got to the bottom of the can, the remains tasted warm and flat and became really, really hard to swallow.

But I persevered, because gagging down warm beer made me happier than watching Adam point out stars to Decklin and watching her giggle and elbow him playfully in the ribs, offering him a bit of her hot dog while a smile spread across his face.

That buzzed, giddy feeling made me forget that Brandon's sister had died. That my father had disappeared. That I wanted to share that fact so badly with someone who might understand.

"Mira, can you help me with this?" Brandon called from the picnic table. I swallowed the last tepid sip of beer with difficulty and grabbed another. If Adam could have fun, I could too. Serial killers be damned, Conduit be damned, bears and spirits, all of it. Funny the things that didn't matter after I drank a couple beers. Like a lot of things. All things.

Brandon screwed in the propane.

"I would have thought you'd go for Decklin." I slid the sides of the stove into place, popping them into the metal clasps so the lid would stay up.

"That's not fair," he said.

"Well, look at her. And, I mean, you've seen her in her underwear." I forced a laugh. "I've seen her in her underwear, and even I wouldn't blame you."

His face fell. "So she told you." His eyebrows furrowed. "It really wasn't a big deal."

Something went cold inside me. "No, not a big deal."

"I swear." Brandon put a hand to his heart. "I looked away."

"Right. You looked away. I may not be as experienced as Decklin, but I'm not stupid." I snapped on the burner a little too hard and blue flame shot straight up. I flinched backward and scraped my hand on the metal.

Decklin rolled onto her stomach and propped herself up on her elbows next to Adam. Even across the campsite, I could see her cleavage.

"Mira, I… Is that blood?" Brandon asked.

"What?" I turned and saw him looking at my hand in shock.

"Your hand." He lunged forward and clicked off the stove. "Let me see."

When I turned my hand over, a stream of dark red blood dripped onto the ground. Brandon scrambled for a paper towel and pressed it to the wound, but the blood kept coming, soaking it through. I'd felt a little heat, but that was it. I thought it was just a scratch.

"I'm okay. It doesn't even hurt." I tried to pull my hand back, but Brandon held onto it, ripped off another paper towel, and told me to apply pressure while he looked for the first aid kit.

"You're going to need stiches." His voice stayed cool and flat, as if he were removed from the situation. As if he had gone cold. It made me wonder if he was thinking of his sister.

"No, really. I'm okay." Guilt swept through me. When he opened the trunk, the car light came on, and I got a better look at the deep gash. *Oh, shit.* This would not be easy to explain.

"What happened?" Decklin called from the blanket. Adam sprung from his spot and rushed to my side.

"I must have sliced it on the stove. It's fine, I swear." I hid my hand behind my back. "Let me just run to the bathroom. Wash it off."

"I'll go with you." Brandon held a white plastic box with a red cross on it. "I don't want you to pass out on the way. I've got bandages. Gauze. A needle and thread."

"What?" I backed away.

"I'm prepared for anything," he said. "Let me go with you. That's a lot of blood."

"It's not that much," I lied. But once Brandon snapped on the lantern, I saw traces everywhere, darkening the boards of the picnic table, splashed on the stove, down the front of my yellow sweater.

"What about the fire? You should stay with the fire." My teeth began to chatter.

"Who cares about the fire? We have to get you safe."

"No. Listen. Adam can come with me. I'll be two seconds. I'm fine, trust me." God, I hated blood. That familiar nauseous feeling knotted my stomach, and I leaned on the table, lightheaded. But despite the hurt look in his eyes, I couldn't let Brandon see the wound. I couldn't let him see how fast it healed. He would ask questions I wasn't prepared to answer.

Chapter Nine

I turned the flashlight off and stopped at the edge of the field. We were out of the way of the campsite, out of the way of their ears and eyes, practically invisible to everything. Fireflies floated and blinked against the dark like white lights. Adam held out his hand and one landed on his palm. Then two, then three. One landed on my forearm, flashing its light. Around us, there were hundreds now, hundreds of tiny lights.

The lightning bug traveled up my arm to my collar and crossed the boundary of my skin before I gently flicked it off. The heaviness inside me lifted, and I felt like I could breathe.

"It's in search of a mate." Adam stood next to me. "The male flashes, and the female flashes him back in response. It's how they communicate."

I unwrapped the paper towel from my hand and balled it up. Washing off the blood would be easy, but I had to try explaining why such a small cut had bled so profusely. And why, in the morning, there would be no trace of the wound at all.

I watched the flashing bugs, fascinated and a little repulsed. "Is that one of your powers? The ability to control fireflies? Because it's too late in the season for them. You should be more careful."

"I didn't do it on purpose." With a wave of his hand, one by one, the fireflies departed from the swarm and headed for the trees like lazy buoys afloat in a sea.

"Impressive. You could form a firefly army if you wanted."

"That's true." Adam thought about it for a second. "They're too single-minded though. They wouldn't make a very good army."

He stood too close to me. We breathed each other's air.

"Can you do anything about the mosquitoes?"

"No," he said. "It's blood they're after. They're single-minded in a different way."

I told him we should continue on to the bathroom, so we headed across the field toward the silhouette of it. He walked right next to me, not saying a word, which I liked. Brandon talked constantly. Though Adam barely said anything, his presence filled the silence.

"I love clear nights like this. Look, it's Altair." I pointed to the star.

"Yes, and Pavo," Adam said. "And Octans, Apus, Ara, Telescopium, and Indus."

"Show off." I chastised the swoon inside of me. "Is that what you were pointing out to Decklin?" He stood so close it would have been easy just to slip my hand into his. I moved away since he obviously preferred her. Good, because I had Brandon…if I wanted him.

"Yes. I find it interesting that humans have names for everything." He took a step toward me and lowered his head. His eyes never once left mine.

"Not everything." I stepped back and searched around for something, anything. My brain was fuzzy, but my heart beat loud and clear. "Not these blades of grass." I reached down and yanked a handful out of the ground.

"Is a star more worthy of a name than a blade of grass? They're both visible to the eye. They both have weight. Like you and I." As he spoke, he closed the distance between us.

"Blades of grass don't have any significance." The words left my mouth, but I could barely form them. The closer Adam got the more muddled my brain became.

"Maybe naming them gives them significance." He stopped just inches from me.

My lips trembled as I looked up into his eyes. "Then I'll call this one Josephine."

"Lucky Josephine." He put his hand under mine and blew the grass from my palm. His touch sent an electric charge through my whole body, his breath on my skin dizzying enough to upset my balance. I drew my hand away and turned from him.

"I bet you find a lot of things interesting about humans."

"Yes."

"Especially particular humans." I kept my voice low.

"Yes."

"It's obvious." I was glad for the cover of night. I could never have said those things in the harsh daylight. He would have seen me shaking. "You laugh at everything she says."

"Who?"

I turned around to face him. I struggled to control my tone. "Decklin. She's got you wrapped around her little finger. Be careful though. She's been around the block if you know what I mean."

There. I'd said it, and it was out there. I might have sounded like a jealous psycho, but I didn't care.

"You have to remain vigilant. Don't forget why you're here." I forged ahead, the light of the bathroom a swirling blur. I concentrated on putting one foot in front of the other.

"I'm not sure what you're talking about." Adam kept pace. "But you told me to have fun. You said, 'Enjoy it.' I believe those were your exact words. So I'm enjoying it. Decklin is nice to me. To her, I'm just a regular human being. Not bait. Not a part of the plan."

I swung around and glared at him. "It's not *my* plan. It's not *my* fault we're in this situation. Me and Larry and Hal, we're just doing what we were assigned. I'm on guard constantly. You're the key to this whole thing, and you're flirting your head off and having fun. The rest of us have a job to do."

"Constantly on guard?" Adam folded his arms across his chest. "Like, with your eyes closed and your lips against Brandon's?"

So he had seen. The satisfying tingle of victory burned within me. Underneath that, though, a seed of guilt sprouted in my gut.

"I don't have to explain myself to you."

Two yards away, the bathroom called to me. I couldn't get away fast enough. I needed a reprieve from the heightened nerves, the breathlessness.

"Wait. Stop. Close your eyes." No trace of anger or accusation lingered in his voice. I wondered how he switched off so easily, while my thoughts continued to tumble and clunk like sneakers in a dryer.

"Why should I?"

"Trust me."

Those words hung between us. I rolled my eyes and closed them to humor him, putting my hands on my hips. First came darkness, then dizziness, so I snapped my eyes open. Everything remained; nothing had disappeared into some weird vortex like I half expected. The bathroom, the pine trees, Adam's jawline, his Adam's apple, and his wiry arms sticking out of his t-shirt.

"This is stupid. The world is spinning." I concentrated on the ground in front of me to keep from falling over.

"The world *is* spinning."

"I have to sit. I think I'm a little drunk." I sat on one of the large rocks just outside the bathroom. He sat next to me, and when he rested his knee against mine, I didn't move away.

I sighed. "I didn't mean those things I said back there. I'm just worried that Decklin is going to distract you from your real purpose. You can't let that happen."

"Decklin doesn't distract me." He spoke softly, close to my ear, and shifted even closer to me. "You do."

This time, it wasn't the beer that spun me off-balance. My heart pitched forward, and my face burned like I had leaned too close to a flame.

"You don't know what you're saying." My skin radiated heat where his leg touched mine. I imagined how it might feel if our entire bodies were pressed against each other.

"Try again. Close your eyes. Tell me what you feel."

He rested a hand on my knee and studied me in a way I recognized from a long, long time ago—when everyone told some version of the truth and I didn't have to run from anything. He studied me with pure innocence. With fascination. Resistance was futile.

I did as he asked and closed my eyes. A hard rock jutted into my left thigh, and damp coldness seeped through the seat of my pants. When my lips parted to speak, Adam slid his fingertips up my bare arm, from my wrist to my elbow. Bolts of electricity shot up and down my arms, a tingling, tickling sensation that made me squirm.

"Don't open your eyes," he commanded.

"What are you doing?" I couldn't take it anymore. On the verge of exploding, I jumped down off the rock and stumbled to get my feet under me. My weak knees barely supported me; my breath came in quick gasps.

"I wanted to show you." His voice remained steady, but under the floodlights outside the bathroom, I could see that his cheeks had flushed crimson.

"You wanted to show me what?" Just a few minutes ago, Brandon had leaned in to kiss me. Now Brandon didn't even exist.

"You asked me once what it feels like to be in a human body."

"I know what it feels like to be in a human body. I've been in one my whole life." Larry and Hal would never forgive me for getting involved with an Initiate. And if my mother found out…

I headed for the bathroom, pressing my fingers against my temples. I had to stop things before they spiraled out of control. Before *I* spiraled out of control.

"Mira, come back," Adam called behind me.

I whirled around to face him and took a deep breath. When I stared into those eyes, I struggled to speak. "This isn't a game."

His eyes grew serious; his mouth turned down. "No one knows that more than me. If this doesn't work, there will be nowhere for the rest of us to go. Nowhere."

Moonlight cast a warm glow on his skin, his human skin. How was he any different than me? Since Adam had initiated, I had struggled to think of him coldly, as I might a machine. A very good-looking machine, and I had failed miserably.

No one would know just by looking at us that he wasn't human, or that I was only half-human. On Earth, no one else knew about the existence of his species, of Orientation, or any of the rest of it. But we did, and we all—Adam, me, Larry, Hal, my mom—had a job to do. Save the Senders. The survival of their whole race rested on our shoulders.

I exhaled and tilted my head back to look at the stars and thought instantly of my father. The night before his disappearance, we had bundled up in our coats and hats at midnight to watch the Taurids— his favorite meteor shower. Just when I had given up hope, a bright fireball had streaked across the sky, taking my breath away. My father had picked me up and swung me around. From that point forward, everything I did was for him.

I wiped a tear away as I felt Adam approach. I didn't even have to face him to know he was looking at me. If I brought myself to meet his eyes, I knew I would let everything go. And I couldn't fool myself into believing Adam didn't matter to me, didn't speak to some part of me that no one, not even Brandon, had ever spoken to before.

I took a breath and turned toward him. The last layer of my willpower peeled away and floated to the ground, leaving me helpless against the pull of him.

"Did you two get lost?" Decklin appeared out of nowhere, with Brandon close behind, and slid between the two of us, breaking whatever magic had stolen us from the world. Disappointment shot through me, drew me back into myself, and morphed into alarm. If they hadn't shown up…

"See, I told you they weren't being ravaged by grizzlies." Brandon raised his can and took a swig. "Decklin was convinced—"

"Shut up, Brandon." Decklin shifted her glance from me to Adam. "I had a bad feeling; that's all."

"How's the hand?" Brandon's concern only increased my guilt.

"It's fine." I held up my hand. "See? Stopped bleeding. No stitches. Thanks to you."

"That was a lot of blood." Decklin studied my hand. "Looked like a massacre happened."

"What were you guys doing out here?" Brandon ended his sentence a little too sharply but then softened it with a smile. I searched my jumbled brain for words but could find none.

"Yeah, Mira. All alone with tall, dark, and handsome in the middle of the woods, what could you possibly be doing?" Decklin's hair fell in front of her face, casting her eyes in shadow.

"And what about the two of you huddled in front of the fire?" I shot back. "That's more romantic than a disgusting campsite bathroom."

"Oh please, me and Brandon?"

Brandon stood as still as I'd ever seen him, bouncing his gaze from me to Decklin and back, trying to read the situation. "What? You think you're out of my league?"

Decklin opened her mouth to say something then shut it again. Brandon crushed his empty can under his boot. Adam avoided my eyes. I could have sliced the tension in the air with a machete.

"I didn't mean that." Brandon clapped Adam on the back before turning to me and Decklin. "What happened? This is supposed to be fun, guys. We've got more beer, more food. The night is young and so are we."

Decklin folded her arms. "I'm cold. Let's get back to the fire."

We hiked back single file. No one said a word until we arrived at the campsite, where the flames had died down. Even Brandon's energy had plummeted. My mind raced to find ways to lighten the mood, but everything I thought of sounded desperate and forced.

~~Brandon kicked~~ ash onto the embers. "I don't know about the rest of you, but I'm beat. Let's call it a night."

I paced back and forth next to the dying fire. It was the moment I'd been dreading: sleeping arrangements.

Brandon and Adam took the outsides, squeezing me next to Decklin in the middle. Barely an inch existed between anyone, and within seconds, Brandon made sure that inch grew smaller and smaller until he lay flush against me, his fingertips working their way under the blanket to play with the area where my shirt met the waist of my shorts. His forehead rested on mine, his breath a mixture of beer and hot dogs. Decklin shifted behind me and brought her knee up to press into my back. On the other side of her, Adam's existence filled the entire tent.

"Can I kiss you?" Brandon whispered, too loud. He didn't wait for an answer. He tipped his head, and I froze, thinking immediately of Adam. Brandon missed my lips and planted a wet kiss on my chin. Everyone must have heard the slopping sound. I coughed and turned away, squeezing my eyes shut, wishing I could disappear.

"There's a bug in the tent!" Decklin flew out of her sleeping bag and cowered in the corner, tracking the movement of the bug with wide eyes.

Thank god for that bug. Brandon sighed and pulled back. I drew the blanket up to my neck, covering every bit of skin possible.

The bug fluttered against the walls, bouncing off the nylon. I could hear it, but I couldn't see it.

Then the bug lit up.

"Oh. It's a firefly." Decklin sighed and lay back down.

Of course. Under the cover of darkness, I smiled, knowing Adam had sent the bug. *His army,* defending…what?

I tried to breathe through my nose as quietly as possible, feeling myself pinned between two bodies, and crossed my fingers under the blanket that Brandon wouldn't try again. Not two minutes later—though it felt like an eternity—he rolled over and passed out. Morning couldn't come soon enough. When I closed my eyes, everything spun.

But I must have drifted off at some point because I woke to Decklin zipping the tent and crawling back into her spot next to me.

"I don't advise getting up to pee," she whispered. "Jesus, make some room." She pushed me away from Adam. "You two are practically on top of each other."

She smelled like cigarettes, or campfire, or both. Only half-awake, I rolled away from the warmth of Adam's back and fell back to sleep.

Chapter Ten

I stirred the embers until they glowed, tented some sticks to catch the flame, threw on a couple logs, and hooked the propane to the camping stove to boil water for coffee. All things my father had taught me as a young girl, things I had carried with me through the years. I remembered him as I lit the burner with a match. A broad back and crazy hair. How had he learned? Why had he taken to some things and not others?

By the time Brandon crawled out of the tent, I had coffee brewing and a fire roaring, not to mention a pounding headache and a dry mouth. Brandon surveyed my work with a blank face.

"We should have brought a bb gun. I'd pick off those crows one by one." He slipped his arm around my waist and whispered in my ear. "I'm sorry about last night. That's not me, I swear. You make me so nervous."

I ducked out of his grasp but summoned up a smile. "I'm hungry, aren't you?" I patted him on the arm like one of his soccer friends. Or his mother. His face fell. He turned his back to me and walked to the cooler while I covered my face with my hands.

"Wanna fire these babies up?" I looked up to see Brandon holding a sopping Ziploc of hot dogs he had pulled from the cooler. He raised and dropped his eyebrows a few times in quick succession. I made a face, but the knot in my stomach loosened. Maybe last night hadn't been the disaster my overthinking brain had made it out to be.

"On second thought, I'll stick with coffee." I gave him a thumbs up.

"Your hand." Brandon dropped his arms, concern drawing his mouth into a frown. "How is it?"

I held it up to show him. "Told you it wasn't bad." The pink, faded scratch ran from my wrist up the back of my hand to the knuckle of my middle finger.

Brandon's eyes widened in disbelief. "So much blood."

"I've always been a bleeder." I shrugged and smiled, turning my attention to Decklin dragging herself out of the tent and rubbing her eyes. She drew Brandon's eyes as well. Why did her hair look perfect? Infuriating.

"Sleep well?" I snatched my hat from my back pocket and pulled it down over my ears. My temples pounded, and I had a horrible taste in my mouth.

"I was up a few times." She knelt close to the fire and warmed her hands. "The darkness is unsettling. I mean, if you think about it, we're all alone up here. No one knows where we are. What if there's a colony of psychotic inbreds living in these hills? Or worse?"

"What's worse than inbreds?" Brandon slid his hot dog onto the tip of a stick and dangled it over the fire. My stomach lurched.

"I don't want to talk about inbreds." I glanced up at the crows fluttering and cackling in the trees. "We've got another night here. Possibly. If it doesn't rain."

We all looked up at the graying sky. I slid into a dew-covered camp chair and rested my head against the flimsy fabric. The coffee tasted bitter, but it warmed me. I kicked at a pile of twigs next to the fire pit to avoid casting my gaze toward the tent.

"What are we going to do all day?" Decklin chewed on her meal-on-a-stick. "Sit around and stare at the fire? Can't we go on a hike or something? I want the full camping experience."

She settled across from me, and though my eyes stayed on her, in my periphery, I sensed movement. I stood and threw another log on the fire, fighting the urge to vomit. *No more beer*, I promised myself. *Ever.*

"We could hike," I suggested.

"Yes." Decklin took a sip of coffee and grimaced. "I want to hike. Hiking is better than this." She swirled the coffee in her mug. "Are you sure this is coffee? It tastes just like sewage smells."

"I could say the same about you." Brandon laughed and started on hot dog number two.

In the background, I heard the sound of the tent zipper. I drew in a quick breath. All morning long, flashes of the previous night had interrupted my thoughts: the fireflies, the feel of Adam's leg up against mine, the softness in his eyes as he stared right through me.

I hadn't thought of kissing Brandon at all. And that told me everything.

"Morning, sunshine," Decklin said as Adam ducked out of the tent, zipped it closed, and joined us at the fire. His dark hair curled slightly at his neck, and his shirt clung to the smooth slope of his chest. I turned casually back to the fire as if it didn't require great effort. He'd said I distracted him. The soft way he'd whispered those words played in my head.

"Adam," Decklin said. "I hope you brought your hiking shoes."

"Don't worry." Brandon smiled through his hangover. "I have extras in the car. What size are you?"

Adam looked down at himself in confusion and shrugged. Everyone laughed, but only I understood why it was funny.

✱ ✱ ✱

We found a trail sign and an arrow pointing in the direction of what they labeled the Jump Off.

"The Jump Off," Decklin declared. "Sounds perfect."

I had a shitty night's sleep and no solid food for the last twenty hours, so a hike to the Jump Off didn't exactly appeal to me. But it was better than sitting around the campsite with my nerves on fire. We headed down the narrow trail, brushing away branches, swatting mosquitoes, no-seeums, and black flies, and stopping intermittently to check the trail markers. Some of the red markers had faded or gone missing, and several times we had to double back and reroute ourselves. Brandon stayed in front, narrating, with a can of beer in hand and another stuffed in the pocket of his vest. Adam walked directly behind him. He turned occasionally to look back, as if to verify Decklin and I hadn't run off.

I had definitely thought about it.

"Tell me it's not going to rain." Decklin looked up at the gray sky. The thick air threatened to open up, but maybe it would hold off.

"God, these bugs are annoying." She slapped at herself and the air around her. "Also, I'm pretty sure we're completely lost."

The clouds hung low and ominous, the sun barely visible. The sagging pines bent toward the trail, enclosing it. I heard what must have been squirrels digging in the leaves and birds flitting in the branches, but I didn't see them. The feeling of being watched stayed with me, even as we trekked deeper into the woods. Because, after all, someone was watching. Larry and Hal for sure, and likely the Conduit too. Somehow, I'd let him, and my mission, slip to the back of my mind amidst all this teen drama.

Decklin stopped complaining and sidled up to me. She looped her arm through mine. "Do you think he likes me?"

I glanced quickly at the boys in front of us and then focused on the roots, rocks, and uneven ground, planning my response.

"Of course. Why wouldn't he?" I was sick of the whole thing, and my head still throbbed in the aftermath of the beer. I willed something to happen to distract Decklin from the conversation: a tree falling in our path, a torrential rainfall, a family of startled deer darting out in front of us.

"He hasn't tried anything." Disappointment tinged her voice.

Phew. I'd finally received the answer to a question I couldn't bring myself to ask. I struggled to keep myself from smiling. "He's not American. They have different rules, I think. Just give him some time." Lots of time.

We both jumped as a crack of thunder tore through the air. One of those loud cracks that sounded like the world was breaking in half, that made me question everything I knew about the origin of thunder. How could a puffy mass of condensed air possibly make a noise so earth shattering? Ahead of us, Brandon and Adam stopped and looked up, as if the next clap would announce itself in the sky at any moment. The light faded.

"We should head back," I said to Decklin. "Pack up before it gets really bad." We had seconds, at most, before the clouds unloaded. I scanned the forest for signs of Larry and Hal. Just because I didn't see them didn't mean they weren't there, watching. I wondered how two old guys could be so stealthy.

Decklin frowned. "I don't think he likes me at all. I think he likes you." She narrowed her green eyes.

Thunder rumbled overhead. Either Decklin didn't care about the weather, or she was so wrapped up in this situation with Adam that she didn't notice her surroundings. I could relate.

"We're going to get caught in it." I started backing away, toward the campsite.

Decklin held out her hands in resignation. "We're already caught in it. Now it's a matter of riding it out."

The rain came. Hard. We stared at each other.

"Ladies!" Brandon yelled through the thunderous downpour. "Follow me!"

Adam stood with his arms at his sides, grinning up at the sky. Wet strands of hair plastered to his forehead, and his clothes clung to him, outlining the muscles in his—

Decklin gripped my arm. "All right, let's go!"

Rain soaked my shoulders and ran into my eyes. Decklin was right. It was a matter of riding it out. Accepting I was going to get wet. Letting it soak me and dealing with it.

Decklin kept talking as we ran, pausing every few seconds to pant and wheeze. "I was always *that* girl, you know? I had the hardest crushes. But they never chose *me*. That same thing happened over and over again. It really starts to take a toll on a girl's self-confidence. At Meryton, I thought things would be different. But nothing is ever different. Story of my life. Again and again."

"I like Brandon," I yelled close to Decklin's ear, forcing the words out even though they rang false. I did like Brandon. I did. Just not the catch-in-your-throat, heart-hammering-through-your-chest kind of like.

As if on cue, Brandon turned to look at us. Maybe he wanted to make sure we hadn't been washed down the trail in a landslide or something. He finally stopped and waited for us to catch up.

"Are you two nuts?" He pulled me by the hand up the path before I could protest.

Brandon ran *fast*. Tree branches whipped against my naked arms, and my boots kicked up mud that splashed across the back of my legs. I wiped the rain from my eyes, let go of Brandon's hand, and sprinted ahead of him. I focused on pumping my legs, on breathing steadily. I could have run forever. Each branch, each twist of the path, each slippery rock, I anticipated, tackled, and overcame. My mother had always told me I had to stay agile. For when things ran after me.

Through the pouring rain, I saw a sign nailed to a tree in the distance. *Jump Off: 35 feet.*

I stopped. Adam arrived two seconds after me, not even breathing hard. It was the first time we'd stood face to face since last night, since I had done my best to ignore him all morning. His blue eyes sparkled. My pulse raced, but not from the sprint. He opened his mouth as if to say something, but just then, Brandon jogged around the corner.

"I found the path. It's right up here," I yelled. Adam clamped his mouth shut.

"You should run track. Wow." Brandon walked up and stopped between us, patting himself down while he caught his breath. "The rain let up, but I lost my beer." He tapped his empty pocket and sulked.

"Jesus." Decklin arrived last, out of breath and finally disheveled. "If I have to go much farther, I'm going to vomit."

"Look." I gestured toward the signage that warned: *Steep drop! Stay behind the railings! Do not approach during inclement weather!*

"I would call this inclement weather, wouldn't you?" Decklin twisted the front of her shirt to wring it out. Her silver bellybutton ring shimmered in the light. Brandon stole a glance but then averted his eyes. I didn't dare look at Adam.

Decklin groaned. "Oh good, the bugs are back."

The Jump Off was just as advertised. Nothing separated us from an impossibly steep drop except a rusty metal railing. Way, way down below where we stood, a narrow whitewater river cut through the middle of the valley. Up the other side, green pines, and the red and yellow of the changing leaves of the deciduous trees, covered the hill. A few houses—tiny from here—sat nestled in the greenery.

As I peered over the edge, to the bottom so far below, part of me wondered what it would be like to jump. In those final seconds, freefalling through the air, would I feel total and absolute freedom? Or terror, knowing I couldn't go back?

"Whoa." Brandon searched the ground, picked up a fist-sized rock, and launched it over the railing. We all watched it disappear into the abyss. I shuddered, backed away, and adjusted my hat and the elastic in my hair. Adam took the stone steps down to the lower railing and disappeared around the bend. I wanted to join him but couldn't think of an excuse.

"There's no service up here." Brandon slipped his phone in his pocket. "I hope nothing bad happens."

"Nothing bad ever happens." Decklin leaned over the wall and looked down. "Nothing good either."

"Mira," Adam called from below. "Come down here."

There was my excuse.

"Go ahead, Mira." Decklin's face remained emotionless, but her voice sounded strained.

"Mira, wait." Brandon rested his hand on the small of my back. "Can I talk to you for a second?"

Decklin took the hint and moved to the other side of the lookout, but not before she shot me an reproachful look. *Relax*, I told myself, tensing for an uncomfortable conversation.

Brandon looked out across the valley. "Don't tell anyone what I told you, okay?"

I replayed our conversation around the campfire. "You mean about your sister?"

"I mean about any of it. You make me feel safe. Like I could tell you anything. But I don't want everyone knowing my secret. I don't need everyone knowing I'm not who I seem."

I swallowed hard. Brandon liked me. He trusted me. My stomach clenched. I wasn't worthy of any of it.

I reached out my hand to lay it on his shoulder but stopped halfway and drew it back. "No one is who they seem."

I wanted to give him more, but I found myself incapable of it. In this quasi-relationship, he'd done nothing wrong. In any other circumstances, I would have thrown myself into his welcoming arms. But these weren't any other circumstances. I had to finally admit what I'd denied since that moment in the quad: I was falling for an alien. It was meant to be on a cosmic level, and straining against it was futile. Some interstellar force had brought us together, something bigger than either of us. Brandon couldn't compete with that.

He faced me. His mouth turned down at the corners, only slightly, as if he were battling a frown. "I get it."

I held his stare and nodded. My chest ached to see him hurt, but I couldn't draw this out. "I'm going to see what he wants."

Brandon closed his eyes for a moment. When he opened them again, his lips curled into a grin, and he gave a half-hearted shrug. "Be careful. It's slippery."

With a heavy heart, I followed the stone stairway as it curved downward, just inches from a terrifying drop. Halfway to the bottom, my foot skidded on the slime-covered surface, and I grasped the railing, shot through with adrenaline. *Nothing bad ever happens.* Nothing worse than skinned knees or bruised tailbones anyway. I started down again, with a death grip on that railing. Vultures circled in the wide chasm of the gulch, their wings outspread to catch the air currents.

On the bottom landing, Adam stood in one of the puddles that had formed in the cracks. I rubbed my hands together, a lightness filling my chest. I walked toward him on unsteady legs, thinking of what I wanted to say. He was still drenched from the downpour, every gorgeous inch of him.

Adam didn't look at me when he spoke. "Stop. Listen, but don't look, and don't say a word."

I paused where I stood, chastising myself for where my thoughts had been. Out of the corner of my eye, I saw the brush move. Hal, all six-foot-seven of him, emerged from behind it. Larry huffed and puffed next to him. They'd taken a chance, showing up here, with Decklin and Brandon only yards away. Which meant...

My stomach dropped. Something bad had happened after all.

"Another Initiate was evacuated," Hal told us. His eyes were bloodshot like he'd been up all night. "Just last night. Over in Edgefield, not five miles from here."

I let out a sigh of relief. "So Brandon's not the Conduit. He was in the tent all night."

"No, but it must mean the Conduit's close," Hal said.

A scream broke the silence. I spun around just in time to see Brandon tumbling down the stone steps. Time halted, each second progressing in slow motion: Brandon's arms flailing overhead, his legs shooting out from under him, his face contorting in pain and fear. My brain searched for comprehension, but every beat of my heart offered a different theory.

His jealousy had gotten the best of him, and he'd come to confront me and Adam.

He'd heard Hal and Larry, and suspicion had launched him down the steps.

He'd been pushed.

A strangled groan escaped my lips as he landed, twisted at our feet, on the stone platform—legs splayed out, one arm behind him like he'd posed for a chalk outline. His eyes stared straight up into the sky, and he gulped at the air. Decklin crouched at the top of the stairs with her fist to her mouth, her eyes wide like a deer's.

"What happened?" I raced to Brandon's side, my blood ice cold in my veins. I didn't care that Larry and Hal had shown themselves. I suddenly didn't care about anything.

Brandon blinked erratically. I knelt next to him and put a hand on his chest. His heart beat like mad. The leg looked bad, but the angle of his neck looked worse. Brandon opened his mouth and whispered something so faint I had to lean in to hear him.

"He said his legs are stuck," I said. But his legs weren't stuck. Realization hit me like a brick in the chest. I fell back on my heels, clutching my head in my hands.

"His neck is broken. We need to get him to a hospital." My throat, tight with panic, barely eked out the words.

"We don't have time to bring him anywhere," Larry said.

My skin burned under my wet, sticky clothes. My body pulsed with my heartbeat, which hammered strong and fast as I put my hands on Brandon's chest and took them away again. His breathing came in quick rasps. His eyes rolled back in his head.

"Brandon?" I choked.

This was all my fault. I shouldn't have gone camping, shouldn't have dragged him into this. I shouldn't have been so distracted by Adam. If Hal and Larry hadn't shown up when they did, if Adam hadn't called me away...

"Don't move him," Adam said. "He's broken."

The way he said *he's broken*, as if Brandon were a wind-up toy, caused something inside me to snap. Brandon wasn't a *thing*. He was a living, breathing, human being, complete with a soul and a purpose. Didn't Adam see that? Didn't Adam care? I leapt to my feet and pointed a finger in Adam's face.

"This is your fault! All of it. We wouldn't be here if it weren't for you and your *Senders*. And now Brandon's going to die." Giant, wracking sobs stole my voice before I could blame him for my father's disappearance and for every other terrible thing I could think of.

He stared at me calmly the whole time, which ripped a hole straight through the center of me. A hole through which the truth poured in: Brandon was going to die because of *me*. Not because of Adam. *I'd* led him on. He'd brought me here to impress *me*. And this was the price he'd pay...

When I looked back, Brandon's damaged body lay still on the stone. The heat of my anger rushed out of me, and the cold, bitter wind of agony swept into its place.

"Do something." I implored Adam, then Larry, through my teeth. "Do something. Help him. Bring him back. Now." I had the urge to grab Brandon by the shirt and shake him, shake him until he woke. He didn't look dead. His cheeks were still flushed, and his eyes stared straight up as if contemplating the vastness of the sky. A scream bubbled to the surface and escaped my lips as anguish coursing through my veins.

"He slipped," Decklin whispered from the stairs. Her face had gone pure white. "It should have been me. I went first. The rock was slick. I tried to keep my balance but… then he reached out and caught me, and he slipped and went down. You should have seen the way he went down. Is he dead Mira? Oh my God, is he dead?"

I shivered like crazy and watched Decklin as she cowered on the steps, her knees caked with mud, her face streaked with tears. I buried my face in my hands and wept through my fingers. Of course Brandon had tried to save her. Brandon tried to save everyone, except himself.

Chapter Eleven

I backed away from the body, farther and farther until my back hit the stone wall, and I paused, blinking hard. Blinking like I was trying to wake myself up from a nightmare.

"Oh God," Decklin moaned. "I'm gonna be sick."

As soon as she said it, I felt it too. I watched Brandon's eyes for a sign, a twitch, anything. I watched for a full minute, for an eternal minute, repeating *Please don't die. Please don't die.* His chest rose and fell. Slower and slower. Rose. Fell.

Rose.

Fell.

I waited and willed from the very bottom of my soul for his chest to rise again. To take in air. For him to look at me with those mischievous eyes. But his chest didn't rise. His eyes didn't open. The hard slap of reality knocked the strength from my muscles, wilting me like an under-watered plant.

Brandon was dead.

"No," I whispered. Our short life together flashed before my eyes and threatened to crumble me. It couldn't be. Brandon looked peaceful. Strong. Not dead and gone. I wiped at the stream of tears with the back of my hand, but they kept coming. Adam stood completely still and quiet, looking down at the body.

"It was just a camping trip." I pushed off the wall and hurtled toward Brandon. "This does not happen." My knees smacked the stone as I went down. I lifted him by the fabric of his shirt, drew him to me, and shook him. "Wake up," I begged. "Wake up."

A strong hand gripped my shoulder, and Larry cleared his throat from behind me.

In the background, Decklin kept repeating, "*It was an accident. It was an accident.*"

I set Brandon down and placed my hands on his neck. I bent over him, imploring the healing powers inside me to work on him, to revive him. Fix the broken neck and make him whole. My pleas were as urgent and unhinged as a runaway train barreling down a track.

When I opened my eyes, I expected to see him looking back at me with those chestnut eyes, that crooked smile. I was *that sure*.

"Don't do this," I whispered into his ear. "You can't do this." What about his sister? His parents? Did I seal his fate when I chose Adam over him? Was his fall truly an accident?

He had become just a body, a boy's body in a t-shirt soaked with rain and mud. A body like Orientation would choose to house a Sender's soul…

An idea hatched in my mind, almost too insane to consider. I rose to my feet and faced Larry.

"You cannot let this happen."

No one breathed. Hal put his hand to his head. Larry opened his mouth to say something, but before he could, I ran at him and pounded on his flabby chest. "Do it," I screamed. "Do it!"

Decklin buried her head in her knees. I didn't care. I didn't care if it was right or wrong or who thought what. Larry nodded slightly and held my hands tight in his, his face set and stern.

"Mira, we can't. Not in front of…" He nodded toward the shivering mass Decklin had become.

"This is bigger than her! This is bigger than you." I pleaded with him, pulled at him. "Please. This is our opportunity. We can initiate another one so Adam's not alone. Think about it. It gives us more of a chance to find the Conduit. I would do it myself if I could, but you know I can't." My stupid talent was useless here. I couldn't bring the Senders in. I could only reverse what the Conduit did.

Brandon's body lay there, all the life gone out of it. I struggled to hold on to consciousness. Part of me knew having another body meant another chance for a Sender to escape extinction, another chance for Orientation to draw out the Conduit. But mostly, I just wanted to see Brandon get up and smile again.

Hal's voice broke through my quaking pleas. "Shame to waste a perfectly good body," he said softly. I could have kissed him.

"It ain't supposed to be," Larry said. "They didn't plan for this one. Whoever comes in to Brandon's body might not know how to operate as a human."

Adam spoke up. I had forgotten about Adam. "I agree with Mira and Hal. There are only so many of us left. Whoever comes in will be fine. They trained all of us in preparation."

"You don't need Larry," I said to Hal, dropping my hands from Larry's.

"Now wait a minute. He can't do that," Larry said. He held my eyes for an eternity before he sighed and knelt down on Brandon's right side. Hal followed suit. From my place by Brandon's head, I swayed back and forth, wrung my hands, and watched.

Deeper and deeper inside me, my thoughts chased after each other. If I hadn't been so enthralled by Brandon's good looks, his charm, his confidence, his normalness, I never would have agreed to this camping trip. I never would have tried to drown my nerves in all that beer. It seeped from my pores. I could still taste it in the back of my throat. Nausea started to overtake me, and for a moment, I thought I might spew this morning's bitter coffee all over the wet rock.

Larry closed his eyes. Hal tipped his head back, his own eyes wide and unfocused. Sweat poured from their foreheads. I forgot the world around me, forgot Decklin cringing in the corner. I concentrated with them, for them.

I wanted Brandon back with the same voracity that I wanted my father. The tears came for real then, a wall of them, like they had been building up forever behind the dam of my eyelids and had suddenly broken through. The air erupted with birdsong, and the bugs resumed their onslaught. Or maybe those things had been there the whole time, and I hadn't noticed. They didn't fit the mood. I wanted funeral dirges, thunder, rain.

Larry withdrew first. Then Hal. Both of them fell backward in the mud, spent.

Initiation was rough work; I knew from my mother's accounts.

Brandon lay motionless. No one said anything. Behind me, I could hear Decklin's teeth chattering. Despite what I knew of the world and the afterlife, I still prayed. I watched Brandon's chest, my fingers digging into my palms, my fists pressed against my forehead.

His foot twitched.

Followed by a sharp inhale.

He bent his leg suddenly, as if his knee were attached to a string, like a marionette. All the breath gathered inside me, but I couldn't let it out, not yet. My gaze traveled from Brandon's muddy sock up his leg to the dark hair on his calf, to the scars on his shins from years of soccer, and finally up to his face.

He lifted his head, scanned his surroundings until those eyes—alight and aflame—caught mine and held them, staring at me in astonishment. His chest rose and fell unevenly.

"That's it?" I whispered. I'd always imagined what it would be like to watch Orientation do their job, to see them bring a being into a body. I'd imagined some kind of magic—a lightning strike, a puff of smoke. At least, I'd expected a disturbance in the natural state of things. Something more like Frankenstein's monster, with wires and jolts of electricity. The subtlety of this made it seem so much less magical than I'd imagined.

"Did it work?" He spoke with Brandon's voice, but different. I detected no sign of recognition in his eyes. Instead, he looked confused. Helpless. Not like Brandon at all. I loosened my fists and let the tension out of my shoulders.

"Yes," I answered. It had worked, but it was no cause for celebration. I trudged over to the railing in case I needed to vomit, while Larry and Hal helped the new Brandon to his feet.

"Like a newborn horse," Larry said in awe while Brandon rocked and swayed and struggled for balance. He looked exactly like Brandon, but he wasn't Brandon. A blankness overtook his eyes. Lack of history, perhaps, or context, or experience, or whatever makes people human.

He was new to the body too. Not familiar with the controls. At first, his movements came off awkward and jerky. Like when I drove for the first time, all reaction and overreaction. His arms swung next to his body as if they didn't belong to him. He stood slightly stooped, leaning too far forward and then correcting too far backward. I realized I was staring, all my muscles tense.

"We should go." I choked back the rest of my tears. Brandon was gone, yet his exact likeness tottered before me. Even though it had been my idea to initiate him, my brain couldn't process it, and I was too exhausted to try.

"Brandon," Larry said. "Meet Mira. Adam's your kind. That's Hal. And I'm Larry."

Decklin sniffed loudly, and we all turned to her. She wiped her nose with the back of her hand and then stood twisting her fingers, entirely pale.

"Who are you people? What did you do to him?" She could barely speak. Her wide eyes darted from Larry to Hal, then to me, and finally to Brandon.

Oh God.

"Decklin." I took a step forward, my hand outstretched.

"Stay away from me." She inched up the stairs as if backing away from something big, something dangerous.

"Wait, it's not what you think." My words stuck on the tip of my tongue. What explanation could I possibly give? That Larry and Hal were recruited by a race of endangered aliens to provide empty human bodies for them to occupy?

Decklin darted up the steps.

"I'm on it." Hal lumbered past us to chase her.

"Bring her back to school," I called after him. I needed to be the one to talk to Decklin, not some giant, old, strange man clamoring after her through the woods. What a disaster. What a total and complete disaster. When I'd pushed for them to initiate Brandon, I'd been too distraught by the loss of him to grasp the consequences.

"This is bad." Larry flung one arm around the new Brandon's waist. "Decklin will tell someone."

"Who will she tell? Who's going to believe her?" I said. "Give her a little while to process. She'll convince herself Brandon wasn't dead. I'll tell her you guys are chiropractors or something. I don't know. We have bigger things to worry about. Brandon isn't Brandon, and he has to be. For his parents, his friends, his soccer team."

For me.

"We have to bring him to the hospital," Larry said. "Concussion. That will explain the memory loss. Now Adam, help me get him moving." Adam stepped up and put his arm under Brandon's, steering him in the direction of the path.

"All right, kid. Here we go. One foot in front of the other," Larry said, like nothing at all had happened.

By the time we reached the campsite, Brandon no longer needed assistance walking. No one would ever suspect he was so new to it.

"I hope you were at the top of your class in 'how to be a human' school." My voice was flat. "It's going to be a bitch to blend in."

"This doesn't feel like training," he said with that same careful, crisp pronunciation Adam had used at first. His wide eyes lifted to the sky. "It feels strange. These hands. These thoughts. But I don't know if it's strange or normal."

"It's normal. It takes a while to get used to," Adam said.

"He's talking better than you did." Larry looked at Adam and raised his bushy eyebrows.

"I believe it," I said, thinking of how much Brandon had liked to talk.

Not that any of him remained. Just the body. It hit me that his parents wouldn't ever know. Their only son had died and this new one had taken his place, and they would never know. I imagined Brandon as a boy, unwrapping presents under a Christmas tree, his smiling parents snapping picture after picture. I thought of how they must have cheered him on at soccer games, laughed at his dumb jokes, and taped his drawings to their refrigerator.

All of it was gone. Their future with Brandon would be a lie.

I left Larry and Adam to pack the car and entered the tent. Brandon's half-unzipped bag lay where he left it. I picked up the T-shirt he'd worn only yesterday, held it to my face, and inhaled. The scent brought me right back to the way he'd looked when he leaned in to kiss me. My heart shriveled. If only I could curl up under the blanket and sleep my grief away.

"Mira, in the tent there, that's your girlfriend," I heard Larry say.

T-shirt still in hand, I burst from the tent.

"No," I said. "I am not that thing's girlfriend. I don't know him at all." The tears came again, but this time, they were angry. I started taking down the tent. What was the last thing I had said to Brandon? Something inane, no doubt. Inconsequential. Something typically Mira.

I yanked out the stakes, rolled up the tent, and picked up the empty beer cans, trying not to imagine Brandon's hands gripping them last.

We waited as long as we could, but there was no sign of Decklin or Hal. We left the security truck for them, and Larry drove Brandon's car to the hospital, coaching him the whole way on how to act human. I sat with my face in my hands, too numb to do anything.

Chapter Twelve

I walked through the hospital doors and inhaled antiseptic, linoleum, ammonia, and bleach. Soft-shoed nurses hurried down the hallways, lights hummed, and machines whirred all around me.

I told the lady at intake that Brandon had hit his head and we suspected he had a concussion. She helped him into a wheelchair and directed Adam and me to have a seat in the waiting room. Larry took off down the hall to call my mother. I couldn't bear to talk to her.

"Act normal," I whispered in Brandon's ear before they wheeled him behind the curtain.

In the waiting room, a television flickered in the corner with voiceless newscasters and images of fighting in some foreign country. The clock read four-thirty. My body wanted sleep, but I had to stay awake because Brandon's mother and father were on their way.

Adam reclined next to me, the picture of calm. A bearded man with a ripped jacket snoozed in the seat across from us, and an ancient lady in the corner kept hacking into a tissue. I rested my head on Adam's shoulder and tried to disappear into the news.

"Where is he?" A voice asked from behind me.

I shot up in my seat and turned around. Brandon's mother, I assumed. She rushed over, clacking heels, swinging purse, and flushed cheeks. I pointed to the curtained area, my heart a coiled black lump inside my chest.

"You're Mira? Larry said you were there with Brandon when it happened." She took my hand. I nodded. "Who's this?"

"This is Adam," I said. "A friend. He was with us." Hard swallow.

"You're at Meryton too?" She glanced between us. "Where are your parents?" Neither of us had a chance to stumble through an answer before she moved on. "Jim's coming. He's parking the car. He should be here in a minute."

She took the kind of breath someone takes after not breathing for a long time, and she peered around and clutched her purse tightly to her chest with her free hand as if she thought someone might steal it. Brandon had spoken highly of his mother, of her seventy-hour workweeks and designer shoes. To me, she appeared to be cracking under the surface.

"I hope they're taking care of my boy." Mrs. Tate's thin, cold hand still grasped mine. I hoped she didn't feel me shaking.

"He's over there." I pointed to the curtain. "But I don't know if you're supposed to go in."

"Bullshit. This is my only child we're talking about." I thought briefly of Brandon's sister. She'd had already lost one child.

Two children.

A thin piece of fabric wasn't going to stop her. She threw back the curtain and rushed in. I followed behind her.

"Oh God, Brandon." She choked back a sob.

Thick, white gauze covered his head, and bruises framed his eyes. Underneath the hospital gown, his bare legs stuck out with dirty white socks pulled up to his calves. Next to him, clear liquid dripped from an IV, running down the lines into the thick blue vein in his forearm.

"How do you feel?" I raked my fingernails up the inside of my arm, hoping he wouldn't say anything incriminating.

"Head feels heavy." Brandon inspected the clear tube coming out of his arm.

"Did someone punch you?" Mrs. Tate draped herself across his bed, kissed him lightly on the forehead, and drew back to shake her head.

"No. I hit my head." Brandon looked at me. I tried to relax, but every muscle stayed taut.

"How did you do that? Were you drinking? I smell alcohol." Mrs. Tate took a whiff of the air.

"It's probably the antiseptic." I rushed to his bed to smooth the starched white sheet, some innocuous activity to draw Mrs. Tate's attention away for just a second.

Brandon's dad drew back the curtain and ducked in. He removed his cap and smoothed down his hair, which grayed at the temples. His eyes—the same color and shape as Brandon's—roamed from the bandages on Brandon's head to the IV, to me, and then to Adam.

"Where's the doctor? What in the hell happened?" He perched on the edge of a chair and then stood right back up again.

"We just came in." Mrs. Tate still clutched her purse. "I don't know where anyone is."

I handed Mr. Tate Brandon's keys. Now that his parents had arrived, I itched to get out of there as soon as possible.

"He's kind of out of it," I said, recalling my rehearsed lines. "The steps were really slippery, and he fell. He hit his head pretty hard, and we think he's got some memory loss."

Mr. Tate patted Brandon on the shoulder in this really awkward way that told me they probably hadn't touched in years. *And what was the last thing he said to his son?*

"Was there a railing?"

"Oh, Jim. Not now. You're not suing anyone. It was slippery. It had been raining."

"It's negligence, Deborah. Who's going to pay these medical bills?" Mr. Tate's smooth and hairless forearms reminded me of my own father's arms. For a moment, I envied Brandon, that he should have a father standing right there. Then I remembered again, and again and again continuously, that Brandon was dead.

"Never mind him, Bran. What do you need? I threw some raisins in my purse. It was all I had time..." Mrs. Tate trailed off and dug around in her purse until she produced a box of raisins and set them on the table.

"Raisins?" Brandon glanced at me as if asking my approval. I frowned at him and wished he'd stop doing that, stop drawing attention to me and to his own awkwardness.

"You used to love raisins," his mother said.

"I did?"

"Both you and Annabelle did. Do you remember Annabelle?"

Brandon shook his head. I wanted to scream out of frustration. Mr. Tate cleared his throat.

"Deb, that's enough." Mr. Tate eyed Adam and me. "Who are you?"

"That's Mira. That's Adam." Brandon wore a look of accomplishment on his face, like he'd remembered *something*.

Mrs. Tate shook her head and launched into how we shouldn't have been camping without telling anyone. "What if something worse had happened?"

Something worse *had* happened.

"Are you sick? You look a wreck yourself," Mrs. Tate said to me.

"We got stuck in the rain." I patted my hair, which had frizzed out to three times its normal size.

"Are you hungry? I can go pick something up."

"You saw the town, Deb," Brandon's father said. "What are you going to find? A day-old tuna sandwich from a gas station?"

"I don't like the idea of him eating hospital food. He might as well chew on cardboard."

"Maybe he's not supposed to eat." Mr. Tate ran his finger down one of the tubes coming out of the fluid bag. "They must have him on drugs. What's in the IV? His eyes are glazed. He's swoony. He's got a game Tuesday."

"What is going on?" Brandon shifted in the bed. He reached up and tentatively fingered the gauze on his head.

We all turned to him. It seemed we'd forgotten the reason we were there. Except the machines. The machines stayed vigilant. They beeped steadily from the corner.

Mrs. Tate touched Brandon lightly on the head. "You're in the hospital, honey. You're fine now. It could have been much worse." She stroked his cheek. "You could have broken your neck."

I cleared my throat. "Well, we should get going." I started to back out of the room and motioned for Adam to join me.

Brandon touched his fingers to his neck. "The woman said it used to be broken. They showed me a picture."

"I'm sure you would remember breaking your neck. It's not like a paper cut," Mrs. Tate said.

"Are you sure they were looking at the right x-rays? You never know in these backwoods hospitals." Mr. Tate ran his hand along the top of one of the monitors and looked at his fingertips as if inspecting them for dust.

I nodded my agreement. "Yeah, they probably don't know what they're talking about."

Cue the nurse. A fireplug of a woman, dark-haired with serious eyes. She glowered at us in a way that made me think she might kick all of our asses.

"You're not supposed to be in here." She pushed past Brandon's mother and aimed a small bright light at Brandon's eyes. "How're you feeling, Mr. Tate?"

He blinked a few times. "I'm not sure."

"I bet. You cracked it good. Got a minor concussion. Nothing to be too worried about, but concussions can cause all kinds of problems." The nurse poked and prodded at him, adjusting his head wrap. "That's why we like to monitor people for about twenty-four hours, to watch for symptoms. Vomiting, seizures, hallucinations, that kind of thing."

She turned to Brandon's parents. "He's got slight memory loss, it seems. That should come back. And he's dehydrated. You do some drinking?"

Brandon's mother raised her eyebrows. Brandon didn't answer.

The nurse shrugged. "Most likely he'll be fine, but he should stay overnight."

Brandon seized the nurse by the wrist. She didn't expect it and jumped back about a foot.

"I want to go back," he said to her, though he looked past her to me, to Adam. My heart seized and blood rushed to my face. The new Brandon would ruin everything. He would—

"He's a student at Meryton," his mother explained, charging forward to hold his hand.

The nurse nodded. "You can do what you want, technically, but the doctor's advice is to stay. Let us spoil you a bit. Monitor you, make sure everything is okay, and you can leave tomorrow."

"Then I can go back?" Brandon said.

"Back to Meryton?" his mother asked.

Brandon didn't answer. He didn't mean Meryton at all. I inched closer to the door, waiting for the right time to make my exit.

The nurse shook her head. "Concussions are serious business. You should stay at home for a week. Let your parents take care of you," she said. "And no exertion of any kind." She turned to me and glared. Heat rose to my cheeks.

His dad folded his arms across his chest. "A week? And what about soccer? When can he pick that up again?"

"Jim," Brandon's mother snapped. "Our son is in the hospital, and you're thinking about soccer?"

"I'm thinking about him being one season away from a free ride; that's what I'm thinking about. Kids get concussions all the time. They play through them."

If the nurse had glared any harder at Mr. Tate, she would have melted him.

Rain pounded against the window, drawing my attention away from the bickering. The parking lot lights blurred into orbs of yellow. I focused on the bleary-eyed, disheveled girl with the frizzy hair. Adam watched me in the reflection.

"All right then." I announced from the doorway to no one in particular.

His mother scrutinized me. "You're not going to stay the night? Aren't you his girlfriend?" I sensed a hint of disapproval in her voice.

The nurse answered before I could, thank god. "He'll be transferred to a room if one becomes available. But chances are pretty slim. We're booked up. You're welcome to stay, but you'll have to sleep out there in the waiting room." She glanced at Brandon's dad. "With the rest of the backwoods folk."

Aside from reeling inside about everything, I really wanted to go home. Or, the Meryton version of home. I wanted to crawl into my bed and sleep for the rest of the weekend.

"No, you shouldn't stay." Mrs. Tate clicked her tongue. "You look exhausted. Jim will drive you kids back to school."

"That's okay," I said. "We have a ride."

Mrs. Tate pursed her lips. "Okay. Well, we saw a motel down the road." She turned to Brandon. "Dad and I will get a room and see how you're doing tomorrow, Bran."

Mrs. Tate spoke with such authority that none of us dared to question her. She left to find "suitable" food, and his dad went to speak with the doctor. As soon as the three of us were alone in the room, I dashed across the room to Brandon's bedside.

"You need to keep your mouth shut." I knew it was harsh, but now we had another Initiate to worry about, another potential target. "You have to heed the advice Larry gave you in the car. Don't mention Orientation. Don't act like you've never eaten, never heard music, never watched TV. When in doubt, blame the concussion."

Adam seized my wrist and gave me a hard look. "Mira. Don't be so hard on him."

I jerked my arm away. "It's for his own good. You know that."

"I think there's been a mistake." Brandon rolled his shoulders, stretched his neck, and grimaced with pain. "This body isn't working very well."

Adam patted Brandon on the arm. "You got hurt. Give yourself a chance to heal. It will get better." He spoke from experience.

"And stop saying you want to go back," I added, still miffed at Adam's reprimand. "You can't go back. Right? Tell him, Adam."

Adam studied the monitor with his hands folded in front of him. "You can't go back," he said flatly.

"Rest." I tucked the sheet around Brandon's shoulders, conscious of my own trembling hands. "Your team needs their star player."

I pulled my damp sleeves down over my wrists. The fluorescent lights buzzed over us, and I counted each drip of the IV. If I had to listen to these machines any longer, I'd need a one way ticket to the psych ward.

"Remember everything we told you." I strode past the end of his bed toward the door. "You'll be in Brandon's room at home. Absorb what you can. His interests are your interests. Watch how people act. You'll pick it up. Don't give them any chance to question who you are."

I ushered Adam through the door, glancing down the hallway for anyone suspicious.

"Who am I?" Brandon called after us.

I peeked back into the room and regarded the boy on the bed, choosing my words deliberately. "You're Brandon."

"No, he's not." Adam edged up next to me, wearing a grave expression. "That wasn't the plan. We aren't here to assume someone else's identity. He wasn't trained to do that."

Why did he keep correcting me? I clenched my jaw to keep my voice even. "Change of plans. He's here so you won't go extinct, right? He needed a body, and now he has one. That's the situation. Deal with it. Come on." I pushed past him into the hallway.

Adam didn't move. He watched Brandon, his brow furrowed in concern.

"Adam," I said. "Larry will keep an eye on him. That's what we agreed on. We have to go. Larry is—"

"He's a target, just like I am."

My shoulders slumped. "He doesn't know that. And he shouldn't. He'll have it easy. His mother spoils him. She'll be practically spoon feeding him. It won't be a rough life." I pictured him in Brandon's clothes, driving Brandon's car, smiling with Brandon's friends, using Brandon's body. Something squeezed me from the inside.

"You make it sound so easy." Adam brushed past me, his jaw set.

His anger threw me off, and for a moment, I couldn't move. Just last night things had been so different between us. Now, I watched him storm down the hallway with his shoulders squared and his fists clenched. Before he reached the corner, he stopped and looked back. I took it as a sign and ran to catch up to him, hoping to lighten things up with some kind of apology. But the look on his face kept me quiet. Frustration had replaced the awestruck stare I'd grown accustomed to. The one that made my heart beat faster.

I dropped my gaze. There was nothing I could say.

"You've made it clear you don't see us as human," Adam said. "We're tools for your agenda. I get it. You want to get your father back. When you look at me, that's all you see. That's all anyone sees, anyone who knows what I am anyway." He tilted his head. "Has it ever occurred to you that once I entered this body, I became just as human as you are? Same feelings, same needs." His eyes moved to my lips. I struggled to keep the blush at bay, wanting to kill myself for reacting like a giddy schoolgirl in the midst of all this devastation.

"You watched your friend die. You begged them to repurpose his body. And they did. He's lying there newly initiated with no clue what is going on, and you just want to brush him aside because he's an inconvenience."

He spoke steadily, didn't raise his voice or show any emotion. I stood staring at him, speechless, flexing and unflexing my fingers behind my back. He didn't know how I felt. His father wasn't ripped away from him when he was ten years old. He hadn't spent the last seven years of his life dedicated to hunting down the Conduit. He'd only just gotten to earth, only just gotten a body. He didn't even know how to use it properly, yet he had the nerve to criticize *my* actions, to judge me for how *I* handled Brandon's death.

"Hal's got Decklin." Larry approached us from behind. I spun around, caught off guard. My hands shook and my cheeks burned. Larry frowned. "You okay?"

"Do I look okay?"

He paused a moment and drew an extended breath. If he attempted to comfort me, I would jump out of my skin.

He studied me for a moment and then continued. "He's takin' her back to school. Adam, Hal will wait for you in the parking lot. He'll have to keep you with him for a bit for your own safety since I'm gonna have to stick around here. Mira, try and talk to Decklin, won't ya? She's all sorts of shaken up."

I must have nodded. But inside, I had gone somewhere else. Somewhere far away from all of this, one particular track played over and over again in my head: *I am part of something bigger.* I couldn't let go of the feeling that Brandon had been an unintentional sacrifice in this cloak-and-dagger quest to save a species. I needed to believe his death wasn't for nothing, that it fit somewhere in the broader picture.

"We should go," Adam said.

I glanced back toward Brandon's curtain as we trudged down the hall. Brandon would have no funeral, no eulogy, no closure. But I would remember him. I would make a point of it. I was tired of people disappearing from my life.

Chapter Thirteen

I should have timed it better. The hallway bustled with seniors back from dinner. Though I kept my head down, I felt their eyes roaming over my mud-soaked sneakers, my ratty hair, my lips moving as I went over and over what I planned to say to Decklin. I slid my card and opened the door, ready to convince her it was the heat, or low blood sugar, or something.

But she wasn't there.

Her duffel bag sat wadded in the corner of the closet. Her clothes were still in her drawers. A notebook lay open on her desk filled with geometric doodles. Her bed was unmade, a five point penalty. All signs of Decklin, but no Decklin.

I slouched against the door and let my head fall back. Part of me was relieved—I wouldn't have to have *the talk*. But what if Decklin didn't come back at all? What if she had gone to the police? I spun around and peered through the peephole. Any minute now, they would bust down my door and arrest me for…what?

A thought jabbed its way into my mind. Decklin might go to the police, but that wasn't the worst thing that could happen. What if the Conduit followed her, or had her followed? If he'd managed to create a mole in Orientation, he had to have other henchmen somewhere. And what if they'd infiltrated the police?

My head spun as my conspiracy theories built, one on top of the other, until I'd managed to make the Conduit into an all-knowing deity and freak myself out. I traversed the room and collapsed on my bed, clutching the metal railings and concentrating on the frayed rug to keep from passing out. Every time I closed my eyes, I saw Brandon lying twisted on the rocks. I needed a distraction before I drove myself crazy.

The showers were empty, thank god. I stood under the jet and let hot water stream down my back. Alone, I allowed the tears flow freely as I washed the mud from my ankles and hands. I scrubbed until my skin glowed bright pink. But no matter how many times I lathered and rinsed, I could not wash off the image of Brandon, and I could not silence the whirling thoughts.

Back in my room, even in my warm fleece pajamas, I shivered. In my bed, with the lights on, I stared blankly at my phone for a half hour trying to figure out how to respond to the barrage of texts from my mother. Finally, I settled on an answer. I texted:

I'm fine, good night.

I stared at the door for a while, and then I got up, moved my desk chair across the room, and jammed it under the knob.

❊ ❊ ❊

Decklin didn't come back. On Monday morning, the top bunk sat empty and undisturbed. The tight ball of dread in my stomach expanded, filling me. I walked bleary-eyed to calculus, jerking my head left and right like a paranoid street person. I slid into my seat and watched the door, but Adam didn't show up. Though I didn't expect him to, it still deflated me. I hadn't talked to him in two days, and I couldn't stand that he might still be mad at me.

Identifying slopes and vertical intercepts took all my concentration. Every once and a while, as I chewed on the end of my pencil, I glanced around at the kids in class bent over their calculations, and the ones staring toward the windows, and I wished I were one of them. How would it feel, just for a little while, to be in someone else's body? How would it feel to be someone with an established life, regular concerns, straight hair, and maybe even a talent for playing piano or memorizing poetry?

"Ms. Avery?" Dolby stood at the open door holding a note in his hand. "Mira, the Dean wants to see you."

I jolted at the mention of my name. Everyone in class looked in my direction. Natasha snickered.

"Me?" Now what?

Dolby nodded.

I gathered my books and slid out of my chair, my heart pounding, pondering every terrible thing that might await me. In the dean's office, I sat in one of the straight-backed wooden chairs across from the secretary. She gave me a sympathetic little tilt of her head and continued typing. When Dean Snyder opened the door, he smiled at me from behind wire-framed glasses. The frantic butterflies in my stomach settled; he wouldn't have smiled if it were that bad.

He motioned for me to sit in the chair across from his desk and then took his seat. "Miss Avery, I don't usually talk to students alone about matters like this. But I couldn't reach your mother, and this is urgent. Can you verify this is your mother's correct number?" He slid a piece of paper across the expanse of his desk. I read it, nodded, and pushed it back at him. Though she switched phones all the time, I recognized the number. My throat went dry. Why would he need to contact my mother?

"You came to Meryton as a senior." He tapped the point of a pencil on my records. "That's unusual. Looks like you've moved around quite a bit. Your father in the service?"

"Was." I hung my head. I had used that excuse all the time. Before.

"Ah." He adjusted his glasses. "Of course. Your grades speak for themselves. Maintaining that kind of academic excellence in the course of…" He paused to count, flipping pages.

I really needed him to get to the point, so I helped him out. "Five."

He looked up. "Five? Five different high schools?"

I dug my fingernails into my thighs. "Am I in trouble?"

He flashed me patronizing smile. "Not at all. I should have started with that, I suppose." He gave a quick little laugh, but it did nothing to dispel my nervousness. If I wasn't in trouble, I couldn't figure out what he wanted with me.

"Unfortunately something rather alarming has taken place." At this, he removed his glasses and set them down on the desk.

I lowered my head and pressed my fingertips together.

"Miss Avery, did you know Cassidy Ellis prior to attending Meryton?"

My head snapped up at the mention of Cassidy's name. I had expected him to say something like, *Have you been fraternizing with otherworldly beings on my campus?*

"Cassidy? No." I shook my head. This was about Cassidy?

"Didn't you get a letter late in the summer introducing you to your roommate? It should have included contact information."

The chair creaked as I shifted. "I registered really late, so I didn't find out until I got here."

"I see." He stared at me from under his overgrown eyebrows. "Well, Cassidy disappeared about two days ago."

My mouth fell open. "Disappeared? From where?"

"From her parents' house. In Syracuse."

"So... she was never here?" I still had Cassidy's ID tucked in a drawer in my desk, but its presence felt bigger than the whole campus at that moment. I placed my palms flat on his desk and steadied myself.

"From what her mother says, they dropped her off at campus the day before orientation. She wanted to get settled in. Cassidy was a very good student. Very prepared. Later that night, one of the housemothers saw Cassidy acting strangely and attempted to talk to her. I won't go into details."

He straightened some papers on his desk. "Let's just say questions were raised about the practicality of her remaining on campus, and in the end, her mother came and took her home. For observation." He tapped his index finger on the folder in front of him. "And that's why you were assigned a new roommate."

"So Cassidy is missing." My throat constricted at the idea that my would-be roommate had joined my father, Brandon, and possibly Decklin—the people who disappeared out of my life one by one. If I failed when the Conduit came for Adam, he'd be gone too. Pretty soon there would be no one left.

"It's quite possible she ran away. But Mira." He leaned forward. "If she contacts you, you must let the police know. Call right away."

"Of course." I slid my shaking hands under my thighs.

He raised his eyebrows at me. "Has she?"

"Has she what?"

"Contacted you?"

"No." My head swirled with this new information. I debated telling him about the ID but decided against it. I couldn't sit in that office one minute longer.

"That will be all." Dean Snyder rose from his chair, so I stood as well. "Oh, and I'm going to dismiss your points. Wipe the slate clean." He smiled like he'd given me a gift, and I returned a mechanical grin. "Even your little foray into Mr. Dolby's classroom to retrieve your phone."

I stopped smiling.

"Keep up the good work." He pointed me toward the door, and I walked out.

As I plodded down the hall, thoughts in a tangle, I contemplated all of the awful things that might have happened to Cassidy. And how, like what happened to Brandon, they were most likely because of me.

Chapter Fourteen

When I'd left the dean's office, I'd fully intended to go to English Lit and wait for Decklin while fending off my mother's attempts at communication. But I'd found myself scrolling through the few texts Cassidy and I had exchanged before I came to campus. Nothing in her messages raised any red flags, so whatever had happened to her must have happened here…at school.

Thanks to the knowledge I'd acquired after years of tracking people down, I did a reverse trace on the phone number and located her address. Getting the information had been easy, but convincing Larry to abandon Brandon to take me to Syracuse had proven much more difficult. He did it though. He hated saying no to me.

An hour later, I stood on Cassidy's front porch between two giant white pillars, fist poised to knock. Her parents probably had a heart attack with every knock at their door, thinking they'd find cops with grim looks on their faces. *We found your daughter,* they would say, and Cassidy's mom would buckle at the knees.

I don't know how long I procrastinated. But the door eventually opened without my knocking at all, as if they had some sixth sense I had come.

"Yes?"

Cassidy's mother stood in the doorway, eyeing me with suspicion. Her red-rimmed eyes, and the bags underneath them, spoke of sleepless nights, but not a hair on her head strayed from the tight bun. She wore a fitted top and a pencil skirt with shiny, cream-colored heels. My faded jeans and thrift-store coat seemed grossly inappropriate by comparison.

"Um," I said.

Cassidy's father thundered down the stairs and stared at me expectantly. I thought about bolting, but I needed answers.

"Do you know Cassidy?" Mrs. Ellis grasped at the pearl necklace around her throat, her eyes wide with a mixture of hope and fear.

I winced, not wanting to give them false hope. "No." Their faces fell. I swallowed and tried again. "Well, sort of. Cassidy was supposed to be my roommate at Meryton."

They ushered me into their foyer. Everything gleamed bright and clean, absent of the chaos and bustle I expected to accompany a missing daughter. A tiny white dog with curly hair yipped at me so hard his little barks lifted him off the ground. I jumped each time and backed into a corner.

"Ben!" Cassidy's mother jabbed her husband in the ribs. He pushed the dog aside with his foot.

I took a breath. "I'm Mira."

They both nodded and waited for more. Right behind them, framed, professional photos of Cassidy lined the walls.

"Have you heard from her?" her dad asked.

"No. Not since before school started. We texted a few times."

Her parents studied me. I tugged at the string hanging off my right sleeve.

"Have you heard from her?" I asked.

"No."

Pause.

"Would you like some tea?" her mother offered.

"No thanks." I rubbed my hands on my thighs, unsure why I'd come and what exactly I'd hoped to gain by doing so. I needed information, and the only way to get it was to ask for it.

"I'm sorry to intrude, but I want to help." I gulped. "The police think Cassidy ran away?"

Her mother shook her head right away. "That's what they'd like us to believe. But she wasn't the running away type. That's what they just don't understand." She sniffled. "They're acting as if I don't know my own daughter. I know her better than anyone."

I looked Mrs. Ellis right in the eye. "I don't think she ran away either."

She sucked in a deep breath and grabbed at her pearls again as I told them about my conversation with Dean Snyder.

Cassidy's parents glanced at each other.

"Why don't we have a seat?" Mrs. Ellis motioned for me to sit on the leather couch in the immaculate living room. Everything in their house was perfectly coordinated, crisp and clean, a stark contrast to the cluttered mess of my thoughts. I sank into the soft leather couch. My stomach tumbled end over end.

Mrs. Ellis twisted her pearls, taking a seat across from me, next to her husband. "Cassidy was acting strange. Not like herself at all. We got the call from the school about it, but by the time we got there, they had Cass locked in Dean Snyder's office. Said she was a threat. I could tell from the look in her eyes she wasn't my Cassie. They were all black, gone away."

Her father furrowed his brow. "Why was Dean Snyder talking to you about this?"

The way they sat huddled together, staring at me, made me feel like I was being interrogated. I rubbed my sweaty hands together. "I guess he just wanted to tell me why I didn't have a roommate and ask me if I'd heard from her. Maybe he thought I could help somehow."

He nodded before swallowing hard and putting a hand on his wife's knee. "They told us she was on drugs, and that drugs were unacceptable at Meryton. Grounds for expulsion."

"Cassie's never done drugs a day in her life!" Her mother's eyes filled with unshed tears.

I stole a look at the photographs of Cassidy. Blonde. Pretty. She didn't look like a drug addict. But then again, looks could be deceiving. I knew that better than anyone.

Mrs. Ellis sniffled and rubbed the tip of her pert nose. "They made us take her home. She sat in the back of the car. Blank-faced. Not defending herself, not explaining herself. No response whatsoever. Like she didn't know us, or know what was happening. Not quite catatonic, but close. We took her right to the hospital."

The more she talked, the bigger the pit in my stomach grew. I wanted them to stop talking. I wanted Cassidy to walk through the front door, all cheerleader smiles and bouncing curls. I shifted on the couch, my mouth dry.

"There were no drugs in her system," her father said. "They ran so many tests and couldn't find anything wrong with her. But she acted really strange."

"What do you mean, strange?" I thought of Brandon, newly initiated, staring in fascination at his hands.

Mr. Ellis looked at his wife. "Once, we found her in the closet, just rubbing the fabric across her face. She didn't want to wear clothes. When we ate, she studied her fork like she had never seen it before. I had to remind her how to chew."

"She had become a different person." Her mother lowered her voice. "She had become something dark. I thought of calling a priest."

"Clara, don't." Mr. Ellis shook his head.

"I thought we needed an exorcism. Everyone thought I was crazy. But sometimes I would hear her in her bedroom. Except it wasn't her. It sounded like she had people in there with her. Whispering. I stood outside the door listening and heard awful sounds." She clenched her pearls until I thought they might snap. "Sounds that made the hair on my arms stand up. When I opened the door a crack, it was just Cassidy, staring at me with those eyes. Her room felt cold. But more than that. The air in there…"

"Oppressive," Mr. Ellis said.

"Something happened to Cassidy at Meryton," Mrs. Ellis said.

Realization thundered up from the pit of my stomach with a loud and terrible roar. I was wrong to compare Cassidy to Brandon. Her parents had described her as acting strange, living a nightmare. They'd heard sounds. And then, the disappearance.

Cassidy wasn't a new Initiate at all.

Cassidy had been evacuated from her body. And replaced with a Shadow—a foul entity from the Conduit's alien race.

I bent over and squeezed my eyes shut.

"Are you okay?" I heard Mrs. Ellis ask.

I couldn't answer. This was the work of the Conduit, no doubt about it. Cassidy was supposed to be my roommate, so maybe the Conduit had mistaken her for me. Or maybe it was a warning. Either way, it didn't make sense. The Conduit evacuated initiated Senders from human bodies. Cassidy wasn't an Initiate; she was a human being.

Oh god. I sat up suddenly. The blood drained from my face.

"What? What is it?" Cassidy's mother reached out a hand to me, her mouth drawn back in fear.

My knees shook when I stood up. "I'm sorry," I stammered. "I really need to use your bathroom."

I shut the door behind me and turned the lock, resting my hands on my knees to catch my breath. *Cassidy was a human being. And now she was a Shadow.* A framed photo of her cheerleading team stared at me from next to the sink. I caught a glimpse of myself in the mirror: wide-eyed, sweating. I looked like a crazy person.

I felt like one.

"Are you okay in there?"

I flew over to the window and unlatched it, stepped onto the toilet, and squeezed through the small opening. Once on the ground, I sprinted for the end of the street where the Campus Security truck sat waiting for me, hidden next to a row of tall bushes.

"It's worse than I thought." I slammed the door, gasping for air, and spun in my seat to face Larry. "The Conduit can evacuate humans."

CHAPTER FIFTEEN

The whole way back to my house, I chewed on this new information. If the Conduit had learned to evacuate living human beings, he didn't need Adam anymore. He could have his pick of bodies, emptying us one by one and replacing us with a whole army of Shadows. I shuddered to think of it. I had never seen a Shadow, but from what Larry had told me, they were gruesome, vacant, merciless creatures who answered to only one master.

"Impossible." Larry pulled into my mother's driveway after about forty-five minutes of listening to me argue just the opposite.

"I know I'm right. What else explains the way Cassidy acted?"

"We have no way of knowing—"

"You've seen a Shadow firsthand. Remember that one you told me about?" I tapped my forehead. "In Columbus, I think. Thomas, that's what you named the Sender when you initiated him. You said the Conduit got to him somehow and evacuated him. You saw him wandering by the side of the road, totally changed. His eyes had gone black, remember?"

"Thomas wasn't a human in the first place. And he wasn't nothin' like how they described their daughter." Larry parked the truck but didn't turn off the ignition. Though heat blasted from the vents, nothing could have thawed the chill that had settled deep in my bones.

"Yes it is! Remember how you described the air around him?"

Larry, who had been looking toward my house, turned to me. "My eyes watered. I couldn't take a breath."

"*Oppressive*. Just like Mr. Ellis described the air around Cassidy."

He frowned. "But Cassidy didn't try and attack her parents. Thomas went right for my throat when I tried to approach him."

I pondered that for a second. "Cassidy had no reason to attack her parents. Thomas went for you because you're in Orientation. You're the enemy."

Larry's jaw tightened, and he glanced away. Whenever we talked about Initiates like Thomas disappearing, he withdrew inside himself. After all, the Initiates were like his children. He brought them into the world. He named them. From the moment they opened their eyes, their well-being rested in his hands. And he had let them down.

"Anyway," I said. "I'm the one who's half Sender. I've got more intuition in my big toe than you have in your whole body. You have to listen to me."

"Oh yeah?" He raised an eyebrow. "Then how'd this whole thing escape your attention til now?"

Because I'm a huge fat failure, I wanted to say, but it wasn't the time for a Mira pity party. I shrugged and stuffed my feelings into their little box.

As soon as he turned off the engine, I dashed out and knocked five times like I always did. Two slow, three fast. All the blinds remained closed, but behind them, I saw lights. My mother peeked out of the curtain and, a few seconds later, unlocked the door.

"The Conduit got Cassidy." I rushed in and spilled everything in one breath. When I finished, I paused to gauge her reaction. In the month I'd been away, the lines in her face had deepened. Streaks of gray appeared at her temples. A dark brown stain ran the length of her oversized wool sweater. Guilt clenched my stomach.

"Humans." My mother sunk into the frayed and claw-shredded recliner that Orientation must have found by the side of the road somewhere. They'd even found a couch for us, and that's where Larry settled after brushing aside the thick pile of my mother's clipped obituaries. He ran his hand over his face and stared at the ceiling, drumming his meaty fingers on his chest.

"It's not that we never thought it was possible, but we didn't think it would actually happen." My mother maintained an impossible calm about the whole situation. Meanwhile, my thoughts raced and I paced the room.

"Nothing's been proven, Lydia." Larry addressed my mother but glared at me. "It's just a whim Mira has."

"Mira's whims are as good as fact," my mother said. "She's half Sender."

I looked Larry square in the eye and smirked. "Told you. So if it's true, what do we do about it?"

Larry dug his phone out of his pocket. "I've gotta call Hal. Get them over here as soon as possible."

"For what? A committee meeting? If the Conduit's turning humans, we have no chance. None." I slammed my fist against the wall. "Seven billion people in the world, give or take the ones already turned. The Conduit could be anywhere. He could have a factory for all we know. Evacuating humans from their bodies and filling them with Shadows until no one remains to fight back."

My mother shook her head. "I just don't understand it. Why would the Conduit change his focus to humans? He's been evacuating Senders from bodies as revenge for the Senders evacuating *his* species out of their bodies. Moving on to humans would be hypocritical, making him just like the Senders he claims to hate. I think you're jumping to conclusions, Mira. Cassidy is one human. I think the evacuation was a warning sign, directed at you."

I opened my mouth to argue but thought about it for a second. That made more sense. Like my mother said, the Conduit was launching a revenge campaign against Senders. Humans had never been involved in the equation. Though I wasn't completely convinced, it settled my nerves a bit.

"Get here as soon as you can," Larry said into the phone. "What's that? I'm losin' you. Hal?" He looked at his phone and shook his head. "He's on his way, I think."

There was nothing to do but wait.

I curled up on the opposite end of the couch, the end with the broken springs. My mother watched me from across the small room, sipping the tea she made that calmed her nerves. Her eyes said, *I'm so sorry about Brandon*. Larry must have told her everything when he called her from the hospital. I didn't want to talk about it. What's done was done, and talking didn't change anything. So I shoved it back down into the depths of me where everything else festered. Maybe one day I would have time to properly mourn. For everything, for everyone lost.

My mother could sense something was wrong. She sat next to me and rubbed my head like she had when I was little.

"Tell me the story." I sounded like a child, but I didn't care. My mother shifted her weight, tucked her legs up under her, and told me the story of the last time she brought in a Sender.

She told me the story of my father.

As she talked, I pictured it in my mind. South Dakota, the middle of a cornfield. I knew the story so well I could have mouthed every detail: Larry's crazy uncle who worked at the county morgue, the weight of what would become my father's body as they loaded him into the back of the flatbed truck, the way they laid hands on him. How he opened his eyes.

Then suddenly, my mind flashed to Brandon, dead on the stone.

My eyes shot open.

"What is it?" my mother said. My whole body had tensed.

"Nothing," I murmured.

I closed my eyes again but couldn't shake the image. As my mother's voice floated around me, I tried to hook onto it, to forget everything else.

She once told me the simple act of stepping out onto the porch filled her with a sudden fear of being sucked out into the universe: flying off her feet, spiraling past the treetops and up and above the houses in a final scream, and disappearing into nothingness. I knew the feeling.

"But that won't happen," I had said, "Because nothing like that ever has."

"Just because it never has doesn't mean it won't. I've seen stranger things."

You couldn't argue with fear like that. So I hadn't tried.

"You know you've always been so willful," she said. "Do you remember, when you were a little girl–kindergarten, I think it was–you absolutely refused to wear shoes to school. I tied triple knots so you wouldn't untie them. But you kept coming home without them. Turns out you were cutting the laces with scissors as soon as you got to school."

I picked up my head and, for a moment, saw my real mother. Through the paranoia and capsizing grief and fear, I saw the woman I had once admired, steel-eyed and strong. The one who used to throw her head back in laughter and put daisies in my hair. I lay back down.

"You've told me that story a hundred times. I don't see what it has to do with anything."

"It means from the moment you entered this world, you knew who you were, what you wanted. And you didn't give up. You always found a way. And you'll find a way this time."

How I wished that were true.

"You have a lot of your father in you," she said. "It's scary. But I'm glad for it. Sometimes it's like he's still with us."

I sat up again. "He is still with us."

"Exactly." She paused to look around the room, her eyes resting on the one photograph we managed to cart from place to place, a silver-framed black and white of me and my father standing at the end of a dock, holding hands, looking out across the mist-covered water. I was five. I remember what it felt like to hold his hand. It made me invincible. Since the day he disappeared, I'd been struggling to recapture that feeling.

Though I didn't know why. My father wasn't invincible. Which meant neither was I.

❈ ❈ ❈

When the front door squealed and clanged, I jolted awake. Hal stood in the foyer, alone.

"Where's Adam?" I asked, rubbing my eyes. How had I fallen asleep?

Hal looked from me, to my mother, to Larry. His mouth turned down. "Oh Christ. I thought he was with you."

A sharp blade of panic pierced my heart, catapulted me off the couch. "Where is he?"

"It was a misunderstanding." Hal stepped back, ducking under the ceiling fan as he went.

"You lost him?" My voice reverberated in the half-empty house.

Larry produced his keys from his pocket, his mouth a thin line. "When's the last time you saw him?"

"I thought he was with you." The way Hal shied away from me—like a sheepish kid in a giant body—made me want to hit him.

"We have to go get him. He can't be alone," Larry said.

"Let's see now." Hal rubbed his head, visibly sweating.

The room spun around me. "You left him alone? I can't believe you left him alone." I wrung my hands. My heart pounded, thinking of all the work we had done to get here. All the cities and towns we had settled in, the cross-country driving under cover of night. Every single lead ended in disappointment. And now…

I could have sunk to my knees and bawled, remembering Adam's electric touch, his penetrating gaze. Thoughts of him tumbled through my head, threatening to overwhelm me. But I chose to go the other way. I used those thoughts to bolster my courage. Sobbing on the ground wouldn't help me find him, and he was counting on me. Determination flooded my body. I turned to Larry, fists clenched, head lowered.

"I'm going with you." I zipped my coat and stepped into the muddy shoes I had left by the door.

"No." Larry put a hand on my shoulder. "You stay here. In case he comes."

"Why would he come here?" My voice bordered on hysteria. "He doesn't even know where we are. You guys didn't give him a phone. Or a car. What's he going to do, hitchhike?"

"He knows where this place is," Larry said. "It's the safe house."

The safe house. The look in Larry's eyes suggested there was a lot I didn't know—about Orientation, about the process of initiating, about all of it.

I ground my teeth. "If he could have come, he would be here already." Their silence indicated they agreed. "Mom can stay. Adam needs me. What if the Conduit..." I couldn't bring myself to finish the sentence.

The way my mother stared at me—furrowed brow, downturned mouth—spoke for itself. She knew exactly how I felt about Adam. I stared right back at her, daring her to call me out. After all, she had fallen for one too.

Hal stepped forward. "This is my fault. Larry, I'll take the school. You troll the back roads. See if you can't pick him up. That was the plan. Mira, it's best you stay here. He might be on his way." The blue-tinged bags under Hal's eyes sagged.

My heart sank, but I knew he was right. I didn't want to leave my mother here all alone, not after what happened to Cassidy. I told myself Adam would come back. I closed my eyes and willed it so.

Larry and Hal rushed out the front door and peeled out of the driveway in their separate trucks. I stood for a long time in the doorway, feeling like Cassidy's parents, waiting for their little girl to come home but terrified she never would.

Chapter Sixteen

Hal came back alone.

As long as Larry was still out there, I couldn't rest. I patrolled the living room and the hallway, peering through every window. My mother had gone to her room, and Hal had splayed out in the recliner, snoring. I didn't understand how they could sleep at a moment like this. But then, their hearts weren't breaking in a million pieces.

On my seventeenth useless slog through the kitchen, I heard a soft tap at the sliding glass door—a barely existent sound, yet one so jarring and meaningful it shot my heart into my throat.

Tap, tap, tap.

Not the agreed-upon entry knock. My muscles tensed, ready for fight or flight. My heart thumped wildly. I flattened myself against the wall, to the right of the Venetian blinds, and contemplated waking Hal or my mother. But the tap came again.

The Conduit wouldn't knock.

I stood frozen in place. The knife drawer was just on the other side of the door. I knew my mother had a meat cleaver in there, but the thought of wielding a knife against such a powerful entity seemed absurd. I inserted an index finger between the slates of the blinds and moved them slightly to the side.

The figure on the other side of the glass moved from the shadows into the moonlight. I gasped, fumbled to unlock the door, and threw myself into Adam's arms.

"Oh my god, Adam. Oh my god." He smelled like Adam, a living, breathing Adam, warm and alive in my arms. "I thought you were dead. I thought..."

He held me so tight I felt his heart through his chest, thudding against my ear. I drew back to look at him.

"Are you okay? Where have you been?"

"I'm okay, but..." He held up his wrists. Under the motion light, I saw his festering skin. Wounds. Blood.

"What happened?" My breath came out in a white cloud. Adam put his hand on my elbow and steered me to the side of the house. The cold siding pressed against my shoulder blades. His blue eyes shined, as bright in the darkness as in the light. He wore the same clothes he'd worn camping. The same mud-caked clothes, ripped now and faintly musty.

"It's Larry," Adam said. "Larry took me."

I shook my head. He must have been confused. "What? Larry? What do you mean?"

Adam put his trembling hands on my shoulders. "Larry is the one. At campus, he took me in the truck, drove me to a place, and told me it was to keep me safe. He put plastic around my wrists and left me there. I escaped. But Mira..." With every word, my eyes grew wider. "Mira, I saw them. I saw their bodies. The evacuated ones."

I clapped a hand over my mouth. It couldn't be. Not Larry. Not the Larry that had oriented my father, or carried me sleeping from a cold car to a new house, or patched up my skinned knee, or a thousand other acts of kindness. Not my Larry.

"No," I said, yearning for him to relent, to explain that it was someone else. "It can't be Larry."

"I'm sorry, Mira. But it is." He gazed down at me with somber eyes.

Memories of the past overwhelmed me, now colored by the lens of betrayal. Larry had been there the night Brandon died. He said there was another initiation nearby, and another evacuation. He must have been a part of it. My stomach roiled.

All those Initiates. All those evacuations. Larry had known about them all. Of course he had. He'd been there.

Just like he'd been there the night I found Cassidy's ID.

Strength left my body. I collapsed against Adam. My eyes closed. He wrapped his arms around me and pressed me to him.

"What about Hal? Hal must be in on it if Larry is." I mumbled into his shirt, feeling the hard muscles of his chest against my cheek.

"No. Hal is not a part of it."

I bowed my head, thankful for that, at least.

"But you saw the evacuated ones." I took a deep breath. "Did you see my father?" My question hung in the air between us.

He swallowed hard. "Maybe, but I'm not sure. There were many."

I looked up and searched his face, trying to decide if he was telling the truth or just making me feel better. After studying him for a moment longer, no closer to determining his motives, I forced my mind to return to the situation—to Larry, the betrayal, and the Conduit.

"How did you get away?"

He massaged the back of my neck with his strong fingers. "I jumped from the fire escape and came to you as soon as I could."

My skin tingled where he touched me. Hope surfaced through the sadness in my heart.

"I don't know what I would have done if you hadn't come back. That night in the woods, all I could think about was getting close to you." I pulled at his sleeve, traced a finger down his arm. "Then that whole tragedy with Brandon happened, and things went sideways. I pushed you away, and you disappeared. I was so worried I'd lost my chance with you forever."

He looked at me steadily and ran his fingertips down the sides of my neck. I shivered with delight, despite my heavy heart.

"I felt the same way. I don't understand it." His eyes shone with wonder as his gaze roamed from my eyes to my lips, my bare arms.

"Understand what?" His touch gave me a sudden heightened awareness of every inch of my body.

"Whenever I'm around you, I have this impulse to touch you, to hold you. To kiss you."

"Adam…" For a moment, I let the world fall away. Only the two of us existed under the moon, in that backyard, against the cheap aluminum siding of that manufactured home. He pressed against me. Our bodies melted together. Just as he lowered his lips to mine, I heard a crash coming from inside.

A cold sweat broke out over my whole body.

"Mom!" I bolted around Adam, through the sliding glass door, across the kitchen, and into the living room.

I skidded to a halt when I saw Larry swinging a bat. Hal went down. Dark, shiny blood clotted what remained of Hal's hair.

"No!" I screamed. My brain struggled to process the scene. For a moment, my heart leapt with a crazy idea. Maybe Adam had it all wrong. Maybe Hal had turned. Maybe *he* was the traitor, and Larry was protecting me.

"What are you doing?" I crept toward Larry, keeping an eye on the injured Hal. "Is he the traitor?"

"You wouldn't understand." Larry kept a tight grip on the bat. I took another step toward him. He shook his head. "Now don't you come any closer." Sweat poured down the sides of his red face. Hal lay motionless on the ground.

I pointed at Hal. My voice quaked. "I knew it. I knew from the day I met him. He's in on it, isn't he? How could you have ever trusted him?" Hoping against all hope that I was right to trust Larry and not Hal, I inched closer.

"Now Mira…" Larry sighed. "Stay where you are, and hand him over." He motioned behind me, toward Adam. The last glimmer of hope left my body in a shudder, leaving an emptiness behind. I clutched my heart.

So it was true after all.

"Mira. I have to go with him." Adam brushed past me, toward Larry. I grabbed his hand to stop him.

"No." My gaze fell to the scissors on the floor. My mom's most prized tool. My chest heaved. "Where is my mother? Mom, where are you?" I clenched my teeth and glared at Larry, my blood boiling. "Where is she? If you hurt my mother, I swear to god…"

He pursed his lips. "Look, I'm taking him, and I don't want to hurt you. I never wanted to hurt you."

"Hurt me? You took me to my first day of kindergarten. You stopped Jimmy Harlon from taking my lunch money in the third grade. You…" I faltered as memories assailed me. Larry, my substitute father. "How could you do this?"

"I'm sorry." He took Adam by the arm and guided him toward the door. Hal lay in a heap on the ground, all six foot seven of him had gone still. I nudged him with my foot, but he didn't move. If only he'd wake up and help me stop Larry.

My mind raced. I had to keep Larry talking until Hal woke up, or until my mother came back. "How could you betray us all like this?"

"Don't say it like that, Mira. You'll understand one day." He cleared his throat. "The others—Cassidy, Brandon—just got caught in the crossfire, and I am sorry about that. But Mira, it's for the *greater good*. Like we always told you."

"Brandon?" I said. What did Brandon have to do with this? My legs quivered and threatened to give out. Nothing made sense anymore.

Hal stirred from the floor beside me and let out a slow groan. Larry yanked Adam a few more steps closer to the door.

"Mira." My mother's voice floated to me from somewhere in the back of the house. As I turned toward the source of her voice, Larry muttered an apology and slammed into me. I flew backward until I smashed against the wall. My hip and shoulder screamed in protest and pain. The air rushed out of my lungs, and I slid down to the tile floor with an ungraceful thud. Through bleary eyes, I watched Larry grab the bat and smack Adam in the temple. Adam crumpled to the ground in slow motion.

I sat there, unmoving, dazed. Tears welled up in my eyes. Not Adam. Not him too.

Larry threw Adam over his shoulder and slammed through the screen door. Adrenaline coursed through me, silencing the objections of my aching body. I rolled over, forced myself to my feet, snatched the scissors from the floor, and propelled myself out the door. Larry moved his heft faster than I could have imagined. He'd already reached the end of the driveway by the time I got down the porch steps. He stuffed Adam into the cab of the truck like he was tossing a bag of garbage into a dumpster. My legs pumped harder than ever. Larry raced around the front of the truck and took off while swinging the door shut.

The heat of the truck's exhaust plumed in my face. I'd come so close only to fail. Again.

As the truck disappeared around the corner, I stood in the middle of the street, holding that stupid, useless pair of scissors. I turned back toward the house to find my mother wavering, stunned, in the doorway. We stared at one another until I broke contact. Disgust and disappointment clawed at me. While I'd confronted Larry and run out to save Adam, she'd hidden in her room, and even now, she couldn't gather up the courage to step outside.

❈ ❈ ❈

I shot past my mother into the house. "Where would they go? I'm going after them."

She followed me inside, her face pale. I'd always known she'd never wanted to be part of Orientation; they'd chosen her. But I always thought she believed in the cause and would fight for it. Now I wanted to scream at her. I didn't want to exist in the same kitchen, the same house, the same family as her, as someone so *weak*.

Hal struggled to sit up. A purple-red clot matted his hair. I swallowed down bile as the whitish gristle of his hacked up cheekbone stared back at me like a skeletal ghoul. I darted to his side and dropped to my knees. "Where? Tell me!"

My mom stepped up beside us and handed him a bag of frozen peas. He pressed them against his face and winced. "Must be back at school. Meryton. That hill where he initiated. That's the only way he'd be able to evacuate him."

I shook my head, digging my fingers into the carpet. Alternating waves of grief and anger cascaded through my body. "All this time. All this time Larry was the Conduit, and we didn't even see it." Though I was half Sender myself, I hadn't sensed anything. I turned to my mother, my jaw set. "I'm going. Hal needs stitches. Do you think you can handle that?"

"Wait." My mother held up her hand. "Did Adam tell you where he saw them? The evacuated ones?"

"No." I moved toward the door. "He didn't exactly have time to pull out the GPS."

Her eyes flashed. "But he must have walked from wherever he was. If it's within walking distance, we can track him. Hal, you can get the dogs."

"What dogs?" I glanced between them.

Hal rolled over onto all fours and struggled to his feet. "Cadaver dogs."

Made sense. The bodies were technically dead.

My mother crossed the distance between us and took my hands in hers. "We can track him and find out where the evacuated ones are kept. But Mira, Orientation can't help once we find them. Only you can kick out the Shadows. This is your time. Once you get rid of Shadows and the Senders reclaim the bodies, we'll have an army of behind us. We'll have a better chance of succeeding. And your father might be there. Your father, Mira."

"Behind *us*?" I snatched my hands away. "You mean behind me and Hal? Because you know as well as we do that *you're* not going anywhere. The only time you've seen the outdoors is when you're running under the cover of nightfall for a van full of our stuff. You're not even part of this anymore, so don't pretend you are."

She rubbed her forehead like she was trying to erase the lines that had formed there. "I'll always be a part of it."

"Whatever." I whipped my coat off the hook and removed the keys from the metal basket by the refrigerator. "I'm going after Adam. Once I find him I'll come back, and we'll go get my father. The least you can do is get Hal some real medical attention."

"Mira."

I shut the door before she could say anything else. Taking a deep breath, I started her car, pulled out of the driveway, turned left, and accelerated toward Meryton.

Chapter Seventeen

I zipped my coat and stuffed my hands in my pockets. With my nose running and stomach churning, I crossed the empty parking lot and sprinted up the path. Through the bare trees, I saw the hills in the distance where the sun peaked over the horizon.

Pine cones, branches, and a frozen mosaic of fallen leaves littered the path. I gasped for air, but my heaving lungs burned in the cold. My eyes watered. I rounded the last bend ready to take on Larry, the Conduit, and whatever else waited for me. But I stopped short as a realization hit me. I would need a weapon. I'd run up here by myself with nothing but anger and justice to fuel me, and neither of those stood a chance against the Conduit. Other than advanced healing, I didn't have superpowers; I only had the strength of a teenage girl.

I scanned the ground, kicking at the leaves, and searched for the right weapon. A rock? A big limb? What would suffice against a revenge-bent alien? My foot hit something hard, a thick tree branch. It would likely do nothing against the Conduit, but holding it restored my resolve. I clutched it under my arm and sprinted the rest of the way up the trail. The ball of anxiety tightened in my stomach.

Two more steps, and the apprehension morphed into relief. Over the crest, I saw him. Adam was alive, unharmed. The lightness in my chest only lasted a moment, until my gaze landed on her.

Decklin.

Wait, Decklin? I stumbled back a few steps, confused.

They stood alone on the hill, facing each other. She rested her hands on his shoulders. With her head slightly bowed, her black hair fell over her shoulders and masked her face. She leaned into him with possessiveness, and my heart pricked with jealousy.

Why was she here? Why was she with Adam? Had they arranged to meet? My brain attempted to rationalize what I was seeing, but there could only be one explanation: he must have fallen for her after all. As the realization came upon me, my world slowly ripped at the seams. I remembered how I felt with his arms around me, like nothing could harm me. And there, on the hill, there he stood with Decklin, so close he might have been kissing her.

First Larry, and now Adam. My heart couldn't take another betrayal. I stepped backwards, yearning to turn and run, but I couldn't. I had to secure Adam, for the cause if not for myself. And I had to report to Hal and my mother.

Deadlocked between anguish and duty, I continued to watch them. Jealousy shrank my heart, took my breath. The way she placed her hands around his neck, how his head lolled to the side like he was...

I dropped the branch. Adrenaline pulsed through my veins. They were not going to kiss, not at all. She was trying to evacuate him.

"Stop!" I stooped down, grabbed the branch, and broke into a run, my stupid polyester coat whooshing ridiculously with each step. Adam didn't turn around. But Decklin's eyes snapped open, and she released him. I slowed my pace, thinking maybe I had made a mistake. Maybe they were hugging after all.

Adam flopped to the ground. A groan emanated from somewhere deep within me when I realized the truth. A shockwave rattled my body, dropping my heart into my stomach.

All this time. All this time we were searching for a "he," but the Conduit was a "she."

I raced toward Decklin, fury grinding through my bones. She braced herself as I approached, her gaze locked on the thick piece of wood. I wielded my branch, poised to knock her down, but when I drew close enough to see Adam, I noticed his eyes blinking at the cloudy sky. I forgot all about Decklin and fell to my knees beside him.

"Adam." I reached out to touch his cheek. My Adam. A sour taste crept into the back of my mouth.

"I wouldn't touch him if I were you." Decklin snickered.

I reared back to glare at her. "What did you do to him?"

"I think you know."

When I looked at him again, I understood. The being before me still had Adam's body. His dark hair and broad shoulders, the jeans and the muddy blue t-shirt he'd worn in the backyard of my house. It was Adam's body down to the socks and canvas sneakers Orientation had provided for him. But this thing lying prone beside me was *not* Adam.

I recoiled and fell backward. The Adam I knew had been evacuated. The sweet, unassuming boy who'd tripped his way into my heart now existed in some plane I couldn't reach, with my father.

I clawed at my throat, desperate for air. My lungs burned with each fetid gulp, and my eyes swam behind a wall of tears. Adam, gone. My father, gone. And Decklin, the mastermind Conduit behind it all.

Whatever had overtaken Adam's body flailed about like an upended bug. I scrambled backward to avoid his thrashing arms and legs. He arched his spine and gasped. His left temple, where Larry's bat had made contact, oozed with congealed blood.

He had the same blue eyes, but they had gone blank. Void. Empty.

I coughed and gagged. The atmosphere dripped with heaviness. Despair beaded like humidity on my skin. The ground tilted in front of me. I put my hands on it, dug into the cold dirt with my fingers, and hung on as everything went spinning.

My mind flew back to that night in the woods. *The world is spinning,* Adam had said. This wasn't the gentle spin I had reeled from that night. This was an out-of-control, holy-shit kind of whirl that pinned me in place.

"Don't be so dramatic. It was only painful for a minute," Decklin said from behind me, closer now. "And it's not like I killed him. I gave him life, if you think about it." When I turned to scowl at her, she grinned. "Hey, chin up. He still looks like Adam. Right? Well, Adam with a massive head wound. Larry got a little overzealous with that bat, don't you think?"

The thing stopped flailing and lay there, arms at its sides, breathing in and out with all the labor of a fish on shore. Deep red cuts ringed his wrists, and a purple welt, the size of a baseball, glistened on his forehead. Larry must have hit him hard. Really, really hard. In my mind, I watched the bat connect with Adam's skull and heard the crack of it.

The thing struggled to his hands and knees. I remembered Larry's words about Brandon, *unsteady as a newborn horse.*

I shuddered. "That's not Adam." It wasn't a Sender. This was a Shadow. Untrained, unearthly, ungodly. A displaced soul with a vengeance. The worst of the worst. I backed away from it, hollowed out completely.

Decklin plunked down on the ground next to me, like we were friends waiting on the sidelines during gym class instead of mortal enemies. "You must be feeling pretty stupid. But don't blame yourself." She shrugged. "I have the uncanny ability to blend in. So do you, apparently. I didn't know what you were until I witnessed that whole scene at the Jump Off."

So Decklin's whole cowering-against-the-wall thing had been an act. I had pitied her, and the whole time she had been plotting my demise. The thought made my skin crawl. I had shared a room with that monster. I had borrowed tampons. I had slept underneath her for weeks, only now to discover she could have woken in the night and bludgeoned me to death any time she chose?

And I could have done the same to her. If only we'd known.

I apologized to my father in my head and to Adam, wherever they were.

"Larry never told me you were the halfsie." She poked my arm, and I jumped back. "Maybe he did have a soft spot for you."

My stomach heaved. I didn't care how Larry felt; I couldn't pull my eyes away from Adam. The settling of a being into a human body. *The evacuated ones,* Adam had called them. Now I saw for myself. The body had remained the same, but the operator had changed. Like Brandon after the transition, the Adam thing struggled to its feet. Wobbly, uncoordinated. Arms flailing to keep balance. Meanwhile, its eyes scanned the surroundings: me, Decklin, the grass, and the sky.

"Adam's not in there," I said. "Whatever is in there, I can feel it." I hugged myself despite the heavy coat, teeth chattering, and eyed the tree branch I had dropped ten feet away.

"Think of the body like a glass," Decklin said. "You pour in milk, or you pour in water. The glass doesn't change, only the contents."

"The contents are what matters." They mattered far more than I had realized until this moment, as I watched Adam's body move around absent of his soul. "So where is he?"

Decklin waved a hand in front of my face. "Duh, he's right there."

"Not him." I struggled to take a full breath. Tiny white stars crowded the outside of my vision. "Where is my father?"

Decklin sighed. "Well shit. That was bound to come up, wasn't it?"

"Don't make this into a joke." I inched backward toward my weapon.

The Adam thing stood there like a scarecrow come to life, something just a bit *off* about him. Someone else would think he was drunk. Or in shock. Staring at him, I felt like puking, but I had nothing in my stomach.

Decklin took her time standing. Once she did, she stretched and cracked her knuckles behind her back. I crawled backwards, watching her.

"In the end, everything worked out exactly as I had planned." Decklin flashed a boastful smile. "You arrived in hot pursuit just moments too late to save your alien boyfriend."

"Don't change the subject. And he's not my boyfriend." I pushed down the anger building in my stomach, though it rose in me like a buoy from the depths of the sea. If I allowed it, my rage would make waves and upset the balance, and I needed to hold onto myself, keep a clear head, for just a bit longer. It was the only chance I stood against Decklin.

"I know you don't like me right now, but I'm still glad you're here to witness my accomplishments. Adam was the last one, so I guess I'm done." She frowned. "It's a bit anticlimactic, to tell you the truth. I feel like we should have a cake or something. To celebrate."

I shook my head. "He wasn't the last." I reached behind me, grasping for my weapon.

Decklin tapped her chin and tilted her head up to the side like she was thinking. "Oh, right. Your friend Brandon." She fake grimaced. "Well...you haven't heard much from him lately, have you? He was a tricky one with all those doctors and nurses and his mother. Gawd, his mother. But I won in the end, like I always do." Her eyes glimmered with amusement. "Poor Mira. Lost two boyfriends at once."

The deep grief I had so neatly compartmentalized, until it barely existed, flowed just under the surface. I steeled myself against it, concentrating on my next move. "I'm not talking about Brandon. I'm talking about me; I'm the last."

She laughed. "A halfsie? I'm not too worried about you. In a couple generations, there'll be no trace of you or your kind."

"I can bring them back." I clenched my fist. A slow burn built inside me. I could bring them back from the place they went when they weren't in their bodies, back from the Dark Eternal. That was my gift. My one and only gift. I could bring Adam back. And, if I could find my father's body, I could bring him back too.

Decklin's eyes narrowed, focused on the branch I had finally gotten hold of. "Don't you underestimate me, Mira Avery. You don't know what I'm capable of." She stood five foot four but cast a shadow that extended to the trees.

I rose to face my enemy, my grip tightening around my weapon, my knees quaking. If I had to go down, I would go down swinging.

We circled each other, with the Adam thing, busy examining his own hands, in the middle of us.

"I know you want information about your father." She toyed with me, batting around my feelings for Brandon, Adam, and my father like a cat would a mouse.

I paused. "I know you evacuated him. Where is his body?"

"I've never met a girl who wanted her father's body so bad." Her smile ignited the spark of my fury, and darkness descended upon me. A darkness apart from the heartache of losing Adam, apart from the despair at having arrived too late, apart from the hatred I felt for Decklin in that moment. Fragments of a bone-cracking anger worked its way through me and found a solid hold. My body itched to fight.

I charged at her and swung, as a faraway scream, like a catamount on a distant mountain, pierced the air. She ducked to the left, fast. I tripped and fell from my own momentum, pinning the branch under me. My wrist bone cracked, an audible snap that echoed through the trees. Even the Adam thing glanced over at the sound. Though searing pain shot through my snapped wrist, I sprung up.

Using Decklin's face as a target in the haze, I surged forth again. Feigning right and swinging left, I connected just below her hip. A sense of pride surged through me until she laughed and swerved around me, uninjured.

"I see they didn't teach you how to fight. Would have thought that was Sender 101."

I came at her headfirst and barreled into her chest, knocking her backward but not off balance. She flung me to the side, and I somersaulted into some brush, snagging my coat.

She was clearly playing with me, but something else shined in her eyes, something hidden past the hubris and taunting.

Fear.

"This is the most exciting thing that's happened in a long time." She danced around like a cheerleader at a homecoming game. "What a rush!"

This time, she didn't wait for me to strike first. She came at me hard and slammed her fist into my forehead. Stars erupted in my vision, like the ones my father had shown me. Bright twinkles of constellations embedded in blackness. I stumbled backward until I landed on my back, gazing upward. Hands freezing. Heart beating. World turning.

Her face floated above me. I saw two of her. "It's a shame. We could have had fun together. It's lonely being the Conduit, you know."

She lifted my own beloved branch and swung it toward me. With a last hurrah, possibly from my inhuman instincts, I rolled to the left, and the branch thudded down on dirt. My foot shot out and caught her on the knee. It snapped, and she howled in anger.

I jumped to my feet, raised my boot, and rammed it into her rib cage. Her "oof" echoed in the still air, loud enough to make the birds take flight.

Her pain centered me. A new calm descended over me. Our next moves played out in my mind like a chess game.

When she tried to walk toward me, her knee buckled, and she dropped to the ground. With my good hand, I wrestled the limb from her and stepped on her hurt knee. She cried out, and using the distraction, I swung the branch at her. Her eyes widened, startled, and I closed my own in response.

Crack. Like when Larry hit Adam.

Crack.

I dropped my weapon, turned, and wiped the blood from my eyes. I had envisioned this moment for years, the Conduit defeated, sprawled on the ground in front of me. I waited for elation to take the place of the numbness I felt inside, but the numbness remained.

The Adam thing focused on me with a steady, curious gaze, like he was waiting for an explanation of how he'd got there, what he was, and what had happened. I didn't know if he understood, but I suspect he did. Already more stable on his feet, he faced me like a caged animal. Shoulders up. Fingers splayed.

Forcing myself to put one foot in front of the other, I staggered toward the thing that regarded me with curious indifference.

"It'll kill you," Decklin croaked from where she lay in the grass. A thin layer of snow coated her black clothes and hair, a contrast of light against dark underneath the gray-blue sky. Deep red blood seeped from her upper lip and nose. She struggled to stand.

This was it. What my father had told me I was made for. Evacuate the Shadow, bring back whatever had been in there before. Bring back Adam. I always thought Larry would be there with me the first time. That was his promise as a part of Orientation. That's why he followed me around constantly, a looming presence. That's why he never taught me how to fight. I was never meant to be on my own. But here I was.

My God. Maybe I could save the world after all. I, Mira Jean Avery, armed with nothing but a powerful crush and a perplexing sense of duty, could save the world. I moved forward with renewed purpose, my throbbing wrist and pounding head no more than background noise.

As I approached, a sound as large and thunderous as a jet engine filled my head. The trees spun around me. I recalled the word

Cassidy's father had used: *Oppressive*. The Shadows were evil beings. Their malevolence rotted the atmosphere around them. I was experiencing it first-hand. I commanded my legs to slog through the thickness until the Adam thing stood directly in front of me.

Decklin laughed deeply, or it might have been the crows beating their wings.

Everything had gone black except for a tiny tunnel of light, like I was looking through a pinhole camera. I saw Adam's wrist, his arm, his shoulder, his neck.

I held out a tentative hand.

"Don't," Decklin's voice surfaced from far away.

Fat flakes of wet snow fell. I placed my hands on Adam's shoulders.

The Shadow screamed into my body and left a black hole in its place, accompanied by pain I couldn't rationalize. My nerves oozed fire. A head-gripping, squeezing agony started at the place I touched him, wormed through my fingertips, and adhered me to him.

My body jerked like I'd been electrocuted. My mind swam until I became lost in the recesses of my own brain. Floundering, I crawled around under a mental rock within the depths of me, but I could not escape. I became pain.

On instinct, I lifted my hands from his shoulders, desperate to disconnect from the source of the torture. But it remained, even though I'd let go. Unable to stand any longer under the weight of such oppression, I collapsed. The sky spun above me in quick, nauseating whirls. I rolled on my side and dry heaved. My body shook with huge, wracking shudders.

After I-don't-know-how-long, a hand touched my shoulder. I jumped, exhausted but still on alert.

"Mira? You still with us?" Hal? He bent down in front of me, his eyebrows arched with concern.

My head throbbed when I tried to lift it. "Where are they?"

He eased me off the ground. "They're gone. You're safe, for now."

Part II

Chapter Eighteen

Darkness came early in December. Freezing rain pelted the windows. Across the quad, blurred by the downpour, multicolored Christmas lights glowed against the buildings. Beyond that, the windows of the boys' dorm shone with dulled light. All but one, which had been dark for months.

Betsy walked next to me, her eyes barely visible above the scarf covering the entire lower half of her face. My teeth chattered, and the tips of my fingers throbbed with cold. The gap between the English building and the dorms created the perfect wind tunnel. I dipped my head against the icy gale and trudged onward, eyes watering, as we approached the steps to the dorm.

"I'm actually glad she's gone," Betsy said as soon as the doors slid shut behind us.

She began to unwrap herself while I stood next to the vent and defrosted. She stripped off her thick red gloves with balls dangling from the wrists. Since I didn't own gloves, I breathed warm air into my hands and rubbed them together. When I rolled my wrist, I felt no pain. My physical injuries had healed quickly, but my emotional ones still ached.

Betsy untangled her scarf. "I never wanted to come to your room. Not with Decklin there. She always looked at me funny." She shivered. "I had dreams about her, you know. In one, she chased me, and she had these black, full eyes."

I opened my mouth to reply, but no words came out.

She frowned. "People must really want to get away from this place. First Brandon got his concussion, then Adam went back to Iceland, and your creeper roommate moved to Des Moines. I almost feel sorry for that city."

"Yeah." Guilt pricked at me. I'd lied to my only friend, but I couldn't have told her the truth. I barely believed it, and I'd been there.

We continued to thaw out in my room. Heat rattled out of the register, but I doubted I would ever feel warm again.

When Betsy opened her computer to study, I just stared into my lap. How could I study for Women's Lit while Adam's soul rotted with my father's in the Dark Eternal and the threat of Decklin lurked around every corner? I'd read the Wollstonecraft and Austen, but only with about a quarter of my brain. My mother had wanted me to ride out this semester. Get my education between intergalactic crises. But I could barely concentrate.

I'd started glancing at my phone so often it had become an unconscious movement, a weird tic I couldn't control, and a swarm of bees had taken up residence in my stomach. They buzzed endlessly. Every minute stretched to forever.

Betsy's things now graced my room. Her pinks and purples, polka-dotted throw blanket, and boxing poster were vast improvements over my drab decor. But even Betsy, with her lilting voice and Valley girl sarcasm, couldn't fill in the silence left by… well, everything.

After a few minutes of clacking away on the keyboard, Betsy turned to me. "You seem distracted. I mean more than usual."

I'd told her I had lost an aunt. Spent a few days out of school for the funeral. Came back five pounds lighter and a million pounds heavier.

"I'm okay." I made a pathetic attempt at a smile. "This year is harder than I thought it would be."

Betsy turned her attention back to her screen, gnawing on the end of a pen, pondering her work. I tried to focus on rereading the notes I had taken throughout the semester, but the words blurred off the page. I had missed classes. I had doodled. Nothing had any context. It didn't seem that important to me. Nothing did.

"I'm going to take a walk." I slammed my notebook shut. "I need fresh air."

Betsy glanced up at me, then out the window, and then back at me.

"You just defrosted," she said slowly, though she had grown used to my walks, even in weather like this.

"I'll be quick," I said. As I stuffed myself into my coat again, my phone vibrated across the desk. I jumped at it. When I looked down at my screen, my heart stopped. Hal.

Betsy had called me mysterious once and asked why I was so secretive. I felt bad shutting the door behind me and crouching in the hallway underneath the Christmas Dance poster, the one decorated with glitter and paper snowflakes, but I didn't want her to hear my conversation.

"Mira," Hal said to my silence. "We've got him."

I had to stay out in the hall for a full five minutes to compose myself.

❆ ❆ ❆

I tucked my hair up in my black wool hat, put up my hood, and braced myself against the wind and driving snow. Even though no one dared to go outdoors in this weather unless they had to, I ducked behind Harris Dining Hall and melted into the cover of trees. I slid across the brick until I reached the basement door. Finding it unlocked, I opened it and stepped in.

I descended the steep stairs alone, into a dark hallway, and followed the signs for the boiler room. My footsteps reverberated in the damp concrete hall, past the hissing water pipes with their small bursts of white condensation, and fell in step with the metallic banging, creaking, and dripping of the pipes. A storm raged inside me, but I kept swallowing it down.

Hal stood in half-shadow between two large copper pipes, his head grazing the low ceiling. "Anyone see you come down?"

"Not that I'm aware of." I rubbed my hands together and clenched my jaw to keep my teeth from chattering.

In the low light, the nasty scab glistened on his head. Though a lot of time had passed, his wound still had not fully healed. He was human, after all.

"He's in there." Hal nodded toward a small, shadowy room off the main hall. "He knows where she is, and he'll tell you." He sniffed. "I'll go in with you. But make it quick; they want at him."

"How did you find him?" I asked.

He folded his arms and rested against the wall. "Contrary to popular belief, Larry ain't that smart."

A grin tugged at my lips. Despite myself, Hal had grown on me. "I guess you'd know where to look."

Hal swallowed, nodded, and smiled. But the momentary mirth slid off his face as soon as it arrived. He ran his fingertips across the scab on his head.

I took a shaky breath and ducked inside. A bare bulb hung from the ceiling in the middle of the room. Larry sat slumped in a wooden chair under the light, his hands tied behind him. He made an effort to straighten up when he saw me approach. When he met my gaze, he smiled. I faltered for a moment, my heart shrinking. I managed to glare at him, not giving an inch.

He cleared his throat. "Mira, I'm so sorry. I never meant to hurt you or your mother." Sweat darkened the shirt under his arms.

I unzipped my coat, removed my hat, and gathered up the courage to ask him the question I needed to know. "Why did you do it?" Heat hissed from the pipes.

"You don't know what she's capable of," Larry said. "I had no choice. She threatened my family. She threatened me. And Hal. And your mother, Mira. It was for your own good."

I kicked a pile of rusty screws and they skittered across the cement floor. "That's bullshit. You should have told us. We could have helped you."

"You can't beat her." Those same kind, gray eyes I'd known my whole life shone up at me under the bright light. "I tried to protect you. To keep you out of it. Everything I did, Mira, I did it for you. You're like a daughter to me."

"Like a daughter isn't the same as being a daughter." Tears streamed down my cheeks as I threw his words back at him. "This is bigger than you. It's bigger than me." Behind me, Hal coughed.

I wiped my eyes and nose on my sleeve. "How could you do it?"

Larry sighed and dropped his head. "I'm weak."

My heart shattered, and my love for him evaporated away like the steam above my head. He'd betrayed me. I'd never be able to trust him again. Unable to stand his excuses, I turned from him. That's when I saw the men.

Three of them, huddled in their coats, hats snugged down to their eyebrows. They stood against the wall in the shadows. I'd never seen them before, but I could piece together why they'd come.

"You'da done the same thing, Hal," Larry's terrified voice carried over the noise of the pipes. "I told you I was sorry. I'm so sorry. You two are my family. Orientation is my family. But I did what I had to do to protect all of you. Please." His last word came out in a squeak.

"Sorry ain't good enough." Hal touched his forehead again. "You betrayed the cause, and the cause comes first. Your cowardice has put the whole thing in jeopardy." He stroked the side of his face, where Larry had split open his cheek. "Ironic, ain't it. You claim you wanted to save your family, but your family's in danger now because of what you did. Dammit, Larry, you coulda killed me." He pointed to his head. "Two inches higher, and you woulda."

"Hal, you know me. There's more to it than you know. I wouldn't have done it if—"

I whirled around to face Larry again, a question burning within my soul. "Did you have something to do with my father's evacuation?"

Water dripped from a pipe. It's constant trickle highlighted Larry's silence. He hung his head.

My knees quivered as my strength left me. "I'll take that as a yes." So many years, he'd been in on it for so many years.

Hal glanced back at the three men against the wall. "Now's your chance to redeem yourself, Larry. Tell Mira where the Conduit is."

Larry examined me. I struggled to see past the man I'd known forever. To see beyond the man I'd loved like a father to the man who'd helped evacuate my real father. I clenched and unclenched my fists. "Yes, tell me."

The overhead bulb deepened the blue-black shadows under his eyes. "I sure do hope you succeed, but you're in deeper than you know." He shook his head. "You better have some tricks up your sleeve. Cause I'll tell ya, the Conduit's not alone in this. She'll be waiting for you, and she'll destroy you."

I swallowed hard. "Maybe, but at least I won't die a coward. Like you."

Chapter Nineteen

Larry had said the drive would take an hour. Snow bombarded the windshield so hard the wipers couldn't keep up. The landscape had lost all definition, washed in gray, mirroring my state of mind. Headlights came and went in blurs.

When I saw the sign—West Cotter—I exited the expressway and hydroplaned my way around the sharp curve of the slick off-ramp. The gas tank was running close to empty. My heart beat fast enough to warm me without the heater. Ice caked the windshield wipers.

Five long miles took me to the heart of a town, laden with boarded up shops. No signs existed, except for the occasional street names. Under a slate-gray sky still dropping fat snowflakes, the houses appeared as barren and lifeless as the trees. No streetlights, no people, no cars. No life.

I gulped when I saw the monstrous building looming in the distance. Three rectangular brick buildings stuck together, fronted by a large parking lot where snow drifts half-covered abandoned cars. I rolled toward them.

Rows and rows of dark windows spread across the three floors. Shards of glass formed sharp mountains in some of the window panes. A thick chain with a rusty *Keep Out* sign blocked the entrance to the parking lot. I parked across the street, next to a field that stretched as far as I could see.

I turned off the truck and pocketed the keys. My fingers touched the phone in my pocket, and I thought of my mother back home, pacing the floor, glancing at her own phone every few seconds. I removed mine from my pocket, stared at the screen, reconsidered, and put it back again. Hal would know where I had gone as soon as he saw his truck missing. And he would come for me. I hoped.

I bit my lower lip. I had misjudged Hal. Misjudged Larry. And Decklin.

A frigid wind swept across the lot, and for the first time since fishtailing out of the Meryton parking lot, I wondered just what, exactly, I was planning to do. I carried no weapon, not even a branch. I was alone. A single target.

I adjusted my hat and pulled my bare hands into my sleeves, chastising myself for stealing Hal's vehicle and driving to the middle of nowhere without a plan. This counted as horror-movie stupid. I should wait for Hal. He would bring people with him. I might be able to evacuate the Shadows—though my first attempt hadn't worked so well—but they had strength in numbers.

Glancing at the building, I sensed movement out of the corner of my eye. I squinted through the falling snow. Curtains billowed out of an open window on the third floor. My breath caught in my throat. A dark figure stood in full view. Tears seeped from the corners of my eyes from staring so intently. I blinked them back and focused as hard as I could.

Adam? My heart leapt at the possibility. All thoughts of waiting for Hal vanished, and I stepped out of the truck, trudging through knee-deep snow toward the apartments. Toward Adam, or his body at least. The body I could put the real Adam back into.

As soon as I pushed the door open, the smell hit me—mold, dirty hair, and bad ventilation lay over the top of *something worse*. I clapped my hand over my mouth and nose, but the stench persisted with each step. Dim light bathed the entrance, but after several feet, the hallway disappeared into blackness. I braced myself for an attack, scanning the darkness, expecting an army of Shadows to greet me. I drew my fists back into my sleeves to keep my hands warm and took another step forward.

A bare bulb flickered and swung in the draft that blew through the corridor. I convinced my feet to keep moving. Third floor. Second window. I sensed him.

I pulled out my phone again. No bars. No service. But somehow, maybe before I entered this dank, dark mausoleum, Hal had sent a text. He was on his way. I took a deep breath and moved forward, past the elevator and through the door to the stairwell, wary that the bodies Decklin had evacuated—emptied of their souls and replaced with an unspeakable darkness—had to be here somewhere.

I turned the corner and came upon the first one.

I jumped back, slamming my spine against the metal railing. The door swung shut behind me, and the clang of it echoed through the building. The woman raised her head. I froze, my heart hammering wildly, waiting to see what she'd do. She had bags under her eyes and pale skin, as if she hadn't seen sunlight in weeks. Months. Her thin, gray hair lay matted against her head. Her white knees poked out from underneath a faded sundress.

My mouth went dry. Though I tried to swallow, I couldn't. I backed up the stairs, running my palms along the cool cement wall. The air in the stairwell floated thick with the presence of the Shadow, making it hard to breathe. She opened her mouth to speak but only managed a small croak. Her glassy eyes roamed over me and pinned me to the wall.

Any minute now, she'll fly at me in a rage.

Any minute.

She itched at her head with a bony white hand but didn't move. The longer we stared at one another, the more I relaxed. My shoulders drooped in relief. I inched forward, my nose and mouth still covered. If all of the evacuated ones resembled her, maybe I didn't have a reason to fear them.

I slid past the thing and shot up the stairs to the second floor, pausing behind the door to listen. When I heard nothing, I cracked it and peeked out, my breath suspended.

I choked back a gasp. They could have been normal people. One wore a business suit. A bald one, with a big round belly that stretched against his Buffalo Bills t-shirt, stared straight ahead. A gray-haired one stuffed his hands in the pockets of his corduroys. All of them remained completely silent. Air whispered through the exposed pipes on the ceiling. I didn't take a breath for a while, for an eternity, and when I finally did, I gulped the putrid air.

I couldn't help it. I coughed.

The one closest to me snapped to attention. He turned his black eyes toward the door and locked his gaze with mine. He curled his lips into a hungry smile and started toward me. The rest of them—at least a dozen—followed. My hand flew to my chest as I jumped backward, one thought knocking the breath from me: they would rip me limb from limb.

My body moved without me. Up the stairs to the third floor, where I heard the sound of the door opening one floor below. They clamored after me, pouring into the stairway, a swell of bustling dead bodies.

With a trembling fingers, I reached for the handle of the third floor door and then jerked my hand back. If they occupied the second floor, they'd be on the third too. My heart hammered. I was trapped.

"Fuck." I smashed my fist against the wall in frustration, glancing around to assess my options: chance the roof or go back down to the second floor. I leaned over the rail to see a group of them making their way up the stairs. Luckily, they were slow. They raised their blank faces and stared at me.

I scanned them for my father. He'd had red hair and freckles, like me. Would I recognize him in that putrescent state?

I didn't have time to find out.

I chose the roof.

At the top of the stairwell, I spotted a large plastic garbage can, and it gave me an idea. I flung open the door to the roof. Whirling snow whipped my bare face. The cold blast of wind pushed me back onto the landing. I felt the things below me, gaining. I slammed the door shut to make sure they heard it. With seconds left, at most, I lifted the lid to the garbage can, climbed in, and scraped the lid back in place.

Inside, I buried my head in my hands to block out the rancid smell, and I squeezed my eyes shut. A sticky, tacky substance covered the inside walls. I did my best not to move and worked on slowing my breathing.

The silence was the worst part. I pictured them gathered around the garbage can, ready to toss it down the stairs, waiting to descend on me when I rolled out at the bottom. I made myself as small as possible, willing myself not to exist. Their clamor shook the floor under me. The garbage bin rocked to the side. I bit my lip to stop from screaming.

Over the raucous drumming of my heart, I heard the roof door open, felt the cold sting of winter air through the gaps in the lid. Had they fallen for it? Did they think I was out there? Underneath my coat, something crawled lightning fast along my spine. Each and every one of its hundreds of tiny legs tickled my skin. I fought the urge to burst from my hiding spot, yet I couldn't risk moving. Not until I heard that door close behind them.

My mind raced with potential possibilities—stay, leave, die. They must have moved past the tiny landing onto the roof in search for me. I listened, waiting for the perfect moment to run. The bug skittered up between my shoulder blades, and I couldn't take it anymore. I burst out of the garbage can, threw my weight forward, and toppled out onto the floor. Through the crack in the closing door, I saw a group of them turned at the noise. As soon as they saw me, they lurched back. I gripped the door handle, swung it shut, and threw the bolt, letting out a huge exhale.

My legs shook so bad on the stairs I worried I might fall forward, crack my skull on a concrete step, and die right there. I made it to the third floor landing and shook out my shirt, shimmying and slapping at myself like a fool while they beat at the rooftop door.

A centipede, dark orange with long antennae, dropped from my shirt and disappeared into a crack at the bottom of the wall. I once again suppressed the urge to scream.

The Shadows had either all congregated on the second floor or some hid in the apartments because when I peeked through a crack in the door to the third floor, I saw only a stretch of worn carpet. Light streamed in from the window at the end of the long, empty hallway. I slid along the wall, my back against the peeling wallpaper, and inched past apartment after empty apartment.

Determined to find Adam, I searched for the room I'd seen him in from the outside. Third floor, second window. It was hard to tell from the inside if I was in the right place. I held my ear against the apartment door and listened, but I heard nothing.

I gripped the knob with a sweaty hand. The door creaked open a crack but then rebounded back at me. Something blocked it from the other side. Not an active resistance though. Not like someone pushing back.

After a glance behind me to make sure none of the evacuates lingered nearby, I dug in my heels and pushed as hard as I could. The obstacle on the other side gave way and slid and squealed across the linoleum. I peeked inside the apartment—empty as far as I could tell. No one by the window. No furniture or decorations or anything else that might suggest someone had lived here.

"Adam?" I tiptoed farther into the room, keeping my back to the wall.

With my next step, I slipped in something and landed on my back with a thud. My head slammed against the floor. I lay there, stunned, blinking at the spider web of cracks in the ceiling. Things wavered and blurred. With great effort, I managed to sit up. Blood coated the floor all around me. I'd never seen so much of it. The room swayed as I struggled not to pass out. God, I hated blood.

In the middle of the room, a blonde girl lay on her back in perfect repose, eyes staring straight up at the ceiling, hair spread around her in flowing platinum waves. I recognized her right away from the photos—Cassidy. Numbness started in my hands and spread through every inch of my body. I scooted backward through the slick blood.

A circle of white bone stuck out from the pulpy stump of her elbow, right where her left arm should have been. Her right leg was entirely gone. And half of her stomach had caved in, wet and dark red.

"Cassidy." I dry heaved and put my head between my knees to block out the sight, to hold onto consciousness.

Right now, elsewhere in the world, people hung Christmas lights. They offered tidings of joy and drank peppermint lattes. People sang carols, hung decorations, and gathered with family around the hearth. But Cassidy's parents searched for their dead daughter. The families of all these bodies missed them this holiday season. And I knew where they were, what they'd become. My stomach roiled and twisted with disgust and despair.

I breathed deeply until the worst of my nausea passed. Though it still came in waves, I peeled myself off the floor, wiped my sticky, bloody hands on the edge of the rug, and backed out of the room. I spun around and ran smack into Brandon.

Chapter Twenty

I stifled a scream as he pushed me back into the apartment. He closed and locked the door and then turned to face me. I backed away until I felt the wall behind me. He wore that same Yankees baseball cap and tie-dyed shirt. He looked too much like the cocky Brandon who had approached me on my first day at Meryton. From across the room, I watched him break into a familiar smile.

I slumped against the wall and motioned toward Cassidy. "Did you do that?"

He didn't stare blankly like the thing in the stairwell. He didn't try to rip my limbs off either. He said nothing, quietly regarding me until my irritation got the best of me.

I pushed off the wall, leaving bloody handprints behind. "Are you just going to stand there? Don't you do anything?"

I hoped my insults would distract him as I searched for an exit. But being on the third floor, in a room with the windows painted shut, left few options. Brandon eyed me from where he stood. As a last resort, I considered launching myself at him. I remembered the way the Shadow ripped through me when I had tried to evacuate it from Adam's body, and I bared my teeth in preparation.

"How did Decklin get to you? In the hospital? At Brandon's parents' house?"

Brandon shook his head and spoke in a completely normal voice. Brandon's voice. "She didn't turn me. Orientation brought me in, remember? You were there."

I paused next to the frosted window. She hadn't turned him? I sized him up, trying to make sense of his words. "You mean you're still...?"

I should have noticed. The air remained clear. My lungs didn't burn like they did around other Shadows. Brandon hadn't been evacuated. I let out a sigh, but my heart continued to ache. He hadn't been turned, but he wasn't exactly Brandon. My Brandon had died, and for all Orientation's power, they couldn't bring back a dead human. Neither could I. Between that thought and the lifeless body splayed in the corner, relief eluded me.

"If she didn't evacuate you, what are you doing here?" After Larry's betrayal, I couldn't be too careful.

A ray of sun illuminated the room, and Brandon's eyes sparkled, holding mine. "She brought me here to wait."

He crossed the room toward me. Seeing him again, fully functional, hit me full force right in the gut. I slid down the wall and sat on the floor. Brandon squatted down in front of me, seemingly unconcerned by the urgency of the situation. He smelled faintly of mothballs and dust, as if he'd been in this place long enough to take on its scent.

I picked at the nubby carpet, trying not to focus on the mouth I had kissed. He would have no memory of it. "She brought you here to wait for what?"

"She has to take me back to where I initiated to evacuate me. Back to the Jump Off. But she won't do it while you're still out there. I heard her talking to them. She's made you a target. That's why they want to... well." He gestured toward Cassidy. I shuddered.

Brandon hadn't flinched at all the blood on the ground. He'd stepped right in it and stained the white rubber on his sneakers red. Blood was just blood to him, a component of the body's machinery. Not a sign of mortality, like it was for me. Poor Cassidy. I thought of her parents and her tiny white dog.

The blood on my hands—her blood—had dried and cracked. I scraped at it with a fingernail, swallowing down my revulsion. "Where is Decklin now?"

"I don't know. Looking for you. Looking for your mother."

My mother. His words plunged through me like a sharp knife. I'd last seen her at the house. Surely Hal had gotten to her, or others from Orientation. They had to know she'd be a target. Unless, they didn't... I shivered, but not from the bitter cold seeping through the window.

I narrowed my eyes at him. "Tell me one thing, why haven't you escaped? If I walked right in the front door, you could have walk right out."

He stared at me with wide, innocent eyes and shrugged. "Where would I go? I'm not the Brandon everyone knows. I'm me, but I can't be me because I'm Brandon." He frowned. "So I stay because I can do something here. I can help my kind; I can help you."

A whisper of hope nagged at me, but I pushed it aside. "How? How can you help?"

When he offered his hand, I took it.

He pulled me to my feet. "I know where Adam is."

❈ ❈ ❈

I followed him down the hall and around the corner. After taking a deep breath, I pushed the door open with the tip of my shoe, expecting to see another dead body, or worse. Brandon hung back, either to give me space or because of the air in the room. As soon as I walked in, I knew I'd found the right place. When I took a tentative breath, my lungs burned, the taste in my mouth turned acrid, and the pungent air burned my nostrils. A rotting, sewage smell. The smell of death. The smell of *them*.

I felt around on the wall for a light switch and flipped it up, then down, and then up again, to no avail. I stood in the doorway, vulnerable and imagining the worst, until my eyes adjusted. A slow, scraping sound emanated from deeper inside the room. I blinked a few times, squinted into the dark, and focused on the huddled mass in the dimmest corner of the room. My skin burned, but my blood ran cold.

"Adam," I whispered. The tight knot in my stomach twisted as I drew closer. I knew it was him, but it wasn't him. Yet, I hoped to God that maybe by some miracle—

He lifted his head to look at me, and I knew there had been no miracle. The Adam thing stared me down. A grotesque sight. Whatever took up residence inside that body had thoroughly ravaged it. Severe gauntness made his face angular. His eyes sunk into dark cavernous sockets, and I saw his bones through the same thin t-shirt he'd worn when I'd last seen him. I gasped and propelled myself back toward the door.

The Adam thing brought one knee up and then the other until he crouched like a tiger ready to pounce. His black eyes fixed on me, holding me in place. His glare sent shivers up my spine, as tactile as the centipede crawling up my back—a creeping, visceral revulsion that flushed my skin. After a brief struggle, he stood. He rocked backward once, unstable in that used body, and then lurched toward me.

I couldn't move. Gulping at the festering air, I tried to hold onto myself. The world tilted and turned and dropped out from underneath me, all dictated by the dark presence in the body only a few feet away. He stumbled toward me, his fingertips closing in on my—

"Mira!" Brandon shouted behind me.

My trance broke. I snapped to attention and grasped the Adam thing around the neck. When I did, hot darkness shot through me.

"I wouldn't do that if I were you."

As soon as I heard her voice, I let go.

Chapter Twenty-One

Decklin stood in the doorway, looming larger than her small stature should have allowed. Dressed in black, like usual, her ebony hair and lithe movements resembled a silhouette more than a person.

"I hope you three had a pleasant reunion." She glided into the apartment, winked at Brandon, and gestured toward the Adam thing. "So, let me guess. This is where you infiltrate the bad guys and save the world?"

My heart lodged in my throat. My legs tensed to dash, but where? Decklin had me trapped. The Adam thing wanted to kill me, and I wasn't sure where Brandon stood. Beads of sweat formed on my forehead.

"That's what I thought." Her pale skin glowed, almost translucent. The Adam thing rocked unsteadily next to me.

Decklin wrinkled her nose at him. "Not quite up to standards anymore, is he? It's too bad. Sometimes it doesn't work out, and I can't figure out why." She smiled at Brandon behind me. "But I still have Brandon, don't I? He'll make a nice substitute." She waggled her eyebrows at him, and I suppressed the urge to gag.

"Brandon is dead," I said through clenched teeth. Electric currents ran up and down my legs. My muscles begged me to move. To take off running and leave behind any part of me that wanted to stay.

"Right. Such a pity." She clicked her tongue like a tragedy had occurred, but her smile revealed her true feelings. "So here's the reality of the situation you're in. There are twenty Shadows outside that door. You can come quietly or not. But 'not' would be more painful."

I wrinkled my nose in disgust. "You're a lunatic."

Her black eyes swirled with madness. "Maybe. But I've honestly grown tired of you, Mira. I should have finished you on the hill when I had the chance. Or even better, as soon as you stepped into the dorm room."

She took a step toward me, and I backed up. Brandon slid over to the door, nodding slightly at me. I knitted my brow in confusion. Was he on my side or hers?

As Decklin passed through a weak strip of light from the gap in the shade, her eyes went fully black. Behind me, the throbbing heat of a Shadow—the Adam thing—crept toward me. Brandon braced himself against the door and mouthed the words *I'm with you*. My pulse quickened with the knowledge that he was trying to help me. She hadn't gotten to him after all.

I knew what I had to do. I had a split second to distract her.

"Brandon, look out!" I yelled, my voice someone else's, someone strong and confident. Decklin whipped her head around. It was all I needed.

I shot an elbow backward into the approaching Adam thing, pulled the keys from my pocket, and pried open the small blade on the rusty Swiss Army knife on Hal's keychain. Then I swung around to face her.

"Oh my." She stopped inches from me, as if someone pressed pause. Her eyes went from me to the knife. "I surrender." She threw her hands in the air.

I thought I had her, until she doubled over with the kind of laughter that rankled me to my bones. And I realized, Jesus, the knife was small. Pretty ridiculously small. It shook in my hand. My heart beat in my ears, and my whole body vibrated with fear.

"There are probably bigger ones in the drawer." Though she'd started to compose herself, her lips still curled into a superior grin. "Help yourself. Though it probably won't matter. You and a tiny knife against a hundred of us?"

A hot flush spread across my face as I thought of the evacuated ones with their dead hands on me, their darkness exploding inside me.

"I will beat you." I raised my chin, exuding a confidence I didn't feel. Brandon stood by the door, poised for battle at my command. Two of us—a half Sender and an alien in my friend's body—against Decklin and a hundred Shadows. It did seem ridiculous. And yet, I had to try.

Her eyes shifted colors like a dollar store mood ring. "You think putting a hole in me will change anything? You think it will bring Adam back? Your father? Okay, Mira dear. Say you go so far as to kill me. What will you do about them?" She gestured to the door.

"The Shadows?" I gulped.

Decklin nodded. "Yes. The *Shadows*. They're waiting for you outside the door. Go ahead Brandon, open it. I dare you."

He hesitated, looking to me for direction. My hand coiled around the pocketknife.

"They're hungry, you know." She waved her hand in the air. "Try feeding a hundred of those things on my budget. And anyway, who's the bad guy here? They lost their souls in the mass genocide perpetuated by *Senders*, don't forget." She tilted her head toward the Adam thing and continued to move toward me.

"Senders needed the bodies," I argued, sidestepping a pile of trash on the floor. "They didn't know the damage they were doing. They're not making that mistake with humans. They're only taking the dead ones now." I swallowed. "They can't change what they did, but they can try to do better next time."

Decklin's eyes widened, and she put a hand over her mouth in mock shock. "Oh, well, it's all okay then." She rolled her eyes. "Don't even try to defend them. They kicked my friends—my family—out of their bodies and sentenced them to wallow in oblivion, in the Dark Eternal. And they'd still be there now if it weren't for me."

I gritted my teeth. "Oh yes, you're the dark hero. You're evacuating human souls, the same thing you're mad at the Senders for doing to your people. Do you not see the hypocrisy?" I waved the dumb, tiny knife in the air to halt her progress. "Don't get any closer."

I glanced over at Adam, willing his body to hold on for just a little while longer. Then I looked back at Decklin. "We live and learn. What the Senders did was wrong, but what you're doing isn't any better. Those Shadows don't belong in human bodies. These are your friends, your family? They can barely function. Is this kind of life better than the Dark Eternal?"

"Anything is better than the Dark Eternal," Decklin snapped. She moved toward me.

I inhaled through my teeth, brought my arm up, and focused on her shoulder. That perfect spot wouldn't kill her, but it would disable her a bit and buy me time.

She halted mid-step, eyes on the knife. *Bring down the knife, bring it down once, hard, like jamming a blade into a watermelon.*

I felt it. My muscles working, the thump of the impact. The satisfaction.

If only, if only I could force my arm to move.

Decklin smirked. "The hero falters in her moment of glory. In moments like this, we find out who we really are, don't we?"

I let my arm drop, and my confidence went with it. So I couldn't bring myself to stab someone after all. It wasn't such a bad characteristic, for a normal person, but it felt like failure to me—half Sender, savior of a whole species. *You were born to save the Senders,* my father had said, standing in the field under a blazing sun a lifetime ago. His wild hair had blown in the wind, red like mine. *You'll just have to trust yourself when it comes time.*

My father was wrong. I couldn't trust myself. I couldn't trust anyone.

A few feet from where we stood, the Adam thing collapsed to the floor, legs splayed in front of him, head lolling against his shoulder. My heart plummeted. "Adam."

"He's pretty much done for." Decklin's mouth turned down at the corners. "I was afraid of that, but sometimes it happens with these guys. The bodies reject them." She blew her hair out of her face, and for a moment, I saw through the rough exterior to the broken soul inside. These were her friends, her family. They meant something to her.

Then I thought of the woman on the stairs, how years in a body ravaged her beyond function. Would the same thing happen to Adam? How could I ever bring him back from that?

Decklin raised an eyebrow at me. "You know, you should thank me for evacuating him when I did. Your mother fell for one, and look what happened to her."

The fire in me roared back to life, her words the gasoline. She wanted me to *thank* her? For destroying my life? My mother's life? Seven years I had waited. Seven long, heart-wrenching years. I was not about to lose this chance at retribution.

It's what you were born for.

Maybe it was what I would die for too.

I surged forward, thrusting the knife in front of me, blindly swinging it in wide arcs. Power radiated through my fingertips to the cold metal. The keys rattled like victory bells.

Decklin and the apartment became a blur through my barely open eyes. The knife settled somewhere and stuck. Decklin drew in a quick, sharp breath, and I withdrew my hand, knifeless, breathless. She stumbled backward and slammed against the window. The shade went up with a loud snap, and sunlight poured in.

Everything looked much different in the light.

I shielded my eyes from the brightness and peered over my arm to see Decklin standing dazed, holding her right shoulder. She looked from me to the keys dangling against her chest. The iconic red plastic of the knife had lodged below her collarbone, a few inches above her heart. The Adam thing sat motionless on the floor. It pulsed there as if catching its breath, not dead after all, but close. I moved my lips to say something but all that came out was a whisper of air.

A sudden clamor in the hallway brought my attention to the door, which rattled on its hinges. Brandon braced himself against it, his eyes wide.

I had forgotten about the others.

I started to shake uncontrollably. Despite the small sense of triumph I felt, I had never been more terrified. I jerked my gaze from the door back to Decklin. The lines on her forehead deepened. Her face changed to a veil of shock.

"Ouch." Her eyes widened in disbelief. She doubled over, one hand on the windowsill. "I can't believe you actually did that."

"It's your fault." I backed toward the corner of the room, my hands out in front of me like a linebacker, ready to fend off attackers. "You left me no choice."

"It hurts." Her breath wheezed out. "I'm bleeding like crazy. I think you hit an artery or something."

Blood sprayed everywhere. That little knife, the one she'd laughed at, had done a lot of damage. Aside from the main wound, a deep slash ran from her ear to just below her chin, and her forearm dripped bright red blood onto the carpet.

"That's for Cassidy. Now call off your minions." I motioned to the door, feeling bigger inside than outside. "And then you will tell me where my father is."

"You know I can't do that. Anyway, who do you think you are?" Decklin straightened up, and wrapped her fingers, with her bright pink nails, around the keychain.

The pounding at the door grew more intense. Brandon struggled to maintain his leverage as his sneakers slid out from under him.

Decklin's grimace turned to a scowl. "I'll feed you to them."

She drew her mouth into a taut frown. With a quick yank, she drew the knife out and threw it aside. The keychain skittered across the floor and disappeared under a chair. She winced as she pressed her hand to her shoulder. Blood seeped through her shirt, ran down her forearm, soaking her collar.

"Tell them to stop." I stood my ground, despite my shaky legs. "You're going to bring Adam back. And then you're going to bring my father back."

Decklin shook her head. "You are dense, aren't you. I can't bring Adam back. It doesn't work that way." She took two steps toward me and then staggered backward. "It doesn't matter anyway. Any second now, that door is going to break open, and then you'll see how easily these sorry excuses for human bodies can rip apart at the seams."

Each bang brought a new crack in the growing spider web in the door, and tiny jagged pieces near the lock splintered off onto the floor.

I clenched my fists, determined to get the answers I needed. Determined to fulfill my birthright. "I know my father is here. Where is he?"

Decklin teetered on her feet. Blood drenched her shirt. She had given up holding the wound and instead steadied herself against the windowsill with both hands. "That was seven years ago, you idiot. Your father is long gone."

"I don't have time for this." I barreled into her, knocking her against the window with an oomph, and both of us crashed to the ground. The hard floor cracked my kneecap and elbow, but it only registered on the outskirts of my consciousness. Her weight forced the breath out of me, but I swung my fists anyway, connecting with bone and the soft parts under her ribs.

She struggled against me and managed to get loose and scramble toward the door. "Break it down! Break it down!"

The pounding increased, and the blows got harder. Brandon couldn't hold them off for much longer.

I grasped Decklin by the ankle, lugged her backward across the wood floor, flipped her over, put my hands on her throat, and closed my eyes. She clawed at me, but I held firm.

Anger surged through me. Everything could have been prevented if Decklin had just left my father alone. My mother wouldn't be crazy. I would have made friends. Brandon would still be alive. But I never would have met Adam…

Adam.

A cold hand clamped around my wrist and dragged me off Decklin, across the floor. A shriek pierced the air. My shriek. The Adam thing had me. Before I could think to react, the darkness took me. With my last bit of energy, I groped at his arm, his shoulder, and finally found his neck. I wrapped my hands around it, and everything went black.

Chapter Twenty-Two

My vision blurred, and my head weighed a thousand pounds. Images flooded back in slowly, in waves. The dark, empty walls of the apartment surrounded me. My knee throbbed where I'd cracked it. My sweat-soaked shirt stuck to my skin under my coat. With each blast of cold that poured in through the windows, I shuddered violently.

"Decklin?" I whispered, hoarse.

She lay unmoving a few feet away.

No response.

I nudged her hip with my foot. Dead weight. No movement in her chest. Legs splayed out, arms at her sides as if she'd fallen without even bracing herself. As if she'd fallen stone dead.

On quivering arms, I crab-walked backward and propped myself up against the wall, half expecting her to pop her eyes open and smile a malicious smile. As I came back fully to myself, I realized the whole apartment shook with the weight of the Shadows throwing themselves against door. Decklin no longer posed the biggest threat. Or any threat at all.

I had no time to find any satisfaction in that.

"Can you hold them?" I yelled to Brandon, pulling myself up on rubbery legs and stumbling to the window.

He didn't answer. Each blow knocked him backward an inch more. His sneakers squeaked on the wood floor as he struggled to get traction.

My shaky arms did little to dislodge the window frame from the paint, which held like glue against the sill. As I frantically deliberated my next move, I remembered how Adam had been in this very spot when I'd arrived. The spot that was now empty.

His absence slammed into my chest with the force of a tractor trailer, knocking the breath out of me. I glanced to the corner where he'd fallen, then around the apartment, but there was no trace of him. He couldn't have left without letting the stream of Shadows in. So where was he?

The front door splintered.

I dashed for the bedroom. "Brandon, come on!"

He quit the door and sprinted after me, jumping over Decklin's body. I blasted down the short hallway, my knee throbbing, and reached for the bedroom door. A figure shot from the dark room and clasped my shoulders, hard, spinning me around. I screamed, terrified the Shadows had caught me. A hand clamped down over my mouth, cutting my scream short. From the living room, I heard the wood finally give. The door busted open.

Brandon stopped just short of running into me. "Adam, take her into the bedroom."

Adam? Cold blood ran in my veins, and my forehead broke into a sweat. The hand over my mouth must have been Adam's. Maybe this had been their plan the whole time. Brandon and Adam in collusion to get me alone. I kicked and moaned, my eyes stinging with tears. He was too strong. I couldn't get away.

He hauled me through the doorway into the bedroom. I struggled against him and broke free, but he pushed me toward the bare mattress with enough force that I fell across it and snapped my teeth down on my tongue. He shut the door behind him and turned the tiny lock. I watched from the bed with horror as he and Brandon scraped the heavy dresser across the wood floor and wedged it against the door, barricading us inside.

I scrambled across the mattress to the window on the opposite side of the room. With a mania I didn't know I possessed, I ripped the shade right off its anchors and strained and pushed against the window. It budged a centimeter. My arms quivered from the effort. My bruised elbow protested, and my knee screamed in agony. Slowly, the window loosened and slid open with a groan. A cold blast of air rushed in, freezing my face as I peered down at the thirty-foot drop. The height made my head spin, but I had no choice. I'd risk a broken ankle over whatever fate awaited me in that bedroom. I didn't even feel the cold. My heart banged in my chest. Clutching the sill, I inhaled hard and swung one leg over, eyeing the bone-breaking, snow-covered concrete below.

"Mira, please. Don't try it." Adam's voice held me where I was.

The place deep within me, which had been overflowing with terror and despair, filled with sudden hope. I spun around and gasped, knowing instantly by looking at him that Adam had come back. The veins stood out on his arms, his torn t-shirt flapped against his skin, and the wound on his head needed serious washing. But when his eyes met mine and locked into place, I saw nothing except the boy I loved.

He smiled. "You did it. You brought me back."

I rushed to him, tripping over the sill and pitching forward. He caught me in his arms and held me up. I threw my arms around him so hard we fell backward onto the bare mattress together. I ran my fingers through his hair, cupped his face in my hands, and stared with disbelief into those eyes I thought I might never see again.

We both smiled. He must have felt my heart soar, for it beat right next to his.

"Am I crushing you?" I whispered.

He shook his head, his smile growing wider. His body shifted underneath me as he raised his hand to push a stray curl behind my ear. For a moment, nothing else existed. In the distant background, I was aware of the pounding against the door, but I didn't care. Adam had come back to me.

"I brought you back?" I remembered wrapping my hands around his neck while he encircled my wrists with his decomposing hands. But after that, everything had gone dark.

He nodded. "It was your touch. You banished the Shadow, and I funneled back into this body."

He touched his forehead to mine. His scent, his skin against mine, made me dizzy. I couldn't take it anymore. I had to kiss him. He must have been thinking the same thing, because he brought his hand to the back of my neck and tilted his head. I closed my eyes, seeing stars already, waiting for his lips to touch mine.

"I could use some help here," Brandon yelled. I jerked my head back, suddenly faced with reality. Through a crack in the wood I saw the faces of the Shadows as they threw themselves against the door with such force it knocked Brandon backward. I jumped off Adam, and we both sprung from the bed to brace ourselves against the dresser.

There were too many of them. They pummeled the bedroom door, a steady, coordinated banging as they launched themselves against it over and over again. Our muscles strained, our faces went red with the effort of holding them back. The door busted open an inch and forced the dresser forward.

"They're too strong." I panted, struggling to keep pushing, though my muscles burned.

"Get under the bed," Brandon commanded, his face shiny with sweat.

I absorbed another blow. This one knocked my head back. "What's that going to do? You think a bed will stop them?"

He shook his head. "No, but they'll think you went through the window. Hurry. They're almost through."

"What about you two?" The dresser slammed into my hip, sending a shockwave down my bad leg. I grunted. "They'll kill you."

Adam squeezed his eyes shut with effort, his outstretched arms straining against the encroaching hoard. "Do what he says. They're not after us. It's you they want."

"But my father might be—"

Another pound popped the hinges loose. I saw their heads: some gray, some balding, some with blonde curls, and others with hair as dark as Adam's. They clogged the doorway, the entire apartment, and pressed us back into the bedroom. The dresser scraped across the wood floor, slamming into the wall as the door flooded with Shadows.

I gasped, dropped down, and inched under the bed, just clearing the metal frame. A putrid sea of legs and feet surged into the bedroom.

"She went out the window," Brandon yelled with such conviction I might have believed it myself.

The springs pressed close to my chest as a throng of them flung themselves across the bed and hopped off the other side to look out the window, down to the parking lot where they believed—God help me, I hoped they believed—that I had escaped. If they had been human, with reason and deduction, they might have searched under the bed.

But they weren't human. Not even close.

I held my breath so long my lungs burned, and my eyes teared until I could stand it no more. My deep, controlled breath brought a cloud of dust into my lungs, and I jammed my lips together to suppress the cough. Every fiber in me taut, I withstood the urgent need to expel what I had inhaled.

Just when I reached the verge of bursting, the springs once again pressed into my chest, and the pressure relented. Footsteps left the bedroom and echoed down the hall.

Adam's feet appeared—his socks gone black with grime. He dropped to his knees and ducked his head to look at me, and I coughed. I hacked until my face turned purple.

When I composed myself, I slid out from my hiding place and straightened up. Adam's eyes wandered over me, from head to foot, and my cheeks flamed. He reached out and stroked my cheek.

"They're gone." His eyes were impossibly blue, and his cheeks had regained their color.

"They'll come back." Brandon appeared behind Adam, disheveled. "We have to go."

"The truck's out front." I grabbed Adam's hand and moved toward the door.

In the living room, Decklin lay where she had fallen, the small pool of blood shiny and dark around her. Adam stopped short but slid a few inches in the blood. He rubbed his temple and stared at her body.

"Adam, come on," I said. "We have to hurry." I followed Brandon through the giant, jagged hole in the apartment door, relieved to see an empty hallway, but at the same time, suspicious.

"Adam," I called again.

He crouched next to Decklin and bent down over her so I couldn't see his face. I thought of them at the campsite, reclined on the blanket, talking softly under the moonlight. How they'd linked arms when they'd walked, how he'd made her laugh even when he'd said nothing funny.

Jealousy clamped its black fist around my heart. Jealousy over a dead girl and how he might have felt about her.

I frowned. "Adam, she's dead."

He flinched at my words but ignored them and folded her hands on her stomach. He brushed her still beautiful, still silken black hair back from her face and paused as if to offer a prayer.

Though Adam's actions distracted me, I heard them approaching. With a strangled cry, I looked past Brandon and pointed.

He whipped his head around. "What? What is it?"

Five Shadows barreled toward us. I glanced back at Adam, who'd risen to his feet and blinked away whatever grief had found a temporary place in his eyes.

"This way." Brandon grabbed my arm and pulled me around the corner.

"No." I shrugged him off and stood my ground. "I'm sick of running."

The light in the hall flickered. Off and on, off and on. Each time it glowed bright, the evacuated ones crept that much closer. The one in front appeared to lead the way—a middle-aged man with thick black glasses and a peppered gray mustache.

This was my time. Screw my bad knee, my elbow, my inability to make wise decisions, and my jealousy over a dead girl. I shot down the hall in their direction. Behind me, Brandon screamed for me to stop. In front of me, the Shadows' black eyes narrowed. Inside me, the naked, animalistic imperative to survive growled and thrust me forward.

Chapter Twenty-Three

Large, calloused hands closed around my throat as the gray-haired one lifted me by the neck. I beat at the sides of his head with my fists. My insides sucked up inside me into one painful point and then radiated outward in an explosion of agony that took my legs from under me. I crashed to the ground with a thud.

The man fell on top of me, his shiny bald spot glistening as he attempted to choke the life out of me. More hands on me, around my ankles, pulling me down the hall with that heavy man-thing riding on top of me. My eyes went up to the fluorescents, flickering on and off. *This is it.* No blaze of glory, just the embarrassment of being choked and dragged down a tacky hallway carpet by a displaced soul in a stolen body. My shirt crept up, and the rug burned the skin on my back.

Someone shouted from behind me. When the lights flickered back on, I stretched my neck and saw a tangle of bodies at the other end of the hall. A flash of Adam's jeans, Brandon crashing against the wall and then springing back into the mix. Cracking bones. Cracking skulls. My vision contracted to a thin circle of black and expanded out again. My face constricted, so hot and tight I thought my eyeballs might pop out. Wheezing for breath, I clawed at the thing's hands and brought my own up to his neck.

These might be my last few moments in this body. If there was ever a time to perform, it's now.

I stopped fighting. The thing raised its head to look up at me, to look right into my eyes, and it shot me full of blackness. The blackness poured through my pupils like hot needles. I couldn't take a breath to scream. The heat barreled down my neck, into my shoulders and my chest, and radiated down my arms to the tips of my fingers. It swelled in my heart and, in the next beat, burst through my bloodstream and into my every part of me—my esophagus, my mouth, my nasal cavity. If the pressure increased any more, my head would explode.

In an instant, like a balloon popping, the pressure relented and only darkness—darkness, and my wrecked body—remained.

Somewhere in my memory, I heard my father say my name.

Recollections flooded through me. I had run through a meadow as a child, on a day so bright that the blues and greens glistened with a brilliance that stole away all sadness. The memory pushed up through the pain I felt now and warmed my skin with the sun from that glorious day.

I clung to the flashback, to the glow of the sunlight.

But a new memory pushed its way to the surface. In it, I saw Saturn's rings for the first time through the telescope in my backyard. My father stood next to me smoking a pipe, the sweet smell filling my lungs. I breathed it in. The smell took the place of the pain.

My heels dragged across the coarse carpet, grounding me in the present when the past threatened to steal me away. But my mind continued to grasp for memories.

I thought of my first goldfish, Jack, with his bubble eyes and long, transparent fins.

The sweet taste of crème brulee with a caramelized, slightly burnt top.

Freshness and light took the place of the darkness rushing through me. The memories faded, and a stillness settled over me. I opened my eyes.

The evacuated one lay across my chest. He blinked up at me from behind thick glasses, his eyes sparkling green, and his cheeks flushed.

"Get off." My throat burned.

He rolled right off and straightened up, patting himself down like he'd forgotten his glasses and smiling. The decaying smell had vanished.

My first deliberate evacuation.

Pride swelled my chest, but just as soon relented. One held my ankles, a younger mustached man in a filthy t-shirt, black jeans, and heavy work boots. Black soot or ash smudged his face.

A miner. One from the article my mother had clipped only a few months ago.

He eyed me, his lids heavy and swollen to match the rest of his face, and then peered past me down the hall.

"What are you waiting for?" I managed to eke out the words despite my pulsing, swollen throat.

I rose to my feet with a surge of confidence. I knew how to do it now. Eye contact, skin contact, concentration. And since I knew what to expect, how to drive out the darkness, I wagered I could probably bear it. Maybe it got easier each time.

The thing backed toward the door, sliding its hands along the wall. When it got to the stairs, it took off. I turned around to see what had spooked him. Brandon, Adam, and three more Shadows occupied the hall behind me. One Shadow lay still on the ground, one bent over himself with his hands on his knees, and one slunk off down the hallway sporting a significant limp.

Had we done it? I touched my fingertips to my neck and winced. The light above me flickered one last time and shorted out, leaving me disoriented in the dark. But the light down the hallway stayed on, illuminating Brandon, Adam, and the evacuated ones like actors on stage.

"So this is it, right?" I hobbled toward Adam. He opened his arms, and I fell into them. Tears of relief pricked my eyes. "We did it. We stopped her. I can bring them back. All I have to do is turn the rest of them." The hard knot in my stomach loosened, and I smiled.

Yes, I would have to evacuate each and every one of them. I thought about hunting them all down and enduring the agony of the evacuation. Time and time and time again. My smile disappeared as weariness saturated my bones. At the edges of my vision, bright white dots swam and darted like sparks from some invisible fire.

"Yes." Adam rubbed my back. "But Mira, you can't do it here. There are too many of them."

I stepped out of his embrace. "But my father."

He rubbed my cheek with the pad of his thumb. "We'll come back for him. I promise." His soft voice calmed the storm inside me. "But it would be suicide to try right now. We know where they are, and they're not going anywhere without Decklin."

Adam put a firm hand on my back, and I let him lead me to the stairs. I concentrated on putting one foot in front of the other and on nothing else. We took the stairs down to the first floor. Our little party had increased by one—the middle-aged bald man whom I'd had the pleasure of being crushed under. He didn't speak except to thank me. He trailed behind us, inspecting everything with his new eyes.

Brandon opened the door, peeked out, and waved us through to the empty hallway. The door slammed shut behind us, echoing in the silence. No Shadows rushed out to meet us, though I braced for it. No one blocked the exit. A matchless shoe lay in the middle of the hall. The Shadows must have all disappeared, ducking back into the apartments and shutting the doors.

I dug in my pockets to retrieve the keys to the truck, and my stomach dropped. "Shit. The keys."

They'd slid across the floor and under the chair when Decklin had thrown them. I slapped a palm to my forehead. I wanted to scream. We'd managed to escape the Shadows and make it to the car, only to be thwarted at the finish line.

"Do either of you know how to hotwire a car?" I could pick locks with the best of them, but that's where my talent ended.

They both stared at me with blank faces.

My heart caved. We had no choice but to brave the building once more. I'd have to face the horrible room where my victim lay staring up at the ceiling. I would have rather stuck hairpins into my eyes than go back, but I had no alternative.

"You come with me." I motioned for Adam to join me. "Brandon, you stay here, in case any come down here."

Brandon shook his head. "I should go too. Three of us is better than two."

"No, I'll go with Mira. Someone needs to stay with him." Adam gestured toward the Sender, who stared at the ceiling in reverence.

I pointed to the fire alarm on the wall. "If they come down here, pull this lever. And if that doesn't work, scream your head off."

Brandon looked at me hard, his jaw set, his mouth a thin line. "It's a bad idea." The newly returned Sender gazed out the window at the white snow.

"We'll be quick." I set off down the hall, feeling Brandon's eyes burn a hole in my back.

As Adam and I scaled the first staircase, my legs wobbled like a newborn Initiate. I'd teetered so close to the edge of panic lately, things had become unreal to me—the gaudy checked pattern of the carpet in the hallway, the feel of my own skin inside my filthy sweater and jeans. I had turned into an interloper in my own body.

As I held my breath, Adam opened the door to the stairwell. Empty. We pushed forward.

I leaned in close to him, in need of a distraction from the wild frenzy inside me. "What was it like, being brought back?"

He thought for a moment before answering. "It was like a flash. I was here, and then for a moment, I wasn't here. Then I was here again."

"You don't remember any of it? Nothing about the Dark Eternal?" Our footsteps echoed in the stairwell, every little noise amplified. I expected to encounter that old woman at any second and held tight to Adam's arm.

"No, I don't." He shook his head. "Was this body stronger last time I had it? It feels different." He flexed his muscles, studied his forearms.

"Yes." I nodded. "The last soul to occupy it didn't take well to the body. Decklin said sometimes the Shadows don't adapt."

"They aren't trained like we are. We had bodies where I came from, but the Shadows are coming from the Dark Eternal. All that time without a body withers them up." Sadness tinged his words.

Anything is better than the Dark Eternal, Decklin had said. I slipped my hand inside Adam's and squeezed. He offered me a woeful smile.

We reach the third floor—empty. My trepidation morphed quickly into suspicion. Where were they? As we edged past a few dozen doors, neither of us spoke. We kept our hands clasped as we crept closer to the apartment, closer to the keys and Decklin's dead body.

When we reached the room, I nodded at Adam, took a breath, and stepped through the demolished doorway. I'd planned a quick in and out. Step around Decklin's body, avoid the blood, reach under the chair for the keys, and get the hell out of there.

I glanced at the spot where Decklin went down, and my hand flew to my mouth. Her body had vanished.

Chapter Twenty-Four

The hair on my arms and the back of my neck stood up. I tiptoed backward toward the demolished doorway and back to Adam, expecting something to jump out at us at any moment. My heart hammered. Adam's posture shifted from cautious to tense and alert.

"I swear she was dead." I wrung my hands. "She wasn't breathing. I never saw someone so dead."

I rechecked the room number. Blood pooled in one spot on the floor but didn't leave a trail, so she hadn't been dragged out. My breathing increased as more and more clues pointed to an outcome more terrifying than Decklin's death.

"She's not dead." I nearly hyperventilated as I spoke.

Adam nodded. "Ok. Let's get the keys. We should stick to the plan." When I hesitated, he touched my arm. "I can get the keys if you'd rather watch the door."

"No, no. I'll get them."

I calculated the keys must be about twelve steps from the door to the chair and back again. I put one foot in front of the other, bracing myself.

Each creak of the floor sent my nerves into a frenzy. My teeth chattered though I sweated through my shirt.

Ten steps.

Nine. I gazelle-leap over the puddle of sticky, drying blood.

Eight.

Seven.

When I reached the chair, I dropped to my knees and groped underneath, praying the keys hadn't slipped through a crack in the wood and disappeared forever. My fingertips made contact with the cold metal. I snatched the keys, snapped the knife shut, pocketed the whole business, and retraced my steps. Six steps back to Adam.

"That was a piece of cake." I released a nervous laugh.

Adam cracked a small smile. "Good, now let's go."

The door at the end of the stairwell opened and shut. An eruption of movement followed. Adam and I ducked back into the room and stood flat against the inside wall, our eyes wide with alarm. Adam slid his fingers along the wallpaper until they found mine, and I grasped them so hard I was afraid they might break. I had defeated Decklin once. Exhausted, injured, scared out of my wits, I doubted I had the ability to do it again.

"She's in there." Brandon's voice echoed through the hallway, and I froze. Had he betrayed us after all?

"Mira?" a familiar voice called.

I looked sideways at Adam, my eyes widening. *Impossible.* All the events, all of the stress of my recent past, and the fact that I'd had two Shadows go through me must have rattled me right out of my senses. Because that voice sounded exactly like my mother.

"Mira?"

"Mom?" I dared to peer around Adam, out the battered door to the hallway.

I nearly collapsed at the sight of her. My mother, in the flesh. With her Gore-Tex winter coat, red scarf, and felted wool hat, she shined modern and strong against the dull, antiquated décor of the building. A tear rolled down my cheek. My mother had come for me.

"Mom!" I sprinted toward her.

We crashed into one another halfway down the hall. She hugged me to her so hard she knocked the wind out of me. I buried my face in her coat and wrapped my arms around her, all my anger forgotten. She had come for me. We rocked together while she shook and sobbed, occasionally taking a break to push me away, look at me, and then pull me back to her.

Brandon, Adam, the newly re-bodied Sender, and even Hal—miserable Hal!—stood nearby, waiting for us to join the world again.

I wiped my eyes with the back of my hand. "You did it. You left the house."

"I thought I was going to lose you." She gathered my face in her hands.

Hal cleared his throat. "I hate to break up the reunion, but we should go."

"Wait. Decklin." I filled them all in on what happened. "I thought I killed her, but she's not where I left her."

My mother's jaw tightened. "We have to find her. This is the closest we've come to the Conduit in a long time; we can't let her get away now."

Hal nodded his consent. "We can't let her leave the building."

"If we do, she'll start again, somewhere else." My mother touched a strand of my hair. "And she'll always be looking for you, my Mira."

I put an arm around my mother and imagined how my life would change if we removed Decklin. We wouldn't have to move—her running out of one house, cowering in the back seat, and then running into a new house. We could eat at restaurants, take jogs in the park, blow money shopping, all the things I'd never the chance to do with her. It was just a matter of finding the Conduit. I'd done it once. With my mother at my side, I could do it again.

"Better to hit her while she's weak," Hal said. "Because not even that'll last long."

"Ok." A deep, resolved breath escaped my lips. "Let's do it." Adam and Brandon stepped up beside me. I smiled at them, grateful for their help. Then I turned to my mother and frowned.

"Mom?"

Her mouth went suddenly slack, and she stared, wide-eyed, down the hall. She moved, as if pulled by some invisible force, toward an evacuated man.

"Jack?" she whispered, pushing her hat up her forehead with a trembling hand.

An evacuate with red hair, sprouting in frizzy tufts, staggered toward us. He wore a hospital gown, dirty and tattered. His cheeks sunk deep into his face, and his eyes held the same vacant, dark, cavernous look of all evacuates. Despite all that, I recognized my father.

Chapter Twenty-Five

Time slowed as a hail of memories bombarded me. My father had once solved Millennium Problems—the hardest math problems in the world—with a marker on my parents' white bedroom wall. He'd often forget where he'd put his coffee, and he'd always keep pens in his pocket. He'd plastered his office not only with star charts but with prints from artists that ranged from Rembrandt to Picasso. He'd loved cooking and hiking, and he'd loved me and my mother.

But he'd never lumbered toward us with a crazed look in his eyes.

We'd found my father, only he was not my father.

My mother cut the distance between them and launched herself at him, arms flung wide.

"Mom, no!" I lunged after her.

"Stop!" Hal called out from close behind me.

We both reached out for her, but she closed her arm around my father's shoulders with a delighted cry. In seconds, his hands crept beneath her scarf and encircled her throat. She choked and sputtered, grabbing at the forearms of the thing that used to be my father. A sick gurgle bubbled from her mouth.

I hurled myself at them, knocking bone against bone, toppling the three of us toward the wall. We skimmed off of it and landed on the frayed carpet. He lay next to me curled on his side. The notches in his spine stretched and strained against his white skin. He clutched for my mother, who had rolled a few inches away after hitting her head on the wall. Blood ran into her eye, but she wiped it away and sat up, blinking.

The thing rose off the floor, reanimated and hell bent on destroying her. There was no trace of my father, the man who'd loved her, in this body. Not anywhere.

Hot anger surged through my limbs. My pulse drumbeat a loud, primal tune in my ears. I yanked my father back by his disheveled red hair and frog-leaped over him to stand between them. I would not lose my mother. Not to this thing. Hal and Adam grabbed her by the elbows and whisked her backward down the hall.

The thing turned and challenged me with its eyes. I noticed the scar above its right eyebrow. My father had gotten it from an exploding rock at a campfire. Fury roared inside me. This thing had my father's scar. How dare this Shadow take over my father's body and try kill my mother with it. Not on my watch.

I raised my hands, determined, purposeful this time, and placed them on him. His eyes shot open. I hadn't touched my father in seven years, yet it brought me nothing but pain.

My vision wavered; white light crowded the edges. All of me strained, all six-hundred and forty muscles stressed to their maximum. The Shadow left him and entered me. It flowed through me and out. It dissipated into the air through my pores, lifting like evaporation from my skin and freeing me so the former inhabitant of the body could come home. My father's soul rushed through me like a warm wave.

This time, I didn't black out. But the effort took my strength. Both my father and I collapsed.

My hearing returned, and my vision withdrew from the tunnel. I wrapped my arms around my knees and stared at him, waiting to see if I'd been successful. My mother raced to my side and grasped my hand. Her pulse pounded in her fingertips.

She brushed back my hair. "Mira. Are you alright?"

I nodded but couldn't speak. My father lay still on the floor where he had dropped. Did it work? I willed him with everything inside me to open his eyes. I willed home the man I remembered.

My mother touched his arm. "Jack?"

He didn't react. It had been seven years. His long absence had ravaged his body, grayed his skin, and dulled his eyes. Maybe he couldn't come back. Maybe it had been too long.

My mother released a strangled cry. A stray tear rolled off her cheek and dropped onto mine. That one droplet freed the torrent within me, and I started to sob. All this time, all this effort. For nothing.

Hal shook my arm. "Mira."

I pushed him away. "Not now, Hal."

"Listen." He pointed toward the stairwell, toward a heavy, metallic, rhythmic clinking. Like a bottle against a concrete wall or a wrench against a pipe. The clinking stopped. Hal and I watched the door. My mother remained fixated on my father's body.

"It could be her." Adam offered me his hand. "We have to find out."

Not now, I thought. I wanted to stay on the floor and wallow in my exhaustion and heartache. But my father had believed in me. He'd believed I'd been born for a cause that spanned the galaxy. And though I'd failed to bring him back, I could still succeed at ridding the universe of Decklin.

I took Adam's hand and stood. My bad knee had begun to heal, but I limped along between Brandon and Adam toward the stairwell. Before we entered, I turned back to see if my father had gotten up or moved at all. To see if he stared after me, proud. But he stayed on his back, my mother crouched by his side. I hung my head.

Adam leaned into me and spoke in a reassuring voice. "He's been a gone a long time, so it may take him a while. But he will come back."

Tears seared my eyes. "I hope you're right. Don't worry, though. I don't need the false hope of my father returning to defeat Decklin. I was born to do it."

Chapter Twenty-Six

The clinking had stopped. Adam, Brandon, and I stood alone in the cold stairwell.

"It's strange, isn't it?" I asked. "That they haven't shown up again? That they've left us alone?"

Adam frowned. "Yes, I suppose so." He took a few steps forward and peered over the edge. "There's blood."

Brandon and I joined him at the railing. Dark red stains the size of half dollars left a trail from the bottom few steps to the second floor landing.

My heart picked up its pace. "Do you think...?"

Brandon started down the stairs. "I'll go see."

I grabbed his arm. "But what if it's a trap? What if she squeezed out a few drops to get us to open the door. Then *bam!* They're on us. Her army of zombies."

"It may be. Which is why I should go." Brandon descended a little farther. "You and Adam stay here and wait. If it's nothing, we'll keep looking. But if her army attacks, you run."

"I'm done running." I crossed my arms.

Brandon's gaze bore into me. "If the army comes, you run."

With that, he disappeared down the stairwell. His heavy footsteps echoed up throughout the corridor.

I looked at Adam, aware with my entire being that suddenly, the two of us were alone. Knowing Brandon could be back in seconds, I stepped up next to him. I had lost chances in the past, and I wasn't about to let this one slip away. Especially if death-by-evacuated-souls waited for me.

Our foreheads, our eyes, and our mouths hovered just inches apart. The space between us buzzed with electricity. His gaze never left mine. He didn't move. I didn't move. Time slowed completely, in contrast to the rapid beating of my heart.

Our fingertips found each other and connected. A thousand fireworks filled my body, exploding through me like shards of glass through silk. He leaned forward, and I closed my eyes.

He exhaled a slow, trembling breath, pressed his lips against mine, and leaned in with his full weight, urging me backward against the wall. I weaved my hands through his hair, overcome with the sensation of falling, falling.

My toes curled in my shoes as he slid his tongue lightly across my bottom lip. His heart pounded against my chest, each beat matching my own until we melded as one. His kiss lit up places in my body I'd never known existed. Shockwaves rolled across every inch of my skin, piquing the interest of every unexplored nerve. Breathless, I pulled him even closer, pushing my body against his. Powered by my zeal, we stumbled backward until his back hit the railing. And the jolt bought me back to the present—the stairwell, the Shadows, our mission.

I guess he did too because he drew back, face flushed. "That was better than pizza."

"Don't ruin it." My whole body buzzed. I dropped my hands from his hair and shoved them in my pockets, blood pumping like I'd just run a marathon.

Brandon's footfalls echoed at the bottom of the stairwell. Adam and I separated and looked over the railing. Brandon had made it to landing and opened the door. Which meant that in a few moments, the Shadows might be upon us. In a few minutes, we could all die, right here in this stairwell.

If that was going to happen, I was glad that kissing the boy I loved would be one of my last memories on this earth.

Brandon poked his head out of the door and glanced up at us. My breath caught in my throat as I waited for the evacuates to stream through after him, but nothing happened. He nodded and waved us down. We caught up to him, and the three of us stepped into the second floor hallway, following the blood trail that stretched down the faded carpet. Adam kept glancing over at me, his cheeks glowing, and I smiled despite my terror.

Brandon pointed to a nearby door. "We have to check the apartments."

The blood trail stopped and started up again the farther we got down the hall. I bent down and wiped it with my fingertip. Dry. It could have been ages old.

I jiggled the cold metal doorknob of the door beside me. "It's locked."

Adam motioned for Brandon and me to move. "Step away."

He took a running start and rammed against the door with his shoulder. It broke loose of its frame, tipped slowly inward, and landed with a dusty thump. Though Adam fell and splayed on top of it, he jumped right to his feet.

I gave him an approving nod. "You've healed up nicely."

"I'm motivated." Mischief twinkled in his blue eyes.

My face burned. I stepped past him and surveyed the empty apartment. Newspapers littered the floor. Yellowing curtains hung in the windows. To my left, in the kitchen area, one glass sat alone in the sink.

Brandon headed toward the bedroom. Adam walked down the hall, dragging his fingertips along the wall and occasionally glancing back at me. He peeked around the corner into the bathroom. For a brief, agonizing moment, he disappeared. A door opened and closed. I held my breath.

"Empty." Adam emerged from the shadows.

Brandon appeared beside him. "Empty in the bedroom too."

We left that apartment and continued on to the next. We checked all the corners, walked side-by-side down the narrow hallways, drew back shower curtains, swung open the door of each dusty bedroom, and looked under stained, lumpy mattresses and rodent-chewed box springs. After fifteen or so apartments, the search became less cautious, more rote. I lost heart in apartment after empty apartment. Adam ran a hand through his tousled hair.

Brandon huffed out an angry, frustrated breath. "Maybe she left after all."

I stopped in front of apartment two-hundred, the last one on the floor. "We still have the whole first floor to check. She could be anywhere."

Brandon sighed. "You two rest. I'll check this one, and then we'll start again on the first floor."

Adam and I huddled close together while we waited. He slipped his hand into mine, and I drew comfort from the warmth of it. Time ticked on, both too fast and too slow. I thought of my father, a broken-down mass on the carpet.

"What's taking Brandon so long?" I peeked around Adam into the apartment.

"I'll go check." Adam released my hand. Before he entered, he paused in front of me and bit his lower lip. "Before Decklin evacuated me, I wondered if I'd ever see you again." He stared solemnly into my eyes. "You were the last thing on my mind before I went, and the first thing when I came back, Mira Avery. They say you forget, but I didn't forget. I'm sorry." He trailed his fingertips down my cheek. "Whatever happens, remember that. Remember how sorry I am."

"Don't be sorry. None of this is your fault." I melted into his touch.

He blinked, turned, and disappeared around the corner.

I counted the minutes until he returned. But he stayed gone for too long.

"Adam?" My heart beat at full speed as I inched my way into the apartment. When I started to round the corner toward the bedroom, I heard his footsteps, his jeans swishing together at the ankles.

My shoulders relaxed. "Did you find Brandon? What took you so long?"

He didn't respond. I edged around the wall. He stood there, beside Brandon's prone body, staring at me. A figure stepped out of the shadows and stood next to him.

"Decklin." Her name stabbed me like a sword through my chest.

"Speak of the devil." She flipped on the hall light, fully illuminating her face. "And she shall appear."

Chapter Twenty-Seven

Aside from the copious amounts of blood staining her clothes, Decklin seemed ridiculously fine. Completely recovered. She'd morphed back into the Decklin I'd first met at Meryton—shiny black hair, quick fiery eyes, flawless skin. I planned to change that, and quick. I brought my fists up just as she flung an arm around Adam and brought a cigarette to her lips.

"So, the Three Musketeers, together again. Huh?" She nudged a lifeless Brandon with her toe. "Why am I always left out of the party?"

My hands dropped to my sides. Nausea twisted my stomach. Adam just stood there beside her. Brandon lay there, unmoving, potentially dead or somehow evacuated. I struggled to make sense of it.

"Adam?" I waited for some sign he'd understood me, that he was playing along with her to benefit me. He glanced away, and my heart sank. "What did you do to him?" My voice cracked.

Decklin grinned, a lopsided, triumphant grin that left me seething.

I sprung at her with renewed energy, a raging scream issuing from my throat. She ducked to the side and out of the way. Adam surged forward and wrapped his steel cable arms around me. I struggled to get out, straining against him, and sunk my teeth into his forearm. He didn't flinch and only tightened his grip. His strength far surpassed my own.

"Mira." He cooed at me as I kicked and flailed. "Mira." Soft and even. The tone a mother uses to try and calm her child's tantrum. He planted a soft kiss against my temple. But instead of melting me like before, his lips singed my skin with the bitter acid of betrayal. I jerked away.

Adam spun me around to face Decklin, lifting me off the ground. My feet dangled. Strands of hair hung in my face. He squeezed me so tight I could barely pull in a breath.

Decklin stepped forward so her face was inches from mine. "Where are the rest of them?" Tiny drops of her spittle showered my cheeks. I wrenched my face away from hers.

"I'm alone." I went limp in Adam's arms, pulling all my weight toward my feet in an attempt to get him to drop me. But he held me up easily, like I weighed nothing. I glanced back at him, pleading. "Adam, please let me go."

"Bullshit you're alone." Decklin stepped even closer. "He told me everything." When Adam adjusted his grip, his breath grazed my hair. His heart beat against my coat. I told myself this wasn't happening.

"Okay, I'm not alone." I thought fast. "But no one is coming. They're waiting for us downstairs."

Decklin took a long, slow drag and exhaled smoke through her nose, blowing it into my face. I coughed at her. Hatred burned within me. She'd somehow turned Adam. The same Adam I'd kissed only minutes before with all the passion in the world. And now he held me captive, for her. I'd been stupid enough to care about him, and she'd used that against me. Just like with Larry. My body sagged. What an idiot I'd been.

"Are you thinking about when you kissed Adam?" She smirked and tsked at me. "Making out in a stairwell when you're supposed to be hunting me down. Humans are so single-minded." She rolled her eyes. "Wonder what your father would think. Good thing he didn't live to see the disappointment you turned out to be."

"All my father cared about was how this whole thing ends. How *you* end." I raised my chin and strived to look haughty and proud rather than foolish and defeated.

"Let's make this fair. Just you and me." Decklin motioned for Adam to release me, and he relaxed his grip. As soon as my feet hit the stripped hardwood floor, I spun around and barreled into him headfirst, knocking him against the wall, raining punches down on his shoulders and chest. Tears flowed as a litany of shouts and accusations poured from my mouth. He didn't fight back.

When I'd exhausted myself, I stepped back, panting. He slowly brought his arms down and peeked at me from under heavy lids. My heart contracted hard enough I had trouble breathing.

I swiped at the wetness on my cheeks. "Why? Why are you doing this?"

"Mira." He hung his head like a kicked puppy. Was I supposed to feel sorry for him?

"Tell me. How could you do this?" He had the same blue, blue eyes, same black hair falling over his forehead, same broad shoulders, same shirt. Yet I had never known him. A chill started at the base of my spine and worked its way up to my neck. "You kissed me. You said you thought of me when you evacuated and when you returned."

From behind me, Decklin snorted but said nothing.

He tilted his head. "I can explain."

"I don't want to hear your explanations!" I smacked his chest and then smacked it again. "You've been with her the entire time? From initiation?" He didn't answer, but he didn't have to. The red flush of his cheeks revealed the truth. I shook my head. "I can't believe you did this."

"Ease up, Muhammad Ali." Decklin stubbed her cigarette out on the bottom of her boot. "Adam was just bait for you. You were using him to get to me. For you, he was just a means to an end."

"No, he was so much more." Behind me, Adam drew in a ragged breath. When I turned to him, he couldn't meet my eyes. "After everything, do you honestly believe you were just bait to me?"

"I had to do it." He muttered the words.

"You didn't have to do anything!" I dipped my head down to try and force him to meet my gaze, but he wouldn't. Or couldn't.

Decklin laughed. "All's fair in love and war, Mira dear." She glanced at her bare wrist like it had a watch on it. "As much as I'd love to stay and watch this little lover's spat, I don't have much time. If Brandon's not dead, he'll be waking up soon, and unlike Adam, he actually cares about you. So, that's a problem for me."

In the whites of Decklin's eyes, I saw tiny red veins, and in the inky black of her pupils, my own reflection stared back at me. Everything faded from my view except for Decklin, her red lips, her pale cheeks. A vein pulsed in her forehead. Somewhere in me, my heart kept beating, my lungs kept pulling in air, but in a deeper place, beyond the flesh and bone that encapsulated me, an unfamiliar beast sharpened its claws and bared its teeth. I wanted to destroy her.

"To the victor go the spoils." Decklin's voice floated through the windstorm of my own thoughts. Just before she flew my way, the beast inside me took over. When she pinned me against the wall, I drove my knee up and connected with hers. The crack resonated through the empty apartment. In the split second she took to recover, I arched my back and pushed off the wall. We tumbled to the ground, landing on our sides. My elbow and my hip took the brunt of the fall, and they cursed me.

But I didn't let go of her.

She squirmed and shook. I gripped her ears to hold her steady. Under my hands, her skin burned and pulsed, as if I had reached into the cavity of her chest and taken hold of her black, smoldering heart. Through the thundering charge of my wrath came Adam's voice: *Mira, stop. I'm sorry. I'm sorry. Don't.* His frantic footsteps circled us. But he was outside the heart of the fight. A bystander. I ignored him.

Decklin's dark eyes flashed. She located the soft part underneath my jawbone and began to squeeze. I growled and twisted, anger pushing fear far into the background.

We glared at each other. My arms grew heavy and useless and dropped to my sides. The perimeter around me went white. Decklin and Adam disappeared, replaced by the face of my father…a memory.

What is a Conduit? My seven-year old self had asked him.

A channel through which something flows from one place to another. He had smiled, the corners of his eyes crinkling.

I fell into Decklin's black eyes, no more need for breath. At the same time, her presence scorched and throbbed inside me. We moved the same distance, at the same acceleration, same velocity, tunneling directly toward each other—an equal and opposite reaction.

We met in the middle and collided. Her powers against mine.

Beyond me somewhere, the apartment door rattled on its hinges, and moments, or an eternity, later, someone's body flew against mine. The impact knocked me back, breaking the contact with Decklin.

Too late.

Farther away still came the muffled sound of my mother's shouts. Cold hands on my cheeks. I scattered like confetti and spiraled so far away I became that star—Mira, *Omicron Ceti*—traveling along at 291,000 miles per hour, three-hundred and fifty light-years from Earth.

A blink, a flash, a streak.

Like my namesake, I disappeared.

Chapter Twenty-Eight

When I opened my eyes, Hal's fuzzy outline hovered over me. He breathed out a long sigh and leaned back. "It worked."

I snapped to attention and fixed my eyes on him. My back hurt and the floor pressed at my bones. The dangling metal pull of a ceiling fan clicked against the overhead light.

"Mira?" My mother's voice swelled my heart. I struggled to sit.

"Mira, is it you?" Streaks of tears ran down my mother's cheeks, and worry lines creased her forehead.

"What?" My voice croaked. I cleared my throat. "Of course it's me."

"It is you. I can tell it really is." Her arms closed around me. I hugged her back and rested my still swimming head on her shoulder.

When I glanced down beside me, I almost jumped out of her arms. Decklin lay sprawled on her back, her black hair fanning out behind her, the remains of a surreptitious smile on her face. Her cheeks had gone sallow. One hand remained balled tight in a fist, and the wounds I'd inflicted had turned to pink scars.

She looked more like a sleeping teenager than a malicious entity bent on world destruction.

I relaxed again when it was clear no life stirred within her. I rested my head on my mother's shoulder and waited for my heart to slow down. Everything settled inside me like dust after an explosion.

Across the room, Brandon leaned against the doorframe. He sported a nasty welt on his forehead, but other than that, he appeared to have escaped Decklin unscathed. He watched me with a troubled look on his face. I smiled, grateful he'd been a true and loyal friend. He may not have been Brandon anymore, but he had found a place in my heart.

As the events of the day continued to stream back into my consciousness, I remembered my father. The last time I saw him, he was curled up, lifeless, in the hallway. I didn't want to ask, but I had to. "Where's dad? Is he…"

"In the hallway." My mother rested her forehead against mine, and we both exhaled deeply. She shook so hard that I rattled with her. Her thin hands found mine and held them tight. "I thought I'd lost you." Her voice trembled with either terror or relief, or a mixture of both.

"I'm sorry I failed to bring him back." I sniffled.

"Failed to bring him back?" My mother lifted her head. "Honey, he's awake."

My mouth went dry, and my heart beat went from calm to erratic as the idea sunk in. "What?"

"He's awake." My mother stroked my hair. "You brought him back."

Adam had been right. My father had just needed time to adjust after so many years in the Dark Eternal. I clutched my chest, the thought of having my father back too much to bear all at once.

"See for yourself." Hal gestured toward the hallway.

I stood on shaking legs, ready to face my father after seven years. Brandon came over to help steady me. He flashed me his telltale, cocky grin. "Welcome back. We thought we'd lost you."

Things blurred when I moved and when I turned my head. I squeezed my eyes shut and focused on stabilizing myself, wishing I could remember exactly what happened. Brandon kept one strong arm around my waist to support me.

I started to venture forward, toward the hallway, toward my father, but paused. Before I saw him, before the reunion I'd imagined for the last seven wearisome years, I had to complete my mission.

"Where's Adam?" They knew nothing about his betrayal, about how he hung back and let Decklin try to evacuate me. He could be lurking around any corner, ready to ambush us all.

"I'm here." Adam appeared in the bedroom doorway, his head hung low, arms dangling at his sides.

Adrenaline gave me strength I shouldn't have had, like a deer that darts for the woods after it's hit by a car. Despite my dizziness, I charged at him, screaming. He raised his hands to block my attack, but I still managed to dig my fingers into his neck. We pitched backward, straight through the bedroom, and landed against the far wall. His eyes bulged as his smooth throat collapsed under my grip. I squeezed until my eyes watered, the agony of his betrayal fueling my determination.

"Mira, what are you doing?" My mother appeared next to me, seizing my arms to try and stop me. Hal and Brandon gripped my shoulders and heaved me backward. I brought Adam with me. The four of us crashed to the floor. I refused to release my grip. I could not, despite the hands prying and pulling on me. Despite the desperation and resignation in Adam's steel blue traitor's eyes. I would not stop until I vanquished the life from him.

"Stop!" My mother appeared over me.

"He's a traitor!" I yelled, tightening my grip.

Hal and Brandon yanked my hands from around Adam's neck and pinned them the ground. My mother wrenched Adam from the melee and dragged him to safety. She collapsed on the floor beside him, breathing heavily. I strained against Hal and Brandon, but they kept their grip tight. And they were strong.

"Mira." A voice came from the doorway. Memories flooded through me. *I had run through a meadow as a child, on a day so bright that the blues and greens glistened with a brilliance that stole away all sadness.*

I snapped my head around. My father leaned against the doorframe. His eyes were still as blue as I remembered, and his hair remained the same Dorito shade of red as mine. "Dad," I tried to say, but no sound came out. Because for seven years, I hadn't called anyone that.

I wriggled free from Hal and Brandon and ran to my father. I threw my arms around him and buried my face into his neck. Finally, the moment I hadn't dared to imagine had arrived.

In his arms, I inhaled the scent of him. Beneath the musty rotten filth of seven years in this place lay the spice of open fields, sunshine, and pines. I burst into tears and pressed my cheek against his shoulder, inhaling him again and again.

"Sorry to intrude, but they're out there." Brandon's voice interrupted my revelry.

As my father and I broke apart, I noticed Adam slipping out the door.

I motioned for Brandon or Hal to get him. "You can't let him go. He's one of them. He was working with Decklin this whole time. He betrayed us all." My breath came in gasps, my emotions skating right there on the surface.

Hal shook his head. "No, Mira. He broke you and the Conduit apart. When we came into the room, you two were locked in a death grip, and Adam tried to pry you apart. He ended up having to crash into you and knock you senseless to get you to let go."

I pursed my lips, frustrated he didn't understand. "Adam didn't do it for me. He did it for *her*."

Hal raised an eyebrow. "Mira, there's something we didn't tell you about Adam."

Brandon cleared his throat. "Guys? They're coming." He pointed to the hallway.

"Right. We have to get out." Hal started down the hall.

I seized his arm. "But Adam... We can't let him get away."

"Let's go." Hal wrenched his arm free and moved toward the door. My mother nodded and latched hands with my father. The five of us rushed out of the apartment, past Decklin, and into the hallway. Dozens of evacuates congregated at one end of the hall.

Their black eyes settled on us. Their stench filled my lungs. But they didn't move.

I peered over Hal's shoulder. "Why aren't they attacking?"

"Because of him." My father nodded toward the dark-headed figure standing between us and them.

Adam faced the evacuated ones, holding up his hands like a traffic cop. The Shadows glanced from him to us and back again, shifting their weight. They knew Adam. My blood boiled. They knew him because he'd been working for *her*.

Hal spoke to me out of the side of his mouth. "The keys."

I drew them from my pocket and placed them in his hand.

"Run." Adam glanced over his shoulder at me. Directly at me. Behind him, the evacuated ones started to close in.

I blinked in confusion. "But..." He'd been working for Decklin. He'd been on her side. Why was he helping us now? Another trick?

Brandon grabbed my hand and pulled me toward the other end of the hall. He jerked open the stairwell door and ushered us through. Hal wheezed and grunted as he flew down the stairs, but he moved as fast as any of us. Above, I heard the clamor of a hundred bodies coming for us. *Adam*. With each step, I waffled between the fear of losing him and anger at what he'd done.

We erupted onto the first floor: my mother and father clinging to each other, Hal barreling down the hall behind Brandon, and me pulling up the rear, looking back. Ahead lay the entrance. The new Initiate, still waiting, welcomed us with a big, clueless grin on his face.

My father got there first, strong on his feet again. After he threw open the door and pulled my mother through, he waited for Brandon and Hal and me. Wind and snow blew into the foyer, and I breathed in the freshness of it. My lungs rejoiced. The cold air kissed my cheeks, reviving me. I stepped out, and the snow crunched under my feet.

The five of them headed for the vehicles parked side by side on the street under a dim lamp, fifty yards away. But I stopped running. My heart pleaded with me to wait. My brain argued that Adam had betrayed me. My jealousy screamed that he'd chosen Decklin over me. But my heart begged me to stay. And even though it made no sense, I froze in place…waiting.

The door banged open, and a throng of evacuated ones charged through. The wind whipped around me and nipped the tops of my ears. The tip of my nose stung with cold. I stuffed my hands in my pockets. Just a few more seconds. *Please, Adam. Hurry.*

The evacuates lumbered forward, not quick enough to do damage…yet. I scanned the crowd for Adam, yearning for him to appear.

"He'll make it, Mira," Hal yelled from halfway across the parking lot. "He's with us. He's always been with us. I'll explain in the car. Now come on, we have to go."

The ice in my veins froze me in place. "What do you mean, he's with us? Tell me what you mean!" I screamed.

My mother rushed across the parking lot and took me by the arm. Snow swirled around us. "He was a plant, Mira. An infiltrator. His job was to cozy up to Decklin. Make her trust him, then bring us information. We couldn't tell you. It was too risky."

I felt the blood drain from my face. My mother wrenched me toward the car, but I resisted, yanking my arm out of her grip. I thought back to Adam's cold stare in the apartment hallway, and suddenly it made sense. He couldn't tell me what he was doing, and he knew he was hurting me. My heart swelled. He didn't betray me after all. Everything he had done had been for me.

With renewed resolve, I stood my ground. "Then we can't leave him."

Hal shook his head. "We always knew it may come to this. He's been prepared to sacrifice himself from the start."

"Mira, come on," my mother pleaded, inching toward the vehicles. But I wouldn't leave Adam behind. Not now, not knowing the truth.

"You go," I said. "I have to wait for him."

The fastest evacuated ones inched closer to me. In moments, they'd be within reach. I choked back the flurry of emotions tearing through me. My parents—my *parents*, such a new concept, one I hadn't even had time to process—launched themselves into the backseat of the car with the new Initiate.

"Mira." Brandon's voice broke as he met my gaze one last time before stepping into the car and shutting the door.

I glanced back at the lurching clog, the gray crowd of evacuates moving as a pack toward me. A flash of blue caught my eye. From the back of the mob, Adam pushed his way forward, fighting through them with his hands up like he was wading through a thick Amazonian swamp.

Over their heads, he saw me. My parents' voices in the background faded away, as did the biting cold and the sound of Hal's repeated attempts to get his truck started.

Hope surged through me and then retreated just as fast.

Adam shot out a fist. He knocked an evacuate sideways and left him lying prostrate out on the ground to be trampled on.

He was fighting to get to me. I watched, unblinking, feeling every blow deep in my bones.

Fists swinging, Adam leveled the ones around him. They flew right and left, sprawled on the snowy asphalt. My own hands curled into fists and ached each time he made contact. He cleared a dozen of them before he doubled over, breathing hard. The remaining Shadows stopped in their tracks, watching Adam with their heads cocked. They had underestimated him. We all had.

"Adam!" I yelled through the white storm. I shouldn't have shouted. The Shadows turned to me. Their black stares locked me in place.

"No, here!" Adam waved his hands, trying to get their attention as they started toward me. For one alarming second, I pictured my own doom at their filthy hands, but they turned their cold stares toward him. I could see their slow brains processing the situation as they turned back to me. With Adam's attack, they had forgotten about us completely.

I bit my lip. That had been his plan. To distract them so we could get away. This was his sacrifice. His offering of love, to me.

And I had to make mine. I had treated him like bait. Hal, Larry, my mother, and I had all been prepared to let the Conduit whoosh him into the Dark Eternal. He wasn't just a vessel. He wasn't just a body. He'd become more to me—more than an alien in a human form—and it had taken me too long to see it. But he'd known from the start. He'd chosen to give his life for a bigger cause, and for me, as he was choosing to do now.

I had moments to make my decision, but I didn't need any time at all. I knew what I had to do. I had to make my own offering of love, to him.

The muscles in my legs burned. Just as I broke into a run, a giant, mallet-fisted Shadow swung at Adam. His fist connected with Adam's throat. I skidded to a stop and whispered, "*No.*" My heart smashed against my ribs.

In the dark winter night, I met Adam's gaze. In the split second before he went down, we stood alone in the parking lot, the only two people in existence, and he immobilized me with his stare, eliminating the distance between us, between our two worlds.

Then all of it shattered.

The punch sent him cartwheeling backward into the frenzied rest of them, and they attacked him. Amongst the clamor, their greasy heads moving back and forth, a churning pit of fists and backs and legs, a hand shot up. Adam's hand. I'd know it anywhere. I didn't know how he'd managed it, not with the feast they must have been having. His fingers splayed, stretched, trembled, and then his wrist went limp. It disappeared.

"Adam." My knees buckled. Before I hit the ground, Hal's long arms wrapped around me. He held me up and dragged me back toward the vehicles as the evacuated ones tore into the boy I loved. The ones on top struggled to penetrate the ones below, to land their own blows. To pull apart, pummel, eviscerate. My gut twisted in revulsion.

"Get in." Hal planted me in the passenger's seat.

"I can't leave him!" I tried to back out of the car. Determination blossomed in my chest. I kicked at Hal, kicked at the door, launched myself onto the snowy ground.

Hal dropped his head. "You can't save him." The words came out strained.

My father opened his car door and stepped out, gestured toward the building. "We're too late."

"What do you mean?" One glance in the direction of the building, and I understood what he meant. In a failed attempt to save Adam, I'd doomed us all.

Chapter Twenty-Nine

The first one had at least a hundred pounds on me. He leapt and knocked me to the pavement. But I went directly for his throat. I bore down so hard his black eyes shot open. He pried at my hands with his own, making no sound. Not one of them made a sound.

"Look at me. Look at me." I wrangled his head until our eyes connected. When they did, the familiar, searing pain tore through me. His breath filled my nostrils, burned its way into my lungs, and burrowed in the cavity of my stomach. I swallowed back vomit. Some of the others peeled themselves off the Adam pile and teetered toward me, their heads cocked.

Strength flowed up from the earth, through the soles of my boots and to my legs, circling my body like it was part of my blood. I squeezed harder. The Shadow entered me, and just as quickly, it left. The body went slack in my grip, and then that familiar lightness came. A spring wind fluttered through me, exited the tips of my fingers, and entered the empty shell of the man through the tiny pores on his neck. It nestled in the center of him, where it rooted and spread. The eyes flickered and turned on. Greenish blue. No longer a Shadow.

Hal helped me to my feet. "Mira, you'll get yourself killed."

My mother pointed to the evacuates, her eyes wide with bewilderment. "No, look. They're afraid of her."

It was true. The Shadows backed away. Slinking toward the building entrance, they moved silently through the snow. Their eyes tracked me as I inched forward to where Adam lay. Only three of them remained on him now. Those three didn't move, didn't blink. He had damaged them beyond repair. His socked feet stuck out from underneath their battered bodies.

Hal and I kicked two of them away, and then we rolled the heaviest one off to reveal Adam's body, face down on the cracked pavement, hands behind his head as if he had been shielding himself.

"Adam." My chest tightened. My eyes stung. I reached out and ran my fingers through his hair, cold and wet with newfallen snow and blood. With shaking hands, I moved his hands to uncover his face. I gasped. Caked blood. Gashes. Bruises, deep purple. Under the pulp, I no longer recognized his handsome face. I lowered my head to his chest and sobbed.

His body heat warmed my cheek, the last remnant of the life inside of him. Wracked with sobs, I clung to him harder, laid my hands on him.

Underneath me, I swear I felt his chest rise.

My eyes shot open. It was the wind, or my own imagination. I watched his chest, his stomach, hope spreading through me like a morning sunrise.

It happened again. "He's breathing!" I cried into the night air. Hal stooped down beside me and rested a hand on Adam's shoulder.

"Adam? You in there?"

Adam's swollen eyelids fluttered. He cracked open one eye. One beautiful, sky-blue eye. I slid my hand into his and squeezed. I never wanted to let go. Tears streamed down my face, despite my soaring heart. "You could have gotten yourself killed."

"I would have, for you." His voice rasped, and he coughed hard into his fist.

I shook my head, drew his hand to my lips and kissed his bloodied knuckles. "Why?"

"You showed me what it means to be human." His eye twinkled beneath the bruises. His bleeding, cracked lips curled into a smile. "You showed me it's more than just a body. It's a heart. *My* heart. But it belongs to you."

His words penetrated the cold. Their truth reverberated through me, nestled right into that inhuman half of myself I'd always kept hidden. I sank into his arms, and the world fell away.

Acknowledgements

This book was a long time in the making, and wouldn't exist if it weren't for the efforts and tolerance of some of the best people. First, the ladies at BookFish Books for taking a chance on a 140-character pitch. Erin Rhew, Jess Calla, and Jenn Herrington, thank you for making my dream come true. To those who read my early first drafts, thank you for not taking a match to the pages. Dad, Ginny, Marri, Jamie, your feedback shaped the work, even if I did want to stab my own eyes out with each comment.

Support and motivation comes in all forms, so thanks to those friends who encouraged me along the way and told me to see it through to the end, which I have.

And lastly: Look ma, no hands.

About the Author

Kama Falzoi Post developed a love of books and writing at a very early age. Her short stories have appeared in a handful of literary magazines and anthologies. *InHuman* is her first published novel. She lives in a small town outside a small city with her husband, son, stepkids, and too many cats.

Made in the USA
Middletown, DE
21 December 2016